# SOME PLACE LIKE HOME

## Sammi Caramela

**Metal Lunchbox Publishing**

*"For my dad - my best friend. Your support is the foundation of everything I have accomplished."*

# PROLOGUE

*Three years earlier.*

"Birthday girl over here gets first dibs!"

I widen my eyes at Jade, my heart hammering in my chest. *Spin the Bottle* is not for someone like me.

"Here, I'll spin for you," Jade says.

"Jade, I don't want to," I tell her, my voice low.

She spins it anyway, and it lands on the guy next to me. I look up at him. His lips are pressed together in a thin line as he stares at the bottle. Messy dirty-blonde hair curls at his ears.

"Well, that's convenient," Jade says.

The boy hesitates, his green eyes questioning me. I recognize him from school. He's a freshman, too. But I don't even know his name.

"If you won't kiss him, I will," another girl says.

"Come on, don't be a prude, b-day girl," one of the guys chimes in.

My face burns, and I push back from the table, rushing out of the room and through the crowd in the kitchen to get out the back door. I don't know where I'm going or how I'll get home. I don't even know what neighborhood we're in.

We weren't supposed to be here. It wasn't part of the plan. Jade told me dinner, just me and her. That was it.

I text my brother for a ride. He'll be mad. I know it. But I'm desperate.

I lean against a car in the driveway, letting myself cry, and suddenly feel a hand on my shoulder. I turn to see the guy I'm supposed to be kissing. I quickly step back, out of his reach.

"It's okay, I'm not—I wasn't trying to do anything."

He keeps space between us, holding his hands up in surrender, like I'm something to be afraid of. Like *I'm* not the one always terrified.

I wipe my eyes with the sleeve of my sweater, turning away from him so he can't see me cry, and try to slow my breathing.

"Are you okay?" he asks. I look back at him, and his eyes are searching me.

"I just wanna go home," I say.

"Do you have a ride? I can call you a car. I'll go with you if you don't feel safe going alone."

"I don't even know your name," I whisper.

"It's Tristan. You're April, right?"

I nod cautiously.

"We have gym together."

Just then, my phone starts to ring. A picture of my brother and me at my eighth grade graduation covers the screen.

"Greg," I say into the phone, but can't manage anything else.

"April, what happened?" Greg asks me. "Where are you?"

Tears threaten to fall again as panic steals my breath. I'm not getting better. That much is obvious.

"April, talk to me," Greg said.

My voice catches in my throat. I try to speak, but every attempt to do so makes me cry harder.

I can't control the tears, can't stop myself from losing it on some stranger's front lawn next to a guy I apparently have class with.

Tristan takes the phone from me. I can see the concern in his eyes as he stares out at the dimly lit street.

"Hey, man. This is Tristan. Uh, Tristan Barelli. April's okay. She's...freaking out a bit. But she's alright." He pauses, listening to what Greg has to say. "No, I don't think so." ... "I'm not sure, to be honest. Some blonde girl, I think." ... "Yeah, yeah, I think that's her name. She was kind of a bitch." He laughs, then listens to what Greg said, nodding. He tells him where we are, an address I don't recognize. "No problem, man. I'll wait outside with her."

When he hangs up, he hands my phone back to me and offers a smile.

"He's on his way."

I nod and take a seat on the driveway behind the car, my body aching as I lower myself.

Tristan stands above me, leaning against the trunk of the car. I try finding a distraction, something to stop the tears and the shame. I try focusing on the night, on the moon and the streetlights, but they all blur before my eyes. I only cry harder, the more I try not to.

"April..."

I shake my head when Tristan says my name, hiding my face in my hands. I don't want to talk. What is there to say? I don't know him. And now, especially, I don't want him to know me.

# CHAPTER 1

"Let's sit outside. It's nice and cool," Jade says once our drinks are ready at the cafe. I follow on her heel and settle at a black metal table on the patio.

"Wow, it's packed today," I say, looking out at the downtown. The street is buzzing with kids around our age, couples kissing on benches, friends window shopping.

"Ugh, I know," Jade says, making a face. She tucks her long blonde hair behind her ears and rolls her eyes, leaning on her elbow. "I can't wait to get the hell away from this place."

"Thanks a lot!" I say, placing my hand on my chest in fake dismay. "You mean you're not gonna miss my beautiful face in college?"

"We're not going to war, April."

"You don't know where we'll end up!" I say, adjusting my glasses. "I'm looking at schools in Boston."

"Please. You and I both know you could never go to college that far from home."

Her cup is marked with red lipstick, and she cradles it like a hand warmer.

I shrug. "It's only, like, a two-and-a-half-hour drive from here."

"From *Connecticut*? I thought it was much further."

I shake my head. "Nope. I mapped it out a few nights ago."

"Well, still. You can barely drive ten minutes on the highway to the mall without freaking out."

I laugh, sipping my coffee and looking past her at the trees lining the sidewalk. The leaves are starting to change color, a mix of auburns and maroons. I watch one sway in the air as it falls to the ground.

"Do you ever miss Catholic school?" Jade asks me. I look back at her as she pulls her feet onto her chair. "I kinda miss the uniforms. Guys love the whole plaid-skirt-and-high-socks, preppy look now. Maybe I'll go to a Catholic college." She winks at me.

"Please, you hated our K-8."

She shrugs. "I'm a different person now. It *was* four years ago."

"I still remember our first day there, when that girl tried stealing my clay and you pushed her," I say.

Jade smirks. "She had it coming."

"How did we last nine years in that place?"

"I ask myself that question every day."

"And yet, you want to go back..." I tease.

Pointing at me, she says, "Hey, just for the uniforms."

"Who do you need to impress with a school-girl outfit? Adam's obsessed with you."

"Oh! Speaking of." She shifts in her chair. "What are you doing tomorrow?"

I swallow a sip of my drink in a gulp. Why do people ask *what are you doing?* without specifying their intentions behind the question? If you go ahead and say *nothing!,* you're trapped. There's no way out, no way to make an excuse if said intentions are to, perhaps, jump off a cliff with them. Or maybe catch a movie, I don't know. "Tomorrow?" I ask, stalling.

"Yes. Tomorrow, as in Friday night. Adam's friends want to hang out with us."

I pick at the lid of my coffee cup. "Okay, yeah. Sure."

"Cool. Brenda and Lindsay are in, too."

Jade scrolls on her phone, so I take mine out and Insta-stalk Brenda. She has luscious golden brown hair and over 2,000 followers, and her page looks like one of those hipster model accounts. If I wore the same clothes she sported in these photos, like baggy jeans and neon halter tops, I'd look like a child trying to be artsy and sensational. But on her, the outfits look like the next big thing.

"Oh my God," Jade says as I make sure I didn't accidentally like one of Brenda's old photos.

"What?"

She looks up at me, her mouth hanging open. "Tristan Barelli is missing."

*"What?"*

I grab Jade's phone from across the table. On her screen is a lengthy Facebook post from Tristan's sister.

**Jenny Barelli:** *Hi everyone. I don't really know where else to turn. I haven't seen or heard from Tristan for a few days now. This is completely out-of-character for him. I've tried reaching out to him, but his phone is home and his car is still parked outside our house. I'm not sure what to do. I'd really appreciate any help. If anyone knows anything, please message me.*

Chills spread down my arms, like a million red ants invading my skin.

I've had classes with Tristan. He was my partner in English all last year. And suddenly, he's missing?

My stomach does a flip, almost like I'm...*intrigued*. Immediately, I drop Jade's phone in the middle of the table. It makes a loud thud.

"What the *fuck*, April? That's the new iPhone!"

"I don't feel well," I say, standing quickly as Jade inspects her phone for damage. I need to walk. Or pace. Or something.

"What's wrong with you?" Jade asks me.

Deep breaths. I need to take deep breaths. In for six, out for eight. I think, right?

"April, you're freaking out."

"I'm really dizzy, Jade. I feel sick."

Jade rolls her eyes, scrolling on her phone again. Scrolling past Jenny's post, as if it's old news. "You're fine. You're getting yourself worked up for no reason. You barely even know Tristan."

"I had a few classes with him," I mutter, though that's not the point right now.

"Plus, he probably just got into a fight with his parents or something. I'm sure he'll come home soon."

I don't remind her that his mom passed away two years ago.

"I just really don't feel well," I say instead, my voice rising like panic in my bloodstream.

She looks at me like I'm crazy. She doesn't know the half of it

*       *       *

Google search: "Feeling excited when bad things happen."

My heart races as I scroll through the results, trying to find what I want, what I *need*, to read. Something that tells me this is normal. This is a fleeting feeling everyone experiences. This doesn't make me a horrible person.

I see the word "schadenfreude." I Google it. The dictionary tells me it's a pleasure you get out of someone else's pain.

That's horrible.

My room is cold, or maybe it's just me. I tug my comforter to my chin and try to get comfortable in my bed as my eyes begin to sting. I'm shivering, my teeth chattering. Maybe I'm getting sick. You know, in the traditional sense. The type of sick that will earn me a day off school or a hot bowl of chicken soup.

I need to try again. I type: "Excited that someone I know is missing."

An article from some girls' magazine pops up, titled "5 Reasons You Might Miss Someone You Barely Know."

I throw my phone across the room. Then get up and retrieve it.

Again: "I want bad things to happen."

This time, I find some forum that features responses from an actual therapist. The question is titled the same as mine. As I read the entire post, I realize the asker has OCD—a disorder I know all too well. One I've struggled with since elementary school.

The therapist responds with:

*"This stems from your subconscious. You know it is inher-*

ently 'wrong' to actually wish for something terrible to happen, but there's also a natural curiosity within us. Your OCD is holding on to that brief reaction, then running with it and twisting it into something so much worse. It's a very common occurrence in OCD sufferers. But it's important you do not seek reassurance or ruminate. Don't judge your thoughts or attach meaning to them; accept them for what they are."

Relief floods me, pouring out of my eyes in the form of tears.

*I'm okay. It's just my OCD. I'm not crazy. I'm not horrible.*

"April!" I hear my dad call up to my room from the bottom of the steps. "Dinner!"

"Coming!" My voice cracks, and I jump up to look in the mirror on the back of my door. My eyes are red and puffy. *How can I play this off?*

I sneak to the bathroom, hoping Greg is already downstairs, shut the door, and turn on the faucet. I splash my face, mascara bleeding under my eyes.

"Sweetie, it's getting cold!"

"One sec!"

Staring at my reflection, I inhale a slow, shaky breath. If my parents ask why I look like I'm crying, I'll tell them I don't feel well. That I have a headache. Simple enough for them to believe. Maybe they'll even let me skip school tomorrow. And then, maybe I can get out of the whole group date Jade has planned.

I smile at the mirror, because I have to, grab my phone off the sink counter, and step downstairs. The smell of pot-roast instantly comforts me.

"Hi!" I try to appear as cheery as possible as I make myself a plate at the marble countertop. The dinner is set up like a buffet, with mashed potatoes and rolls and even a salad, which I won't be eating. My dad always forgets to wash the lettuce. "Looks good, dad." I join them at the table, sitting next to my brother.

"Oh, I made dinner tonight," my mom says, beaming with

pride. "I threw it in the slow cooker this morning."

I collect the meat with a soft baby carrot and dip it into the pile of gravy-covered mashed potatoes, but then I pause. "Um, did you...?"

"*Yes*, April. I made sure it was over 160-degrees, just for you. So if it's dry, you can thank yourself."

I take a bite. "It's not dry," I tell her, even though it is.

The TV in the living room next to us blares with the weather report. I catch a forecaster predicting below-average temperatures into October. My dad and I both make a face.

"Yo, Ape," Greg says. He stares at his phone, eyebrows scrunched. "You knew Tristan Barelli, didn't you?"

My stomach tightens like it did earlier. What *is* this feeling? "Yeah. I heard."

"Heard what?" my dad asks.

"He's missing," Greg and I say in unison.

"*What?*" my mom says.

"He's a senior?" my dad asks me. "Did you know him?"

"Yeah, I had English with him last year."

"Is he the type to pull a stunt like this for attention?" my mom asks, her voice laced with judgement. She can't accept that bad things happen. That life isn't always corporate events and shopping sprees. That sometimes, people hurt. Sometimes, they can't help it. Sometimes, it's not their fault.

"No, mom," I say. "He's a good person."

I'm sure he is. I'm sure he's better than I am. I'm sure he wouldn't experience *schadenfreude.*

I push away from the table and stand abruptly, causing my chair to fall.

"Where are you rushing off to?" my mom asks.

I pick up the chair, ignoring my shaking hands and Greg, whose eyes are boring into me. "I'm not hungry. I went out with Jade earlier." I don't mention that all I ordered was a coffee.

"Are you okay?" my dad asks, though he already knows the answer. They all do.

I nod and walk away so we can keep pretending otherwise.

# CHAPTER 2

I like my town. I like that it's a safe place to roam, even alone at night. I like it for its coffee shops with workers who know my order by heart, for its secondhand bookstore I've been going to since I was four. I like the fact that every house on my street has a porch with rocking chairs.

But Haddon High School is not my favorite place. I have nothing against my peers, but I also have nothing in common with them. The students here can afford, well, most things. Like $300 rubber slide shoes from some designer I always mispronounce. Or monthly haircuts at some high-end salon all the way in Greenwich. Or private soccer training and music lessons at some prestigious school.

I can afford those things, too. I'm just not interested in them.

When I walk into school today, I'm expecting the topics to steer from celebrity pregnancies to something more important. Like, I don't know, our missing classmate? But I guess I shouldn't be surprised.

Suddenly, there's noise over the loudspeaker, announcing itself with static and the shuffling of papers echoing throughout the halls. No one seems to notice or care. *Shocking*.

Principal Bucket clears his throat before speaking. "Good morning, everyone," he starts.

A group of guys and girls in my grade are still talking loudly, grinning and joking with each other as if it's just another Friday morning. A teacher pokes her head out of her classroom and shushes them, which only makes them widen their eyes and snicker.

"As I'm sure many of you already know, a student of ours, Tristen Barelli, has been reported missing. This is a very difficult time, and I understand that many of you are directly affected by this incident. I just want to let everyone know that there will be walk-in grief counseling sessions for the remainder of this week."

Jade elbows me and says, "Counseling? Don't you think that's a little dramatic?"

I haven't told Jade about my therapist, but she could probably guess I'm seeing someone. Or used to, at least.

I told her I had OCD when I was first diagnosed in fourth grade. I'd scrub my hands until they bled in the school bathroom and refuse to eat the sandwiches my dad packed in case someone slipped poison in the ziplock bags. Jade and I were attached at the hip, so she knew something was wrong with me. But when I told her what it was called, she scrunched her nose and said, "I don't know what that is, but it sounds weird." The next day, she told me her mom said OCD means you don't like germs.

At the time, I could agree with that. I couldn't yet understand it myself. But I knew there had to be more to it. I just didn't know how to tell her, or anyone, what went on in my head.

I tried explaining it to her again in eighth grade, when I bailed on our class trip to New York because I didn't want to take public transportation. She was bummed, and a little mad. She said I needed to push myself, to get out of my comfort zone. But she didn't realize that my comfort zone was a lot smaller than hers. Anyway, she ended up bringing me back a snowglobe.

"How is that dramatic?" my friend Kat asks, her voice daring Jade to say more. Her red hair is pulled into a tight ponytail, and she grips the handles of her backpack so tight her knuckles are white. "It's like going to a cardiologist for chest pain. No different."

"Relax, I was joking," Jade says.

I smile at Kat, grateful as always for her presence. We may

have only met freshman year, but it feels more like *she's* the childhood friend.

Principal Bucket continues talking about Tristan, sparing most details but asking that we all keep an eye out and alert the police of any information. I hope this doesn't last long, that maybe he did run away and maybe he'll come to senses and return home this weekend.

When the warning bell rings, Kat breaks off down the hall where the locker rooms are to get ready for gym, and I'm left walking to class with Jade and her theater friends, Brenda and Lindsay, whose outfits are making my jeans and T-shirt look like pajamas.

Jade steps in front of us like the leader of a pack of wolves. "So, you guys excited for later? I can't wait 'til you meet everyone!"

"What's later?" I ask her.

She gives me a look. "The movies? With Adam and his friends?"

"Oh! Right." I force a smile. "I was so focused on the whole Tristan thing that I forgot."

"Were you even close with him?" Lindsay asks, curly black hair framing her face.

I open my mouth to defend myself, but it's not worth it. I've had plenty of conversations with Tristan. It's not like I don't know him. But Lindsay wouldn't get it. She doesn't feel personally responsible for every person she's ever spoken to.

"Don't be a bitch, Lindsay, just because some people have a heart," Brenda says in a sing-song voice. I'm not sure if she means it or just pities me.

"Or some people want sympathy," Jade mutters, smirking. I stop in my tracks, frozen at the trigger. Immediately, I'm like a victim with a gun pointed in my direction, defenseless and still, unable to speak.

"What are you doing?" Lindsay asks, looking me up and down like I'm a freak.

"Oh, come on," Jade says. "It was a joke. Don't get like

that."

But what if she's right? What if I just want attention, even at another person's expense? What if I'm a horrible person who wants bad things to happen?

The illness in my mind leaks into my bloodstream, making my hands shake. I stop at my locker, pretending I need to get books out as they walk away without me, and blink away tears. A few strands of hair fall to the ground as I secure my ponytail.

I lean into my locker and take a deep breath, trying to calm myself. Breathe in for...how many seconds? I don't even remember.

*       *       *

In English class, we're reading *Speak*. Usually, I'm excited to start the day off by analyzing whatever story Mrs. Clark chooses for the month, but I can't focus on anything right now.

I look around the class and notice everyone is writing in their journals. Mrs. Clark is sitting at her desk with her legs crossed, reading through loose leaf papers. She's not paying any attention to me, but in case she does, I have to at least pretend I'm writing.

I'm sick to my stomach, unable to stop thinking about Tristan, about my reaction to the devastating news. I need to help him. Maybe if I find him, I can undo all these bad thoughts.

I turn to a new page in my notebook and record everything I know about him so I have it in front of me for reference.

*Tristan Barelli: 17 years old; senior at Haddon High*

*Friends: Guy from lunch...name??? (I think he graduated last year)*

*Siblings: Jenny Barelli*

*Parents: Dad, owns contracting business; Mom, died in car accident 2 years ago*

*Hobbies: Music (was in Kat's guitar class)*

I tap my pen and bite my lip, trying to think about anything else I know about Tristan. I had English with him. Kat's mom, Ms. Bailey, was our teacher. We were partners all last year. He wasn't one of those kids who made you do all the work and took equal credit.

One time, we had to give a presentation on the art of horror, which was ironic because public speaking is *equivalent* to horror. So, with the OK from Ms. Bailey, Tristan helped me make a video collage of clips from various horror films, explaining each writer's techniques through voice-over, which I recorded in the comfort of my own room.

Everyone ended up loving it, wishing they'd thought of the idea first. Tristan even let me take credit.

"Okay, please write your name at the top and pass it up."

I slam my journal closed so quickly that my pen slides off my desk. I go to reach for it, but Mrs. Clark's black heels step behind it. She crouches down to pick it up and places it in front of me. "Your paper, please?" she asks, hand extended.

I can't give her what I have. She'll know I wasn't paying attention. She'll think I'm crazy. She'll probably make me see one of the school counselors. I already have my own therapist. I don't need two.

*"April."*

I shake my head. "I'm sorry, Mrs. Clark. I didn't get to write anything."

"I saw you scribbling something down. Just hand in what you've got and you'll get full credit. As long as there's something there."

"I wasn't doing the assignment." My cheeks are hot, and even though I'm staring down at my desk, I can sense my classmates' eyes on me.

Mrs. Clark sighs. As she continues down the aisle, her heels clicking, I can't help but wish *I* was the one who disappeared.

# CHAPTER 3

Jade waits until we're at the theater to tell me we're seeing a paranormal movie. I can handle thrillers, especially if there's a mystery packed in them. But "based-on-true-events" ghost stories about possession? No, thank you; I have enough demons of my own.

As we're waiting in line to buy our tickets, I debate faking sick and ordering an Uber home. The theater smells like popcorn, its fluorescent lighting so bright my eyes are stinging. The lobby, which is separate from the actual theater, is far too small for its own good, flooded with roudy middle schoolers whose parents probably dropped them off in a carpool.

I remember when my dad and Jade's mom would do that for us. She'd text me, "my mom will bring if your dad will pick up" at least twice every weekend. Back when it was just me and her, and we were seeing cheesy rom-coms.

I'm paying for my ticket when Adam walks in with three guys trailing behind him. I try to collect my change and stuff it into my purse before they approach us, but I drop coins on the floor like an idiot, and now I'm holding up the line, which is, like, my worst nightmare.

Brenda picks up my change and hands it to me with a look of pity as Adam reaches us.

"What's up, guys?!"

He hugs all of us like we're his fans or something, and his cologne has the audacity to overpower the popcorn. Grinning, he introduces us to his friends: James, a lanky redhead, Kalvin, a stocky athlete with wavy black hair, and Dylan, who looks straight out of an alt rock band with his beanie and Converse.

Okay, if I'm anyone's fan, I'm Dylan's.

"I'm so glad everyone is *finally* meeting," Jade says.

We're standing right off to the side of the box office, and a mom with two young boys shoots us a look as she pushes past us. I'm forced to step closer to Dylan to make room, and to my surprise, I don't feel like a complete giant next to him.

"Maybe we should go to the lobby," I say, but no one seems to hear me. There are way too many people here. Too many voices, too much movement. My head is spinning.

"I'll be right back," I say as if anyone will hear me, and head to the bathroom.

Brenda offers to come with me, and I wish she wouldn't, but I don't tell her that. As I brush past the group, Dylan meets my eye. He smiles, and his cheeks flush like he's embarrassed, which is oddly comforting since I'm definitely red right now.

"Saw that," Brenda says when we're far enough away from everyone.

"Saw what?"

"Dylan checking you out."

"Ha," I say. "You're funny." I walk to the sink right away to wash my hands, lathering them with soap and scrubbing, scrubbing, scrubbing.

"Do you even have to go to the bathroom?" Brenda asks as she locks herself in a stall. Thankfully, it's just the two of us in here.

"What do you mean?"

"Why are you washing your hands first?"

"Oh, I accidentally touched something sticky," I lie, then grab a paper towel and rush into the stall next to Brenda's.

"Dylan's hot," she says right before flushing the toilet. My heart sinks because, well, she's right—he *is* hot. But if she agrees, then there goes my chance with him. "He seems to think you are too."

I laugh as I join her at the sink. "Yeah, oh-kay."

She ignores my comment and strikes poses in the mirror, which is covered in smudges, widening her eyes and puckering her lips, as if trying on the "innocent look." The one I actually embody, but don't pull off half as well she does. I stare at my reflection, at my blotchy face and stringy hair, then glance at Brenda's clear olive skin and thick golden locks. She thinks Dylan is interested in *me* over *her*? I don't buy it.

My phone vibrates in my back pocket, and I check it while grabbing paper towels to dry my hands.

**Jade:** Just heard Dylan ask Adam about you.

"Who is it?" Brenda asks, peeking at my screen as a smile creeps onto my face. "I told you!" she says, lightly shoving me.

When we walk out of the bathroom, Jade waves me over to where they're standing, which is thankfully off to the side and away from the crowd. Her long blonde hair sways over her shoulder as she bounces in excitement.

"You met Dylan, right?"

I glance up at him, hoping it's not obvious how nervous I am. We smile at each other, and his brown eyes crinkle a bit.

"Yes, like, five minutes ago," I say.

Dylan laughs. "It's nice to meet you *again*."

Adam comes up behind Jade as Dylan and I stand awkwardly, me picking at my shirt, him playing on his phone.

"Just waiting on James," Adam says, his dirty blonde hair pulled back into a bun. Each time he snaps his gum, I swear I grow closer to insanity.

I glance over at James, who's buying popcorn with Jade, a long line of people behind them. He's talking to her a mile a minute about something she doesn't seem interested in, and the concession stand worker looks about ready to quit his job. I wonder if she went over there so I could talk to Dylan.

Lindsay, on the other hand, is already flirting with Kalvin, who apparently stole her phone to take selfies. Her hands are all over him, trying to snatch it back as she giggles.

"You guys ready?" Jade asks them when James and Brenda return.

We give our tickets to a worker who directs to Theater 10, which is down a long hall. Dylan and I walk, and he starts asking me how I know Jade.

"We've been friends since preschool," I tell him, staring ahead at Adam and Jade, who are bumping each other with their hips, laughing. "What about you? You're a sophomore like Adam, right?"

"Yup."

"Are you in the same frat as him?" I pray he says no, because I don't think I could ever date a frat boy. Not that I'm looking to date Dylan or anything. We just met.

He feigns offense. "You wouldn't catch me dead in a frat. We play pickup soccer games on campus sometimes." He leans close to my ear, and whispers, "Adam sucks though."

I laugh, and then so does he, and the anxiety decreases a bit.

In the theater, I sit between Jade and Dylan. I almost forgot what movie we're seeing, but now I'm starting to panic. I take deep breaths and lean back in the chair, which is thankfully a recliner. Maybe I can just fall asleep and not have to watch a second of it.

Dylan reclines his seat, too and scoots closer to the side of his chair that's nearest to me.

"I don't like scary movies," he whispers as the lights dim.

"I'm already scared, and it hasn't even started yet."

He laughs and meets my eyes, then looks down really quickly. "I'll try to be brave for you, but I can't make any promises."

I rest my head back against the seat and squeeze my eyes shut as the movie starts. Suspenseful music booms through the speakers. I can feel it in my chest.

I peer up and see Dylan watching the screen with wide eyes and a slightly opened mouth. He already looks terrified, leaning forward and gripping the sides of his chair. Nothing even happened yet. It's just the beginning, where the "survivors" introduce their story.

"So brave!" I tease, and he smiles, keeping his eyes glued on the screen.

I sink back into my seat and close my eyes again. To distract myself, I imagine all of the people Dylan could be. A soft-spoken history major. A well-rounded athlete. A family-oriented boy-next-door.

I wish we were somewhere else, somewhere we could talk and get to know each other. But I guess if it wasn't for this movie, I never would've met him. And maybe it won't be that bad, anyway.

Just as I peek at the screen, a demon doll pops out of the dark and attacks some woman. I scream, and my first instinct is to grab Dylan's arm and hide my face.

His shoulders shake with laughter. I let go, embarrassed, and he watches me with a grin. I am probably ten different shades of red right now. Thank God it's a dark theater. "My bad," I whisper, trying to play it cool.

"I didn't mind."

Next to me, Jade kicks me. I look over at her and she smirks, eyebrows raised. I kick her back.

"I don't like this movie," Dylan whispers to me, slumping in his seat so I can hear him.

"Yeah, I'd rather be home eating ice cream in bed," I tell him, which was my original plan for the night.

He laughs. "I'd definitely much rather be somewhere else." He peers over at me with a sort of longing that makes me giddy and excited, and I instantly think about how I felt when I found out Tristan was missing.

It's not the same sensation I had then, not exactly. So, maybe I wasn't excited he was missing. Of course, I wasn't. Why would I be? Logically, I wouldn't. Rationally, I know that.

But, *what if?*

I smile at Dylan to hide my thoughts, as if he could see right through me and into my mind. Gripping the armrests next to me, I let myself experience the anxiety. I sit with it, like Dr. Glen advises. "Don't feed into it, but don't fight it," she always tells me.

At least Dylan will probably mistake my anxiety for fear

of this terrible movie.

When the film ends, we all walk out to the parking lot, everyone discussing the plot. It must've rained because the pavement is wet, the parking lot lights reflecting off the puddles in the darkness. I keep to myself as I trail behind a bit, wishing Dylan would tag along with me, but he's up with Adam.

When we say bye, he hugs me and tells me it was nice to meet me. *That's it?*

Defeated, I climb into the backseat of Brenda's car so she can drive us home.

"So you and Dylan seemed to have hit it off, April," Jade says.

"Yeah, I thought we did, too. But he didn't ask for my number."

"Maybe he was shy or something," Lindsay offers from the seat next to me, her face highlighted by her phone screen. Is she being nice to me?

"I wish I had your problem. I gave James the wrong number when he asked for mine," Brenda says, eyes on the road.

"Brenda!" Jade yells.

Turning back in her chair to face Lindsay, Jade says, "Kalvin sure seemed to enjoy your company." She nods and stares at her phone. "Are you already texting him?!"

"Yup. We're meeting up when I get home."

"Get it, girl," Brenda says.

"Am I the only one who didn't get a number tonight?" I ask, my heart sinking. I peer out the window, at the cottage-style houses along the road.

"Oh my God! April!" Jade says, whipping her head around from the passenger seat to face me. "Look what Adam just texted me!"

I grab her cell. "Dylan's kicking himself for not getting April's number," I read aloud.

"There you go," Brenda says, smiling.

I beam and send Adam my number to give to Dylan, my heart jumping into my throat. I *knew* there was some unspoken connection between us.

"It's still early. Wanna ask the guys to go to the diner or something?" Jade asks.

"Yes!" I say too loudly. Maybe this time I can actually have a conversation with Dylan.

"I'm out. I can't handle another conversation with James about his stupid frat," Brenda says.

"And Kalvin's meeting me at my house," Lindsay says, sticking her tongue out.

We all laugh, and Jade calls Adam to make the plans with him and Dylan. After Brenda drops us at Jade's house, Jade drives us to the diner.

We get a booth for four, sitting on opposite sides, and wait for the guys to arrive. When they do, Dylan slides in next to me in the booth, our legs brushing. He smells like beer.

"Did you guys drink?" Jade asks, sniffing the air. Adam puts his arm around her, and Dylan just looks down at the table.

The waiter comes around a few minutes later, a tired-looking guy probably in his mid-20s. He doesn't even hold a pen or pad, just nods as he takes our orders. I decide on disco fries and a cheese quesadilla.

"Damn, girl," Adam says, leaning back against the red booth cushions and crossing his arms as he snickers.

"*What?* Being scared made me hungry!"

Dylan laughs. I can feel his eyes on me, and when I look over at him, he opens his mouth like he wants to say something, but doesn't.

My stomach is doing flips. I can't tell if it's anxiety or excitement or what, but—wait, *of course* it's anxiety. *That's* what I felt when I read Jenny's post about Tristan. *Not* excitement. *Anxiety.*

*Right?*

"Hell-ohhhh." Jade's voice snaps me back. I look up to see everyone staring at me.

"What? Sorry."

"I said, I'm wearing sapphire blue to prom, so don't buy a

dress that color, 'kay?"

"It's a little far in advance, don't you think?" I don't have the time or energy to think about prom right now. It's months away. I barely have the time or energy to register what is happening in this very moment, with all the noise in my mind. It's like my brain is a police radio, and I'm the main suspect, the object of discussion for every single crime reported.

"It's never too early. It's *senior prom*."

I hold my hands up like I'm guilty. It's an instinct.

Dylan types something on his phone before placing it on the table and turning to me. "So, have you started looking at colleges yet?"

"Yup," I say. "So stressful."

"Which ones are you looking at?"

"Well, Boston University is my top choice," I tell him, then instantly regret it. That's nearly a three-hour drive from here. "And some other schools here in Connecticut."

He nods his head. "What do you wanna study?"

My lips curl into a smile. "Journalism. I want to be an investigative journalist."

"Wow. That's so...specific." He eyes me, his eyes sparkling as they gaze over my face. "What made you interested in that?"

His question catches me off guard. Usually, people just tell me reporting is a dead-end industry with horrible pay. As if I'd pursue a career solely for its salary.

"I just want to help people," I say, knowing I could never explain the extent of it. How the desire to *do more* and *be better* burns inside me every day. I run my fingers up and down my glass of water. "What do *you* study?"

"I'm undecided." He leans his elbow on the table and rests his chin on it, looking at me. "Soccer was always my priority. I was never really interested in anything else. But I'll figure it out."

"I used to play too, in middle school."

"Nice, what position?"

"Striker."

Dylan smiles. "No shit, me too."

"How long have you played?" I ask him.

"Since I could walk."

"Do you want to go pro, or is it kinda just a hobby?"

He hesitates.

"I wish."

Taking a sip of his water, he looks down at his phone, texting someone again.

Our waiter walks up with our food, and I'm glad for the distraction. As we eat, Jade talks more about prom and, of course, prom weekend. I wonder if Dylan will be my date. I mean, that's months from now. But I guess, as Jade said, it's never too early to start planning.

As we leave the diner, Dylan and I stop by Jade's car while she and Adam walk to his. The parking lot is full of cars, despite how late it is. I glance up at the two of them kissing bye under the streetlight, then tug on the ends of my sleeves.

"So...sorry for being an idiot earlier and getting your number from Adam," Dylan offers. "I didn't want to make it weird if you weren't, you know..."

I smile. "It's okay. As long as you have it now."

Again, he looks like he's contemplating telling me something. But before he can, Jade skips back over to us and jumps on me, her arm around my neck. "Alright, lovebirds! Time to part!"

"We should hang out sometime," Dylan tells me. "Maybe I can hear more about your plans to end crime."

"I might have to get my degree first," I joke.

As Jade and I get into her car, I'm a bit lighter. I'm happy I forced myself out tonight. My mom always tells me that even when you don't feel like doing whatever it is you're being asked to do, you should say yes to the plans. "You'll always be glad you went," she says.

I'm starting to think that maybe she's right. Because by the time I get home, I already have a message from Dylan—and by the time the sun bleeds in from behind my blinds, we have plans to meet for coffee next weekend. And I've only Googled *schadenfreude* once.

# CHAPTER 4

My stomach starts to hurt as I sit in my car outside Dr. Glen's house/office. Parked next to me in her driveway is a maroon Jeep that I recognize from every session.

I don't know the girl who owns it, mostly because we both keep our heads down as we pass each other each week. I don't know her story or her diagnosis or even the color of her eyes, but that doesn't really matter. She's here when I'm here every single week, which means she's probably just as messed up as I am.

*Is it wrong to find comfort in that?*

A few minutes later, the girl walks out, and I take it as my cue to head inside.

Dr Glen's office is a small room in the front of her house, and it smells like lemongrass and lavender, which is supposed to calm you down, but just makes me dizzy. Maybe I'm beyond help.

"Hello, April." Dr. Glen smiles as I settle onto her soft pink couch. She takes a seat on her usual chair, legs folded, facing me. "How's everything been?"

I force a small smile and shrug. "Okay, I guess. A lot happened this week."

She nods like she expected to hear that, encouraging me to go on. My hands shake on my lap.

I can't just put my thoughts out there, into the universe. It might make them true. And I mean, what if it comes out wrong, and she thinks poorly of me and doesn't want to help me anymore?

But she just waits for me to talk, and I can't handle silence.

"One of my classmates is missing," I mutter, avoiding eye contact.

Dr. Glen takes off her glasses and shakes her head. "Oh, April. I'm so sorry." She pauses, and I look down at my Converse, unsure of what to say next. "What's going through your mind?"

"I didn't really know him." That's a lie, but at least she won't pity me so much. I don't deserve sympathy.

"That doesn't mean you can't be affected by it. Especially a caring person like you."

*A caring person.* My stomach clenches at the compliment. "But that's the thing…" I start to explain. "It's like I—" My voice gets caught in my throat as I begin to cry.

Dr. Glen doesn't know who I really am. She only knows what I tell her. Sugar-coated versions of my character. If she heard my thoughts, she wouldn't be saying anything positive about me.

"What if I wanted it to happen?" My voice sounds like it came from someone else. It's so far away, so detached from the girl sitting on this sofa. Because, *God,* I would never want such a terrible thing to happen.

*Right?*

I glance up at Dr. Glen for reassurance. Her head is tilted, and I think she's judging me, even though she's not supposed to.

"That came out wrong," I say.

"What makes you think you wanted it to happen?" she asks.

"I don't know…I got this, like, rush. When I found out. Or, not rush, really. I don't know what it was. I don't know how to explain it."

Dr. Glen adjusts her glasses back on her face and watches me for a moment, waiting. She does this sometimes, making sure I don't have more to say. I *always* have more to say.

"I felt like I was excited, but I wasn't! I don't think so, at least. I would never want something like that to happen. But, I don't know, there was this feeling inside me…that convinced me that I *did* want it to happen. But I *don't*. Tristan was—*is*—a

great person, and I'm honestly really worried about him. I just—
I don't know why I had that feeling."

I lean my head back and stare at the ceiling, tightening my
ponytail and preparing for impending doom as tears run down
my cheeks.

Hearing it out loud confirms my suspicions: I'm a horrible
person.

"Take some deep breaths" is all Dr. Glen says.

*Now is not the time for breathing exercises*, I want to tell her.

It's like I'm at a standstill. I can't see a way past this, if
what I said is true. I'm stuck, and any forward movements will
be tainted, because *I'm* tainted. And there's just no changing
that.

"You want to be an investigative journalist, right?" Dr.
Glen asks me.

I sit up slowly and look at her. *What does that have to do
with anything?* "Yes…"

"Did you ever consider that maybe that 'rush' you're re-
ferring to is really the desire to help?"

"What do you mean?"

"Well, OCD can misinterpret signals. Or manipulate their
meanings."

The knot in my gut loosens a bit. "Really?"

She shrugs. "It's possible."

"But why would I get, like, excited about something like
that?" She gives me a look, knowing not to give me the answer I
so desperately need.

"Don't put more meaning to your thoughts. You need to
let them exist without judgment."

"So, you don't think I'm a bad person?"

"I don't know, April. What defines 'a bad person' anyway?"

I audibly sigh, arms folded. I can't help but be annoyed.
She's not making this much better. Aren't therapists supposed
to *help*?

"You know I can't reassure you, April. Feel the discomfort
and wait for it to pass. You know it will."

"Yeah, in a few years, maybe."

She raises her eyebrows at me. "I'm serious! That's how long some of these obsessions last. I mean, look at my vomiting phobia. We've been working on that since I was ten."

"And you've made significant improvement by doing your exposures."

Exposures. Yeah, because I just *love* spending my evenings watching videos of people throwing up, in hopes that it'll desensitize me.

"But I don't even know if this is OCD. Maybe I'm just..." I don't know what to call myself. There are no words to describe how shitty I am.

I take my glasses off and dab my wet eyes with the sleeve of my sweater.

"I know it's hard," Dr. Glen continues, her voice muffled in my ears as she drains on about not giving up.

But I'm in another world, stuck in my mind. And I might as well be missing, too

\*   \*   \*

As much as I want to go home after therapy, I can't. It's obvious I've been crying, and if my parents see, they'll want to talk. And if we talk, I'll have to either explain to them what's going on, or I'll have to lie, both of which will only make me feel worse.

So instead, I drive to the bookstore. I'm in need of an escape, and reading fiction is the only way I know how to do that. This is my version of retail therapy.

I roll my windows down to cool off and blast *Mosaic* by Cartel, my go-to song when I feel like I've lost all my strength. It's only 6 p.m., but it's already starting to get dark outside. The sky is golden.

*I'm still standing, holding on,*
*stripped of all these chains you've put on.*
*I'm still young,*
*Oh, I'm still free.*
*You haven't got the best of me.*

I sing along, harmonizing with the lead singer. A strange mix of emotions overcomes me. Guilt, anxiety, exhaustion, but also a little bit of hope.

My dad once told me the right music can save your life. I figured that as a music history professor, he had to say that, had to believe in its power and importance in the world. But I have a playlist dedicated to bad days like today, filled with songs that have impacted my life somehow, taught me valuable lessons and made me feel less alone. And, as always, it turns out my dad was right.

I park my car on the street and flip down the mirror so I can see the damage from my therapy session. My eyes are blood-shot and swollen.

*Great.* Maybe I should just sit in the lot and listen to my music, rather than risk running into someone like this. That's the bad part about small towns: you can't avoid people you know.

But then I remember that the next murder mystery novel in the series I've been reading just came out this week, and my mind's made up.

As soon as I walk into the bookstore, I order a coffee at the small cafe in the corner, the same one that first got me hooked on caffeine. Back in middle school, my dad used to take me here every Sunday to shop and grab a cup, as long as I didn't tell my mom, who suspected caffeine was the root of my "anxiety issues." You know, not a chemical imbalance or trauma or anything.

I head over to my usual mystery section in the back of the store to look for the novel as I sip, instantly feeling the coffee's warmth like a hug from a friend.

To get a better look at the titles, I step back from the shelf and accidentally bump into someone.

"Oh my God, I'm so sorry," I say as I whip around. A familiar-looking guy with brown skin and curly black hair steadies me, his hand on my shoulder.

"You're good," he says. "Oh, hey. April, right?"

"Yeah, hi!" The more I look at him, his light brown eyes and the tattoos covering his arms, the more I remember him. I don't know his name, and I've never spoken to him, but he definitely went to school with me. I think I even follow him on Instagram.

I must look confused, because he says, "I'm Zach. I graduated from Haddon High last year."

"Right! Actually, I think we had lunch together."

"Yeah, sixth period."

I nod. I sat with Jade and some random senior guys she was flirting with at the time. Zach sat a few tables away with some kids from my grade. With—

*Oh.*

"You were friends with Tristan."

He hesitates, then nods slowly. And I realize I said *were* instead of *are,* like he's dead or something.

"Sorry, I didn't mean—I meant you *are* friends with him. Or you *were* in high school. But, like you said, you graduated. So, now, I don't know…if you still *are* friends with him. Is what I meant."

He looks at me with a blank face. Why am I so terrible at conversations?

"We still are," he says.

"Oh, well, that's good. I'm glad. I don't really know him that well," I continue, and I know I'm going too far, but I can't stop talking. "I mean, I *know* him. We've had classes together. And we used to talk a lot. In the classes, I mean. But we've never hung out outside of school."

He blinks at me. "Well, he definitely knew you."

"What do you mean?"

He shrugs, then turns to the bookshelf behind me and starts organizing some books. I notice the lanyard around his neck, holding a name tag. He works here? I know every employee in this bookstore, including the baristas. I mean, it's practically my second home. But I've never seen Zach here.

"Did you just start working here?" I ask him.

"Yup."

"Oh. Nice."

My cheeks flush as I turn my attention back to the books and their brightly-colored spines, trying to busy myself instead of making small talk with someone I barely know.

But his being here must be fate, somehow. A sign that I need to help Tristan. I've never had a conversation with Zach in my life, and now suddenly I'm running into him just days after his best friend went missing?

I have to talk to him. Find out more about the situation. *Help* him. But how?

The store is suddenly really hot. I push the sleeves of my sweater up and hope I don't start sweating.

"Do you need help finding something?" Zach asks me.

"Oh, uh...Actually, I was just—I wanted to ask you about..."

He raises his eyebrows.

"Tristan," I say.

Zach looks away, then bends down in front of the shelf to stuff more books in place. "What about him?"

"Do you think he's...okay? I'm sorry, I'm just really worried."

Zach glances up at me, his face softening. He stands back up and sighs. "I wish I had an answer, but I don't know any more than you do."

"What do you mean?"

"I haven't really seen him. He worked full-time for his dad all summer."

"Oh."

"I mean, we talked here and there, but...I don't know. Ever since his mom died, his dad's needed a lot more help with business. This summer was busy I guess."

I remember when Tristan's mom passed away. We were sophomores. I was sitting in the counselor's office when he found out, trying to calm my breathing after a brutal panic attack. My heart was just beginning to slow as Tristan and Jenny walked in. They were both pale and stiff, like they knew something bad was coming. They walked into one of the counselor's rooms, who asked them to shut the door behind them. I could just make out the words "bad accident" and "didn't make it." But I heard Jenny's sobbing from my seat. It made me so uncomfortable that I began to cry, too.

When they finally walked out, Tristan had his arm around Jenny's shoulder, guiding her as she hyperventilated. With tears in my eyes, I glanced up at him. He met my eyes for just a few seconds. His were bright green and bloodshot, but he wasn't crying. He made his lips into a tight, sad smile before looking away.

I wanted to follow both of them out, put my arms around them, be the strong one so he could break down, the way he needed to in that moment. I know he needed to. But I couldn't get my legs to move or stop my hands from shaking. I was useless.

"He'll be okay," Zach reassures me, as if *I'm* the one who has the right to mourn.

# CHAPTER 5

"April, I swear to God, if you bail, I'm gonna kill you," Jade says over the phone.

My car hums as it sits in front of the coffee shop where I'm meeting Dylan. I grip the steering wheel even though it's in park.

"I'm not bailing! I'm already here. I just want *you* here, too."

"Oh my God, you're like...30 minutes early."

I look at the clock on my dashboard and realize she's right.

"Well, I had to get out of the house before my dad found out where I was going. He would've demanded to meet Dylan first."

I made the mistake of telling my mom I had a date this morning while my dad and Greg were raking leaves. Given her excitement, there's no way she won't blab to them. I couldn't risk being around for that..

"Look, I'm not meeting you there, and you should probably drive around a bit so you're not just chilling in your car when he shows up," Jade says.

I groan, leaning back onto the headrest.

"April, really." Her voice is gentler now. "You're gonna be fine, okay? He obviously likes you. Just play it cool."

"I don't know how," I remind her.

She laughs. "Go drive around a bit, until he texts you he's there. It'll distract you. And have fun!"

She hangs up, and I'm left alone with my thoughts again.

I still have over 25 minutes before Dylan is supposed to be here. I don't want to leave my parking spot, because it's the only one that didn't require me to parallel park, and now I'm boxed in thanks to the stupid Mazda behind me.

This shouldn't be so scary. But my heart's racing like it's about to burst its way out of my throat. Can you pass out from anxiety?

I go inside at 6:50 to get us a table in the far corner by a large window which overlooks the rest of the downtown. The cafe is warm and cozy, fairy lights strung across the ceiling. I take out my new mystery novel to try to relax my nerves, but the book only makes me think about running into Zach at the store, which reminds me of Tristan, which sprouts another level of anxiety in the pit of my stomach.

Now is not the time to think about him. Later, yes. But not now.

Instead of reading, I text Kat: Waiting for Dylan...I'm panicking!!!

In response, she sends me every lyric to *First Date* by Blink 182, one line at a time. I laugh as my phone buzzes with text after text. Kat gets me. She has since the day we met freshman year, when she calmed me down from a bathroom cry session and fixed my makeup without asking any questions. We ended up having lunch together that year, which was both a coincidence and a blessing. No one wants to eat lunch alone as a freshman, but everyone else already had their groups, aside from Jade and me, who transferred from private to public. But Jade was good at making friends, and I was good at hiding in bathroom stalls and ruining the winged eyeliner I spent hours trying to perfect that same morning.

Right now is a lot like how my freshman lunch would've been without Kat: me, party of one. It's 7:20, and Dylan still isn't here.

I'm definitely being stood up. Of course, I am. I should've known this would happen.

I'm about to collect my things and save my pride when I see him walk in. He's wearing dark jeans and a black and white flannel, and he smiles when he sees me.

"Hey," he says as I stand up to hug him. He smells so nice I don't want to let go. "Sorry I'm late. There's so much construction on campus right now. It takes, like, 30 minutes to get anywhere."

He asks if I got anything to drink yet, and I tell him I didn't, so we order and he insists on paying for me. The barista hands us mugs the size of soup bowls.

When we sit back down at the table, Dylan shifts around, and I can sense his awkwardness like my own.

*Great, I guess we both suck at this.*

I think about what to say. What do you even talk about on a first date? I've never had one. Just group hangouts. Or casual one-on-ones that definitely weren't this stressful. If it wasn't for Jade forcing me, I wouldn't even be here.

"It's so shitty out," Dylan says, looking out the window at the fog.

"I know. I love it." I take a sip of my hazelnut coffee. It burns my tongue and I try my best not to make a face.

He raises his eyebrows, smirking. "You love it?"

"Yes! Cloudy weather is the best."

"That's interesting. Never heard of someone who prefers clouds over sun."

I open my mouth to explain myself, how I'm more comforted by dreary days than bright ones, which breed too many expectations. But then I realize we're talking about the *weather*. On the first date.

"So…" I say, scraping my fingernail on the handle of my mug. "How was your week?"

"It was okay. Classes sucked. Soccer was fun. My little sister's birthday was yesterday, so I took her out for ice cream, which was cool."

My heart practically melts. "How old is she?"

"Seven."

"Are you guys close?"

"As close as we can be." He takes a long sip of his coffee. "Do you have any siblings?"

"Yes, a super overprotective brother who's four years

older than me and likes to remind me of it every second. But I'm sure you know how that goes."

"Why would I know?"

I pause. "Because you have a younger sister."

"Oh, right."

I look around to make sure no one I know from school is here to witness this.

"Hey, you should come watch one of my pickup soccer games sometime," Dylan tells me, and I'm thankful for the change in conversation. "We play every Tuesday at 5:30. Maybe you can come this week with Jade. She's been a few times before."

I'm about to tell him I have therapy every Tuesday at 5, but that's probably not something you should mention on a first date. "Yeah, that'd be awesome!" I say, already thinking up excuses to tell Dr. Glen.

"Cool." He smiles as he looks back outside. It's starting to rain. "Wanna get out of here? We can go to my apartment and watch a movie or something."

"Sure," I tell him, even though my mind is screaming at me to say no. "But no scary movies."

Dylan's apartment is on-campus. It looks like what I'd imagine any dorm would look like: red solo cups on the ground, fast food wrappers piling out of a small garbage, which is lined with a plastic grocery bag. A tall guy with blonde hair comes out of the bathroom as Dylan's giving me a tour. He's not wearing a shirt, just basketball shorts and Nike socks. He looks wasted.

"Oh shit, my bad. Didn't know we had company," he mutters. He walks into his room before I can even introduce myself. When he opens his door, it smells like a skunk.

"Sorry...he's pretty stoned," Dylan laughs and scratches the back of his head. "Lemme show you my room."

I'm surprised when I walk in. The room is actually pretty clean. I mean, there's a pile of laundry on the floor, but at least it's folded. He even made his bed. Did he expect me to come over tonight?

"What do you wanna watch?" Dylan asks as he plops onto his bed and turns on the TV. He loads Netflix.

I grin. "Oh, I have the perfect show."

He throws me the remote without a question, so I put on *One Tree Hill*, picking up where I left off last night. I'm a sucker for feel-good shows. Plus, I need something sappy to fall asleep to after all the crime stories I read about. And all the dark thoughts that occupy my mind.

"Come on!" he says, laughing. "I pegged you as a *Game of Thrones* type."

"You were way off," I say, sitting next to him on his bed. I lean back against the wall, my heart slamming against my chest.

I look around Dylan's room for a distraction, and for hints of his personal life. Despite how much I like hanging out with him, I still have a lot to learn about him.

There's a T-shirt pinned to his wall. It has a soccer ball on the front and "flight champions" written across it. He has a mini fridge in the corner. A wooden anchor on the back wall. A small ocean breeze candle on his night stand. A picture on his desk of him with some guy at what looks like a soccer game, but none with his parents or little sister.

I glance back over at Dylan, who's watching me, his cheeks tinted pink.

"What?" I ask, letting out a laugh.

"Nothing." He looks back at the TV, but I can tell he's not actually paying attention to the show. "You're just...cute."

"You're funny."

He turns back to me. "Why am I funny?" I shrug, hugging my legs against my chest. Dylan bumps me with his shoulder. "I was serious."

I roll my eyes playfully, but really I just don't know how to respond to compliments. "Well...thank you."

"Well...you're welcome." He grins at me in a way that makes my chest ache. "As soon as I saw you at the theater, I was like, 'Whoa. That girl is beautiful.'"

"Really?" I ask.

"Yes, really."

"Even with the other girls there?"

I cringe as soon as it comes out of my mouth. I don't want to be *that girl*. The one who obsessively compares herself to other girls, as if there's some sort of competition. *How superficial can I be?*

Dylan places his hand over mine on the bed, and it sends chills up my arms.

"I didn't even notice anyone else when I saw you."

He starts to trace circles on the back of my hand, and everything around me goes quiet. We're shoulder-to-shoulder, our faces inches apart. He peers at me and purses his lips together. I break into a nervous smile.

"You're adorable," he whispers, grinning. He runs his other hand through my hair, tucking a strand behind my ear. I really want him to kiss me. I really want to kiss him.

But then the shrill sound of the fire alarm practically sends me over the edge of the bed.

"Ah, shit..." His roommate says outside Dylan's door. "My bad. I just wanted to warm up some pizza."

Dylan bursts out laughing, and I lean into him like it's so normal.

"That scared the crap out of me," he says, his arms around me as I sink into his chest, my palm hiding my face. He pulls back and grabs my hand, tugging me up with him off the bed. "We should probably get out of here."

Dylan opens his bedroom door, and I have to cover my nose to block the smell of smoke as he leads me through the kitchen. His roommate is standing in front of the stove, scratching his head and staring at the oven like he doesn't understand how it happened.

"Dude, you better hide your shit. You know they're gonna check our entire apartment now," Dylan yells as we race out.

*Um. I can't get in trouble for being in an apartment where there's weed, can I? If I wasn't even the one smoking it?*

"I should probably get back home," I tell Dylan as we step downstairs to the parking lot.

"Oh—yeah, of course. No problem."

It's dark outside, and groups of kids are crowding on the sidewalk by the apartment, pissed at the inconvenience. I can't help but feel like it's my fault somehow.

As we get into Dylan's car, he starts the ignition, looking over at me like he's conflicted. I turn away from him. He starts driving and places his hand on my knee as if we've been a couple for months already and it's just something we do.

I really don't want to go home right now. But my dad will send a search party if I'm out late with a guy he doesn't even know. I'm sure by now my mom told him where I was.

Dylan doesn't say anything the entire rest of the drive, so I look out the window and panic about what's going to happen when we get back to my car.

I've never felt like this before. That's so cliché, and I hate clichés, but it's true. I've talked to guys before. I've kissed guys before. At the movies. In their bedroom. At my locker before class.

But those moments don't compare to now. I could never get my mind to shut up enough to let me enjoy being with someone. I always overthought what would come next. The expectations. The commitments. *Sex*. It freaked me out.

But I'm not freaked out with Dylan. I'm not worried about what's to come of this. I'm more worried that *nothing* will come of it. Because how can someone like Dylan be interested in someone like *me*?

I place my hand on top of his as he pulls up behind my car. It's dark outside, and there aren't as many people around as before because all the shops are closing soon.

When he parks, he immediately pulls his hand away and gets out. I'm not sure what to think of that, but I follow him.

He walks me to my car, even though it's just in front of his, and I feel like I'm spinning because I have no idea what to do or what's gonna happen or what he's thinking or if he even had fun today or—

Dylan grabs my hand as I reach for the keys in my pocket. I spin around to face him.

The streetlights are dim, and it's hard to see his expression. My heart is beating so fast that I'm shaking. I lean back on my car for support as Dylan steps toward me, closing the gap between us. He combs my hair behind my ear and leans in.

It's just a kiss. A slow yet short kiss. A respectful, first-date, walk-her-to-her-car kinda kiss. But it's the best kiss I've ever had.

Dylan breaks away and smiles at me, his face illuminated by the lampposts lining the street. It's cold for early October, the air still damp from earlier. I can see my breath as I exhale, and I'm not wearing a heavy jacket, but I don't care. I don't want to leave this spot. I don't want to leave Dylan.

He opens his mouth to speak, but before he can say goodnight, I tug him back toward me by his shirt, pressing my lips to his again.

For a moment, he seems surprised. But then he presses me back against the car, which is still wet from the rain, and puts his hands on either side of me.

He tastes like spearmint and coffee. He feels like long drives and Saturday nights. An escape. An adventure. One I never want to end.

Dylan steps backwards after a few moments, creating space between us as I try to catch my breath.

"You should probably get home," he tells me. His voice is barely above a whisper.

I nod, looking past him at the downtown where the sidewalk is mostly empty, wet leaves stuck to the ground. A few girls around my age are bundled in winter coats, sipping cups of coffee as they walk along the strip. I wish Dylan and I could do that right now, instead of parting ways. But I don't want Greg or my dad to freak out. I have to get home before they file a missing person's report.

My stomach immediately clenches like a fist as I finish

that thought. *Stupid joke.*

"You good?"

I look up at Dylan, whose voice snaps me back to the present.

"What?"

"You look like you're lost in thought or something."

"I'm here," I tell him, grabbing his hand loosely.

Dylan smiles. "I want to see you again."

"Tuesday?"

"You'll really come?"

I swear he's glowing in the darkness. "Of course, I will."

He opens my door for me, and I can tell he doesn't want me to go either.

"Text me when you're home safe, okay?" he says.

"I will."

He gets into his car as I drive away, and I can't help but think how lonely he looks when he isn't surrounded by other people. Isn't next to me. The way his head hangs low and his shoulder slump.

As I pull up to my house a few minutes later, back to the reality of my own world, I can't help but feel that same way.

I'm alone with my thoughts again.

Even after the perfect night, at the end of the day, you really only have yourself. And when you're not happy with who you are, that can be pretty daunting.

# CHAPTER 6

Tristan doesn't live far from me. I know this because Kat's house is only a street over from his, and I've seen him outside helping his dad multiple times while driving to her place.

His house looks the same as usual. White with a stone porch. Dark blue shutters and a black door, which always bothered me. The door should match the shutters.

I shake my head at this trivial quirk, one society would use to deem me "OCD." If only the disorder was as simple as everyone thought.

I don't know what I'm doing here, standing frozen on the sidewalk on a Sunday evening. It isn't my place to pry, and I don't want to elicit any more negative feelings—this family's already been through enough.

But before I can change my mind, I step toward the driveway and walk up to the porch, feeling like I'm trespassing in the darkness. I pause before closing the gap between me and the door, taking a deep breath.

I suck at this stuff. I can barely strike up a conversation with someone I know. I'm the girl who sees a classmate in the store and avoids contact at all costs, ducking down aisles and pretending to be occupied.

But what kind of journalist would I be if I shied away from a source?

"Can I help you?"

I whip around at the sound of a girl's voice.

Jenny eyes me, standing next to the open garage door. I must not have heard her walk out while I was stuck in my head, contemplating my next move. I can be completely oblivious to my surroundings in moments like these.

"Uh, hi!" I say, my voice rushed. "I'm sorry, I was about to knock. I'm April. Uh, April Valentini? I was friends with Tristan. I wanted to see if I could maybe talk to you...about him."

Jenny's eyes widen. There's a flash of hope in them that makes me cringe. "Do you know something? Did you see him?"

I bite my lip and shake my head slowly.

"No, I just—we had a few classes together." I really should've rehearsed what I was going to say. "I can't stop thinking about him, and your family, and I just wanted to see if I could help, somehow."

I realize how stupid I sound. I'm acting like I have the credibility of a seasoned private investigator, when I haven't even graduated from high school yet.

Jenny sighs, her shoulders sagging. Turning from me, she unlocks and opens the back door of her red Honda Civic tosses what seems to be an overnight bag inside.

"You shouldn't be here," she says, her back still facing me.

"I'm sorry. I just—"

"Look." She spins around and meets my eye. Her face is drawn and she looks tired, like she hasn't slept in days. I remember feeling that way when all my issues started. I remember living in sheer panic.

"I—we have enough going on here as it is. I appreciate that you're his friend and all, but unless you know something, then please just go home."

*Ouch.*

"I'm really sorry. I can't imagine what you're going through," I say, though I think I might have an idea. "The last thing I want is to make matters worse for your or your dad."

I brush past her and make my way to my car, hands in the pockets of my army green parka.

"Wait," she says. I look back at her from the end of the driveway, cautious. "I don't mean to come off as rude. I'm sorry. Tristan always spoke highly of you."

I stare at her blankly. "He did?"

"Yeah," she says, slamming her car door. She looks at me before getting into the driver's seat. "I'll keep you updated, if I hear anything. And you do the same?"

"Of course."

Her smile doesn't quite meet her eyes.

"See you around, April."

She says it like she's so sure, despite enduring the loss of her mom and now her brother. She says it like the future is promised. Like it can't be stopped in its tracks at any moment.

# CHAPTER 7

I cancel my therapy appointment without telling my parents. They think I'm going there and then to Jade's to work on a project.

With the amount of shame I feel, you'd think I physically assaulted them. But I try to remind myself that I'm just being a typical high school senior. Lying to your parents is bound to happen from time to time, especially if you're choosing to hang out with college guys instead of attending your much-needed therapy session.

I know my mom wouldn't care. In fact, she'd probably encourage it. All she wants is for me to be "normal." But her gossiping tendencies are too much of a risk.

Jade picks me up on the way to the game because I hate driving places I don't know well. I walk to her car with my head down, avoiding eye contact.

"Heyyyyy!" Jade says as I slide into the passenger seat. She smells like expensive perfume and sweet hairspray.

"Hey. You look cute," I tell her, tucking a loose strand of hair behind my ear. I decided to French braid it since my hair doesn't handle windy nights like tonight well, but now I'm second-guessing it. Jade's hair is bouncy and full of volume, and I look like a little girl at a slumber party.

"Thanks, so do you!"

Jade shuffles show tunes and sings softly as we drive to the campus, which is only about fifteen minutes away. This kind of music always puts me in a weird mood, but I'd never tell her that. Music taste is so personal. It's not just the style, it's the lyrics and the memories and the emotions that come with it, and the artists you identify with. Criticizing someone for that is like taking jabs at who they are as a person.

Plus, music is music. I appreciate it in every form. Even the kind that makes me want to rip my hair out.

"Oh, I forgot to tell you!" Jade says as she turns down the volume a bit. "There's this bar right off-campus that has wing night every Tuesday. I've gone, like, three times already and never been carded. Do you wanna go after the game?"

"Wait, but how would you drive us home?"

"I'm not gonna drink a lot! We'll legit just go for some food and, like, a beer or something. That's all. And I'll obviously wait until I'm totally sober to drive."

I swallow hard. I just wanna stick to our original plans. Is that so hard to do?

It's not that I haven't drank before. A few months after Greg turned 21, he bought me a bottle of wine and let me drink some in his room while watching *The Bachelor* finale because I'd had a bad day.

But I've never actually been *served* as a minor.

I turn away from Jade to look out the window and take a few deep breaths. I can't afford to get in trouble with the law when I'm applying to colleges. Especially when my future career *involves* the law.

"Soooo?" Jade asks. "Is that a yes?"

I look down at what I'm wearing: leggings and a chunky maroon sweater with combat boots. Meanwhile, Jade's in tight jeans, a bell-sleeved crop top, and over-the-knee boots, totally dressed for the occasion

"I don't know, Jade. I just—"

"Don't worry, April! I swear we won't get caught. Adam literally goes every week, and he's not 21 yet."

It's suddenly really hot in the car. Why is the heat on full blast? I shift in my seat and point the vents away from me.

"Here, I'll turn it off," Jade says, spinning the dial so that no air blows out.

"So?" she asks after a few moments. "Pleeeaaaaase, April."

I can feel her eyes on me as I stare at the road ahead.

"Fine, I'll go."

She squeals and swerved the car a bit, and I grab on the door handle for support. What have I gotten myself into? This girl can barely drive *sober*.

When we pull up to the school, Jade parks in Adam and Dylan's apartment lot, which is packed with cars. There are tons of people out, taking walks in sweatshirts and throwing footballs or frisbees in the grass under stadium lights.

A group of girls in tiny workout shorts pass by. Aren't they freezing? It's, like, forty-five degrees out. *I'm* cold, and I just suffered a hot flash for the last ten minutes.

The soccer field is directly behind Dylan's apartment. When we show up, the boys are doing drills, passing the ball around. Their voices echo off the campus buildings. We take a seat on the grass near the team's water bottles and bags on the sidelines, and I wonder which is Dylan's.

"What are you smiling about?" Jade asks, stretching her legs out and flexing her feet back and forth. She leans back on her hands, raising her eyebrows at me.

I hug my knees to my chest. "Shuddup," I tell her, still grinning. I scan the group for Dylan under the bright lights. "I seriously feel like I'm a freshman who just had her first kiss."

"I can't relate. I had my first kiss in fifth grade."

Rolling my eyes, I say, "You know what I mean. I'm just really excited."

"Well, good. You should be. He's awesome, and you're awesome, and you both have that mysterious vibe about you..."

I laugh. "What are you talking about?"

"Nothing." She smirks and leans her head on my shoulder, and I think about all of the times we did this growing up. Sitting on the playground in elementary school watching the boys play basketball. Sitting at eighth grade graduation feeling both giddy and nervous. Sitting on the bus our freshman year of high school, terrified of our new school. So much has changed since those moments, but through it all, I've always had Jade. She's my constant.

"There's my girl!" Adam says when the boys jog over to their bags and bottles. Jade jumps up and kisses him like he just came home from war.

I stand up and pretend to be busy on my phone while I wait for Dylan, my stomach in knots.

"Hi," he says when he sees me. He pulls me in for a hug, wearing a baggy T-shirt and shorts. It might just be my favorite look on him.

"You guys excited to get wasted after this?" Adam asks us, squirting water into his mouth from a Gatorade squeeze bottle.

"Yessss!" Jade says.

"I thought you weren't gonna drink a lot," I say to Jade.

"Hey, why don't you just stay over tonight?" Dylan asks me. "You know, so you don't have to worry about driving home or anything."

"I can't," I say instinctively, ignoring the leap of excitement in my chest. "We have school tomorrow."

"So what, it's senior year!" Adam says. "I made my own skips days every week my senior year."

"Seriously, let's ditch!" Jade exclaims. "Just tell your parents you're sleeping at my place."

"But don't they call home if you miss?" I ask.

She shrugs. "We can tell them we both woke up with food poisoning."

*No way.* I'm not about to jinx myself into an entire day of throwing up. Just the thought of it makes me nauseous.

Dylan grabs my hands and intertwines our fingers. "Pleeeaaaase!" He pulls me close to him.

"I wish I could, but I have a test tomorrow!"

A whistle blows, and the guys jog back onto the field to start their game. Jade and I sit down on the grass. The air is damp and cold, so I cuddle in my sweater, wishing I had a warm coffee.

"You don't really have a test tomorrow." Jade says it like a statement, her voice flat. I don't answer, because it wasn't a question.

She sighs. She picks at blades of grass, pouting. "Well, I'm staying," she says after a few minutes of silence.

*What?* "But you're my ride," I remind her, as if she forgot. "You're gonna make me hitchhike home?"

"Don't be dramatic. I'm sure Kat will get you. Or Greg."

"Greg will murder me if he knew I lied to hang out with college guys."

She shrugs, snapping her gum and watching the game. "You won't have to worry about that if you'd just stay."

I chew on the inside of my lip as my heart rate picks up. I can't even think straight. My thoughts are all tangled up.

*Why did I come here in the first place?* I shouldn't have skipped therapy. I shouldn't have lied to my parents. I shouldn't have agreed to drinking after the game.

"April, I'm obviously not gonna make you get a ride home," Jade tells me. "But I really want to stay, and I really wish you would. I know you want to. I could see it in your face when Dylan asked you. When are you gonna let yourself have fun?"

"What do you mean?"

"You're a senior in high school! This is, like, a rite of passage."

"What, skipping school to get drunk and sleep with a guy I just met in his college apartment?"

Jade smirks. "Pretty much."

I watch Dylan as he steals the ball from midfield. He does some fancy move to get around the last defender and make his breakaway. Then, he kicks the ball into the upper left corner of the goal.

A group of girls on the other side of the field scream for him, doing little dances and raising red solo cups. "Go, Dyly!" they yell.

I turn back to Jade, who raises her eyebrows.

"You gonna let those sorority girls hang with your guy tonight while you're at home in bed?" She watches me, gauging my reaction.

I can practically feel my blood boil. Is it normal to be this territorial already?

"Fine. But you better cover for me! You know I'm the worst at lying."

She squeals and puts her arm around me, leaning on my shoulder again, but all I can do is stare at the sideline girls who are taking selfies and clearly putting on a show for the guys, like personal cheerleaders. I realize they're the same girls from before, the ones in short-shorts and white sneakers. Seriously, how are they not frostbitten?

At the end of the game, Jade tells Adam and Dylan that we're staying the night, and Dylan's breaks into a smile.

"No way!" he says, running his hands through his hair. It's wet with sweat, but he looks like he just got out of the shower. He's about to pull me in for a hug when someone calls his name.

"Dylan!" I hear a female voice say. I whip my head around and see the sideline girls. The short blonde one waves. "You coming to KPs tonight?" she asks.

"Yeah, I'll see you guys there!" he yells, grinning.

"We better!"

Staring at the ground, digging the front of my boot into the grass, I can feel the awkwardness radiating off my body, and Jade watching me.

"That's my friend," Dylan tells me. "You can meet her to-night."

I smile at him.

"Can't wait."

# CHAPTER 8

It's pitch black outside as we walk to the bar, which is around the corner from the apartment. The only light is coming from the dim and flickering streetlights. Adam and Dylan lead the way, talking about their soccer game next week, how "this team's the one to beat," as Jade and I trail behind on the sidewalk.

"So, you think tonight will be the night you finally-"

"No!" I say before she can finish her sentence. I know exactly what she's asking, and I don't need Dylan to hear. "It's, like, our second date."

"Third, if you count the night you met."

"I don't."

I kick a rock on the sidewalk, and it hits the back of Dylan's shoes, but he doesn't notice. "Drunk sex might actually be good for the first time," Jade tells me. "You'll be more relaxed. As long as he doesn't get whiskey-"

"Jade, stop!" I say, but I can't help but laugh. Lowering my voice, I add, "I don't need alcohol to have sex. I just don't want to rush it, that's all."

"Yeah, I can tell. It's been 17 years."

I roll my eyes, trying not to let her joke get to me. I know she's just messing with me, but it makes me feel like a child.

"It's not like I haven't done other things," I remind her.

"Relax, I'm kidding. God, you're so sensitive."

My legs are wobbly as we approach the front of the bar. Apparently, they don't check IDs at the door, and when we make it to the bar in the middle of the room, Adam and Dylan order drinks for us with their fakes.

"What do you want?" Dylan asks me, his hand on my lower back. The lights are dim and I'm already dizzy. Thank God for the high ceilings, or I'd be too claustrophobic to stay here all night.

"Tequila shots!" Jade screams.

Dylan looks at me, questioning. I shrug.

The guys order six, one each for Jade and me, and two each for them. Dylan grabs one from the bar and reaches over a crowd behind him to hand it to me. There's salt and a piece of lime on the rim of the glass.

I stare at it. It's definitely more than one shot, but whatever. I just hope I can get it down without gagging.

Once the guys collect theirs, they step away from the bar and we hold our glasses up together.

"What are we toasting to?!" Jade yells over the music and mess of voices. But Dylan already took his first shot. He downs the other right after, so I follow suit. Might as well get it over with.

I bite my lime, grimacing mostly at the sourness and not the alcohol itself.

"Wow, that actually went down pretty smooth," I say.

Adam coughs, his face contorted like he's in pain. "That reminds me of bad decisions."

We all laugh, and I lean into Dylan. "So, not to be the only fatass here, but are we still getting wings? 'Cause I'm starving..."

"Same!" Adam yells, and we sit down at a table nearby. We order more alcohol and our food. After devouring my plate of ten honey BBQ wings and most of my margarita, I'm feeling pretty good. Full, content, and a little tipsy.

Dylan's nodding as Adam tells him a story. He looks good. Really good. Way better than any guy I've liked before. They were all immature high schoolers. I am now with a mature college adult.

I laugh to myself. I can see why people enjoy being drunk. It's kinda numbing.

"You good?" Adam asks, and I realize he's looking at me.

"I'm great!"

Just then, a small blonde girl runs up to us and jumps into the booth next to Dylan. She's wearing a tight skirt and a halter top.

"Dylaaaaan!"

I recognize her. She's the same girl from the game.

"Hey, Mandy," Dylan says. He looks happy as she leans into him, highlight sparkling on her cheeks. "Mandy, this is my girl, April."

She glances at me for a split second. "Oh my God, no way! She's so pretty." She says it in a flat tone, like I'm not sitting right here, like I'm just a picture on his Instagram page.

"Isn't she the prettiest?" Jade says, pulling me in for a sideways hug. Her cheek smooshes mine, and I can tell she's trying to intimidate Mandy. But it doesn't work. Her eyes don't leave Dylan.

Mandy bounces in her seat and takes a sip of her pink drink. Why is she so peppy? It's annoying.

"Dylan, take a shot with me?" she asks, placing her hand on his arm.

The way he looks at her, drunk eyes and crooked smile, makes my insides burn like they're on fire.

"I'll be right back," he tells me.

They get up together. He leaves me sitting at the table with Jade and Adam. As he follows her to the bar, I feel like calling Kat to pick me up so I can go home and get away from him. I don't want to watch him take shots with her or flirt with her or whatever he plans on doing for the rest of the night.

But I can't get up. I'm too dizzy. I think I'll stay here until that passes. I don't wanna get sick.

*Crap, did I drink too much?*

"Are you okay, April?" Jade asks, hand on my shoulder.

"I'm fine!" I say. "I'm not even that drunk!"

"No, I mean about Dylan...That was messed up." She glances at Adam, who chugs his beer and avoids eye contact.

"I'm fine," I repeat.

But I do need water. Maybe Dylan could get me a glass if he's at the bar.

"Do you see Dylan?" I ask, standing. *Whoa*, okay, I'm pretty dizzy. "I'm gonna go look for him."

"I'll come with you!" Jade springs up and whispers something to Adam before linking arms with me.

"Do you think we could order water?"

"Are you that drunk?" Jade asks me.

"Not really!" I yell. "I mean, not too drunk. Like, I've been this way before, I think. From wine."

She giggles and plops down on a free stool. "I'm a little tipsy. Those shots were doubles."

"What's so funny?" I look up to see a bulky guy standing over me. He's holding a landshark and is smiling at me. But I'm pretty sure he's trying to get to Jade.

"Oh, she has a boyfriend!" I say, pointing to Jade.

The guy furrows his dark eyebrows. I lean into Jade's shoulder and laugh. "You go to school here?" he asks, still looking at me. He has a football T-shirt on with cargo shorts and flip flops.

I push the sleeves of my sweater up. He was smart to wear a T-shirt. It's really hot in here. "No, I'm in-"

"Community college!" Jade cuts me off. "We go to community. We're thinking about transferring though."

"That's awesome!" he says, keeping eye contact with me. "I'm Matt."

"Hi!" I say, and he stares at me like he's waiting for me to say more. "Oh, I'm April!"

He smiles. "Cute name." He sips his beer as we look around awkwardly. I scan the room for Dylan, but I can't find him anywhere. There are way too many people. And I don't like being around people.

Jade crosses her legs and leans her elbow on the bar. "You okay?" she mouths, her hair falling over her shoulder.

I shrug. The whole room is radiating red and spinning.

"So, if you ever wanna take a tour of the dorms or anything, I'd be happy to show you around," Matt yells over the voices and music. He's leaning so close to my face that I can smell the alcohol on his breath. I wish he'd walk away so I could go find Dylan.

Where *is* he? Why would he just disappear with another girl like that when we're supposed to be on a double date?

Matt pulls out his phone and unlocks it, leaning into me. He causes me to stumble a little, but Jade steadies me. "Why don't you just give me your number so I can-"

"Who's this?" Dylan stands behind me, his face bright red. Mandy isn't with him.

"Dylan!" I yell, hugging him.

"Oh, hey, man." He offers his hand like it might prevent Dylan from kicking his ass, but Dylan just stares at it as I cling to him. "I was just offering to show her around campus sometime."

"She doesn't need anyone showing her around."

I look to Jade with wide eyes, and she bites her lip to keep from laughing.

Matt lifts his hands in surrender and backs away, making his way to another group of girls.

"What was that all about?" Dylan asks me.

"What do you mean?"

"I mean, why were you giving your number to some random dude?"

"I wasn't going to!" I say. At least I don't think I was. I definitely wouldn't have texted him. Or met up with him.

I really need water.

"Why are you blowing up on her?" Jade says from her stool. "You're the one who invited her out and then waltzed away with some chick who was hanging all over you."

"You mean my friend?" he shoots back.

Jade shrugs. "Didn't look like a friend."

"Well, she was."

"Well, then this guy was 'just a friend' too."

"You guys don't even know him!" Dylan yells.

"How do you know that?" Jade shoots back. "Maybe we

knew him from high school."

Dylan shakes his head, his features hard. I've never seen him mad before. Then again, I've really only ever seen him, like, twice.

"Seriously, Dylan, what do you expect to happen when you leave a hot girl alone at the bar?" Jade continues. "It's not her fault she got hit on."

Dylan's eyes are bloodshot and narrowed at Jade. I'm growing more sober by the second. "Look, it's fine. I-"

"It's not fine, April!" Dylan yells, running his hands through his hair. "You were about to give him your number!"

"No, I wasn't!"

People around us glance over. The bar is too loud for everyone to hear, but we're still turning heads like one of those dramatic couples who fight every time they go out in public. I always promised myself I'd never like that. "I was looking for you the entire time, but you were nowhere to be found."

"I was in the fucking bathroom, and I come back to my girlfriend flirting with another guy."

Jade raises an eyebrow. "*Girlfriend?*" she asks.

I watch him, waiting for an explanation, but he doesn't say anything. Adam walks up behind us and places his hand on Dylan's shoulder.

"What's up, fam?" he asks as we all stay silent.

"Forget it." Dylan shakes his head and walks toward the exit at the front of the bar and I'm not sure what is going on, but my eyes are suddenly stinging.

"April, do *not* cry. You did nothing wrong," Jade says as I start to follow Dylan outside.

There's a crowd of people by the door in front of the host stand, and I push my way through with tears streaming down my face. *Great.* My first night out at a bar, and I'm the drunk girl crying over her "boyfriend."

The cold air sobers me up even more, sending chills down my arms. I pull my sleeves back down as I scan the parking lot for Dylan.

He's sitting on a curb on the side of the bar when I find him, his head in his hands. I walk over, in a fog. The sounds around me seem so distant. I'm aware of every step I take, my legs wobbly. The cars are all blurry colors. I reach up to make sure my glasses are still on.

I take a seat next to Dylan, stretching my legs out in front of me. But I don't say anything. After a few moments, he lifts his head but doesn't look at me, just stares straight out at the apartments down the road, their lights glistening in the distance.

"I'm sorry," he says so low I can barely hear.

I don't really know what he's sorry for. Leaving me on our date to drink with another girl? Getting jealous and exploding on me because another guy asked for my number? Yelling at me in front of our friends and everyone else around us?

I sigh, knowing I have a lot to think about tomorrow. I don't want to have a lot to think about tomorrow. I don't want to have to think at all.

I rest my head on his shoulder, and we stay there for a few seconds without speaking.

"Look, I know we've only known each other for, like, two weeks," he finally says. "And I know that we've barely even been on three dates."

He pauses, watching a group of drunk friends stumble by, screaming each other's names and laughing. He waits until they pass, lips in a tight line.

"But I also know that I want to be with you," he says, looking me in the eye. "I don't know how *you* feel, but I don't need time to get to know you better or whatever. I feel like I already do know you. And I like you. A lot. I just want to be with you."

His words hit me like the tequila.

*I just want to be with you.*

I snap a hair tie on my wrist a few times, as if it might spark the right words.

"Look, you don't have to say anything," Dylan tells me, dropping his head in his hands again. "I probably just fucked up any chance I had of being your boyfriend." His voice is so muffled I can barely hear him. He looks so defeated, so weak. Like the other night when he got into his car alone.

I recognize that look. I embody that look. And I know that deep down, Dylan is hurting. Because so am I. And not because of tonight—not because of our fight.

I don't want him to hurt, too. I don't want him to hurt alone.

# CHAPTER 9

My head is pounding and my eyes are heavy. I roll over in bed, processing where I am.

It's like I'm waking up on a Sunday before a busy week of tests and papers, knowing I haven't even started studying or researching. Maybe it's the alcohol. All of the anxiety took a seat while I was intoxicated, but they're demanding attention now that I'm sober again.

"Morning, cutie," Dylan says, smiling with tired eyes. He pulls me into him. I bury my face in his neck and instantly calm down.

After our dramatic scene in the parking lot last night, Jade and Adam came out to find Dylan and I making out on the curb. "I guess you made up," Adam said, and we burst out laughing, maybe because we were drunk, maybe because we were giddy, I don't know.

I expected Jade to be skeptical of Dylan after what happened, but she didn't make a fuss over it. As we walked back to the apartments, couples hand-in-hand, we stumbled over the night's events: Dylan's explosion, Jade's snide comebacks, my drunkenness, Adam's oblivion.

I'm glad I made the decision to stay here last night. At 4 a.m., while enjoying a cheesy pizza pie with our boyfriends, Jade called our school, feigning food poisoning. "I've been throwing up all night," Jade cried in a voicemail. Being in theater, she pulled it off way better than I would have, which is why she covered for me and said I was puking in her bathroom during the call.

I really hope I didn't jinx myself and that I won't end up

actually throwing up all day. I lean over Dylan and knock on his wooden nightstand just to play it safe. I know that's "magical thinking" as Dr. Glen would call it, but still. Doesn't hurt to be sure.

"What are you doing?" Dylan asks, smirking. He starts to tickle me, and I kick my legs frantically.

"Stop!!!" I yell, breathless but giggling.

He jolts, eyes wide. "You almost kneed me in the jaw!"

"I am not responsible for any injuries when you're doing that!"

Laughing, he shakes his head and leans back against the wall. His room is freezing cold, as if he left the window open all night or something. I don't want to get out from under the covers.

"What do you wanna do today?" Dylan asks me.

"Well, I could really use some coffee and Advil." My voice croaks when I speak. "'Cause, you know, last night was *mad real*..."

Dylan gives me a look. "You did not just say that."

I wink, shoving him lightly. "No, but really. I have a pretty bad headache."

"I got you." He rolls out of bed and walks to the kitchen, rummaging through cabinets and in the fridge. I take the time to sit up, holding the covers around me and finger-combing my hair into a ponytail. I don't even wanna know what my face looks like right now. I grab my phone from under the pillow and switch it to selfie mode so I can see the damage.

Makeup is smudged under my eyes, my nose is red, and my face is blotchy and greasy. I jump up before Dylan can come back and dart into his bathroom with my purse, not wanting him to see me like this for another second.

The sink is covered with little hairs and dust, and the floor is wet. I cringe as the moisture seeps through my socks. Goosebumps spread down my arms. I really hope it's just water from the shower or something.

Running the faucet, I splash my face and rub off the mascara that's collected under my eyes.

Dylan's sipping a water bottle and sitting on the kitchen counter when I walk out. He offers me Advil and his drink. "So, we don't have coffee here, but I was thinking we could go to breakfast or something. I mean, if you want to hang out still."

"Whoa, Dylan, I don't know if this is gonna work..." He freezes, gripping the counter under him. "How do you *not* have coffee?"

"Wow, thought you were breaking up with me for a second," he says, cheeks pink as his lips curl up. "I don't know, we're not big coffee drinkers here...but I have a feeling I'm gonna have to become one, huh?"

"If you want this to work, then yes," I joke.

"Okay then. Let's see...Deodorant, shampoo, coffee." He counts on his fingers.

I laugh. "What are you doing?"

"That's my shopping list." He smiles at me, his hair sticking up in random places. I can't help but beam back. "So...are you down for breakfast?"

"Always, if there's food involved."

Plus, my parents think I'm at school, so...I *can't* go home.

I don't have an extra change of clothes, and my sweater has a pizza sauce stain on it—*smooth*, April—so I keep my leggings on and borrow one of Dylan's thermal shirts. "You look so cute in my clothes," he tells me as we walk to his car.

Dylan drives a few blocks, then parks in front of a bagel place that's packed with kids around our age. Most of them are wearing sweats or workout clothes and look as hungover as I feel.

It's loud inside, and the walls are painted a bright blue. Also, The Chainsmokers are playing. Not that I have anything against them, but I feel like I'm back at the bar or something. I don't like this place's vibe.

Thankfully, there aren't enough tables for us, so we take our pumpkin coffees and egg sandwiches to the park nearby. Much more my speed.

We grab a wooden picnic table by the lake. The sky is gray, and I lean into Dylan as a cool breeze rushes through my hair.

"It's cute here," I say, unwrapping my sandwich.

"Yeah, it's cool. I practice soccer here with Adam when the fields on campus are taken."

"You were awesome yesterday, by the way. That goal was beautiful."

He grins as he sips his coffee. "Thanks."

"Why don't you play for your school? Instead of just pickup games, I mean."

Dylan tenses. "Don't feel like it."

"But don't you love soccer?"

"Yeah. I love the *sport*. Not all the other bullshit and politics."

I'm a little thrown off by his tone, but I try not to take it personally. Not everything is about me. Plus, I can relate to what he's saying.

"I feel that way about my school sometimes," I tell him, hoping he knows I'm on his side. "I wanted to join the newspaper just for some writing experience, not even for investigative journalism. But the editor was more concerned with celebrity gossip and beauty columns than anything that actually matters."

"Where do you write your investigative stories then?" he asks me, meeting my eyes. "Do you have a blog or something?"

I blush, unsure whether I should tell him the truth.

"For *that*, I have a journal. I'm not sure I'm ready to actually share anything yet."

"Well, have you solved any...I guess, 'cases,' are they?"

"Yeah. A few."

"I wanna hear about one."

I turn to face him, pulling my feet onto the bench and hugging my knees to my chest. I love talking about this, but no one ever asks me about it.

"I guess my favorite case was last year, because it was the first time I felt like I really helped someone. Which is the whole point of being an investigative journalist. For me, at least." A gust of wind blows my hair wildly in front of my face. I tuck strands behind my ears. "So, I was in the nurse's office because I didn't feel well, and this girl came in. She was a senior at the time. She told the nurse she felt sick to her stomach, but I knew it was anxiety-induced. She was *visibly* shaking. She looked like she'd been crying, too. Also, the nurse gave her a sleeve of crackers and she ate all of them really quickly. You don't wanna eat when you're nauseous, usually." I cringe just thinking about it.

"Anyway, the nurse kinda blew it off and told her to wait it out in the office until the period was over, which seemed to please the girl enough for her to calm down. Wherever she was supposed to be at that moment, she did *not* want to be. And it wasn't for stupid reasons or anything, like that she forgot to study for a test or didn't want to see her ex or something like that. This girl was petrified."

I remember the look on her face: her pale skin, bright pink cheeks like she'd been caught doing something bad, wide blue eyes. I recognized the fear in her; I identified with it.

"The girl was usually really put-together," I continue, Dylan watching me closely. "It's a relatively small school, so I'd seen her around a lot. She always wore professional clothes and perfect makeup and all that. You know the type. Mature beyond her years. But she was in sweats when she came to the nurse, so I knew she had to have come from gym class. Meaning, something, or *someone*, in that class was bothering her so much that she felt the need to skip. I didn't want to make it obvious, but I wanted to find out what was going on, so I started asking her questions, unrelated at first, about her hobbies and all that. She played tennis, so I asked if she'd looked at schools where she could play, and she just froze. Then she started crying— like, really crying. And she excused herself before getting up and leaving. That's when I put two-and-two together: the school's tennis coach was also a gym teacher."

Dylan stares blankly at me. "I'm confused...did she get cut from the team or something?"

I shake my head. "No way. She was awesome. Her coach, however...I Googled his name later that day and found him on Facebook. I scrolled through his profile looking for anything weird, and I saw that he was tagged in a photo with a guy who looked just like him. It could've been his brother, that's how similar they looked. Only...they had different last names. So, you know, just for the hell of it, I Googled his first name with this other guy's last name, and—*bingo*. First result was an article about how he'd been fired from his teaching position at an old school in California for sexual harassment claims."

Dylan widens his eyes. "No fucking way."

"Yup. Turns out, he changed his last name to his wife's when they got married, probably to save face."

"Wow. And the school didn't catch that in a background check?"

"Nope. Pretty disheartening, right?"

Dylan's face is of pure disgust. "I fucking wish I saw this happen. They'd have to decide which last name to put on his grave."

I laugh. "You sound like my brother."

"So, what did you end up doing?"

"Well, I pulled the girl aside the next day and told her what I found out. I said I'd happily go to the principal with her, but she started freaking out, begging me not to say anything. Apparently, he threatened to get her tennis scholarship revoked at her top college if she told anyone. Said that no one would believe her. I knew she needed proof if she was going to report it, so we set up a plan: I stayed after school that day and hid in the girls' locker room bathroom, and after acting a little extra friendly with him at practice, she told him she'd be staying late after the other girls left. We knew he'd take that as an invitation. Sure enough, he crept into the locker room that evening and immediately started saying inappropriate things about her body and all this other nasty stuff." I shudder at the memory. "So, she stepped away from him and told him she's going to report him to the principal, and he admitted—on camera, thanks to my iPhone—that he'd ruin her tennis career if she does anything. He started getting really mad, so I walked out feigning confusion and stared at him as if I didn't know what was going on. Then he *bolted*. Like, *sprinted* out of that room."

Dylan stares at me with a look I can't read, and I realize I just babbled like an idiot. I feel like I downed ten coffees in the last five minutes, and I probably look like a crazed conspiracy theorist—an accurate one, of course.

"Is it wrong that your detective skills turn me on?" Dylan asks me.

I playfully shove Dylan with my foot, and he pulls my legs onto my lap. "No, but really," he says. "April, that's some *actual* investigative work. Not that I underestimated you, but...I don't know, that's just awesome."

I shrug like it's no big deal, but I am pretty proud of it.

"So, what happened after that? Did you tell the school?"

"Yeah, she had the evidence she needed from my video, along with the old articles and proof that he'd changed his last name. They 'decided to let him go' a few days later."

Dylan blinks. "That's it? They just acted like he didn't have a record? They didn't apologize for hiring a scumbag? They just tried to cover it up to save their own asses?"

"Yeah, which is something I would obviously include in an article, if I were to publish one. That's where the writing comes into play. It holds people accountable for their bullshit. And provides some sort of reassurance to the victim that, you know, someone's on their side."

"Why didn't you share it then?" He plays with the laces on my boots and tilts his head at me.

"I don't know. The whole 'protecting the victim' thing is pretty serious in journalism. That girl really didn't want it to go any further. And I guess the other situations I've investigated have been...elementary, you can say. Like, no one would want to read about how a local student manipulated her student council campaign, or how the guy my best friend Kat met at a concert was actually five years older than he'd said. Oh, and married."

He laughs. "Well, *I'd* love to read your work. And I think a lot of other people would, too."

"Thanks, Dylan."

"You're welcome, babe."

My heart flutters when he calls me that. I don't remember the last time I was this happy. And I don't want to forget it.

I take out my phone and open the camera so I can capture this moment. "Smile," I tell him. He does, and even blushes a bit.

"Let's take one together," he says, pushing my legs off him so I can sit closer. I turn the camera on selfie mode and lean into him, pointing it at us before tapping the button. I'm beginning to like the girl in that photo.

# CHAPTER 10

I stare at the image of Dylan and me on my phone and catch myself smiling. If only I could've stayed in that moment forever, leaning into my new boyfriend, inhaling the scent of cologne on his neck and feeling the cool autumn breeze, life would be so much easier.

Without even thinking twice, I upload the photo on Instagram and tag Dylan, adding a heart emoji. But then I instantly regret it because the picture doesn't match my Insta feed. It's much darker and less vintage-looking than the others on the page.

Immediately, I delete it so I can edit it, hoping no one saw. I don't know why I care so much, but I do. Call it OCD—maybe it's a part of the disorder, like society assumes. But it certainly isn't the extent of it.

Pulling up my favorite photo editing app, I sip my hot cup of coffee and lean back against the wall, sitting beneath the covers on my bed. The speaker on my desk across the room plays *Time to Time* by Mascots, and I sing along while adjusting tones and adding grain to the image.

My phone buzzes in my hand.

**Dylan:** You deleted our photo. :( Already tired of me?

My cheeks flush with heat as I quickly text back: Omg no! I accidentally deleted it. I'm about to repost. :)

Day one of our relationship, and I'm already lying to hide my crazy.

I do as I said and repost the photo with the proper edits, satisfied now. But as I continue to scroll through Instagram, another picture catches my eye. I immediately stop sliding my finger up the screen to look closer.

It's an old shot of Zach and Tristan. They're sitting in the back of a pickup truck in what looks like the middle of the woods, wearing dark boots, jeans, and flannels. They're both holding fishing poles, grinning.

*God*, they look so young. It must've been taken early in high school.

I place my coffee on my nightstand and tie my hair into a tight ponytail, pulling my knees into my chest as I stare at the photo. Zach didn't put a caption. I don't think there's much to say. Or maybe there's too much.

There's a bunch of likes from people in our school. I look through the list, noticing a few kids from our English class who never even spoke to Tristan. I wonder if any of these people even care that he's gone, or if they're just trying to seem genuine.

I hit Tristan's tag to look at his profile. There isn't much on his page, just a few fishing pictures, some of which are with Zach, and some with random other guys. But he hasn't posted since spring.

*Typical dude.*

I click back to Zach's photo and tap Jenny's name from the likes section, hoping her account is public. It is.

She has a bunch of selfies. Her blonde hair is tied in a knot on the top of her head in most, and she sports concert shirts of all genres, from punk rock to rap.

As I scroll down her page, I see some pictures of her and Tristan. Faceswaps using a Snapchat filter. Candids of them performing music at a cafe I don't recognize. My heart is heavy as I stare at them, wanting to reach out and talk to the people in the photos.

I click the home button on Instagram and stare at the photo of Zach and Tristan. I double tap.

Suddenly, I see the pain in Zach's eyes again, like I did at the bookstore when he talked to me about Tristan. About how he was distant all summer. I wish I could talk to him more. And to Jenny. Be there for them.

I know what it's like to have no control. To have no answers. To live in fear of what might come next.

I close my eyes and take a deep breath, trying to distance myself from the situation. This isn't my business. Not really.

I try thinking about Dylan to calm myself down, but disturbing scenarios play out in my head instead: Tristan getting hit by a car, lying on the side of the street in the dark. Tristan being murdered by a serial killer. Tristan standing on a bridge, contemplating jumping to his death.

I can't make them stop. They're so powerful, so *real*.

I kick the covers off my legs and stand, pacing my room. It's so hot in here, suddenly, and I think I might faint. I open a window for air and sit down at my desk, feeling the breeze on my face like an open freezer.

I know I shouldn't rationalize my thoughts. I know I should just let them be, let them scream without a reaction. But it's nearly impossible when they're so loud that they make my head pound.

Discomfort is the best way to describe it. It's like getting up in front of a courtroom to plead not guilty of a crime you know deep down you didn't commit, expected to provide evidence on why they should believe you, why you are a good person, but not being able to speak. It's like standing there, shrugging at the judgmental faces burning holes in your skin. Who knows, maybe you are guilty. There will never be enough proof otherwise, no matter how much you try to explain yourself.

I can't talk my way out of this. Not even to myself.

My tears are cold on my cheeks from the autumn air. I don't know when I even started crying. I cover my face with my hands as my shoulders shake with silent sobs.

I feel like the worst person in the world—when just a few minutes ago, I felt like I was on top of it.

\*     \*     \*

"Hey, hey, hey!" Kat's already sitting down at our table when I get to lunch. She looks at me expectantly, grinning like a mischievous child. "Way to ignore my text last night…I saw your Instagram pic. You need to fill me in!"

My head spins as I take a seat next to her and pull out a small ziplock full of peanut butter pretzels.

"Is that all you're eating?" Kat asks me.

"Yeah, I'm not really hungry."

"Why not?"

Shrugging, I pop one in my mouth and watch the lunch line shorten against the white brick walls. The cafeteria is so loud, I wish I could put my headphones in and drown everyone out with my playlist.

"April." I turn back to Kat with a pit in my stomach. "What's wrong?"

She knows me so well. *Too* well, today.

"Do you think Tristan's okay, Kat?" I ask her.

She pauses, opening her mouth, then closing it again. Something in her face shifts, ever so slightly, and she looks sad. "I hope so."

"Me too."

"You're pretty worked up about this, huh?"

My cheeks flush. "Yeah, I mean…it's been a while."

She crosses her legs and takes a sip of her apple juice, which she's never spotted without. She carries about four mini bottles in her backpack every day. It's kind of comforting, actually, to see her with it today. It feels routine.

"I'm sure they're doing everything they can to find him. Just gotta trust that."

"I guess," I say.

*But is that enough?* Who knows where he could be by now. It's been a week. Seven full days, each more detrimental than the one before. And the worst part is barely anyone seems to give a shit anymore, aside from Jenny and Zach. It's like it's old news or something.

"So, are you gonna tell me about Dylan or what?" Kat asks me, further proving my point.

I give her what she wants: "He asked me out."

"Aaaaand?" Her eyes are wide in anticipation.

"Aaaaand, I said yes."

Kat squeals, and I wish I could celebrate with her, but I can't feel the giddiness right now. The smell of peanut butter makes my stomach uneasy, so I put the ziploc back in my backpack.

"How did he do it?" Kat asks me.

"We were drunk."

"*You* were drunk?"

I glare at her. "I've drank before."

"No, I know, I just—"

"Why do I keep thinking about him, Kat?" I cut her off.

She looks confused. "Dylan?"

*That would make more sense, wouldn't it?*

"No," I admit in a weak voice. "Tristan."

Her eyes fixate on her apple juice as she peels a part of the wrapper off. "Well...I don't know. It's not like *I'm* not thinking about him. I'm just trying to stay hopeful, is all."

"Do you think something's wrong with me?" I ask.

"What do you mean?"

Sighing, my eyes sting with the threat of tears. "I don't know. I, like, kind of felt...intrigued or something, when I found out that he was missing. And ever since, I can't stop thinking that I'm a bad person who wants bad things to happen. Like, I get these crazy, violent images in my mind that I can't shut off."

As the words leave my mouth, I want so badly to take them back. But at the same time, my shoulders start to relax, the knots in my neck loosening. Although I've already talked to Dr. Glen about this, and Googled it for hours, I don't think I discussed it enough. It only gave me relief for a short period of time.

That's the thing about seeking reassurance—in the moment, it feels like the only palpable solution. But in the end, it just ends up pushing you back.

Kat narrows her eyes at me, probably thinking the worst of me, finally realizing how bad of a person I am.

"You're looking way too much into this. Everyone has weird thoughts."

"Yeah, but like...what if I want sympathy from it? Do you think that's what I'm trying to do? Get sympathy? Is that why I keep bringing it up?"

"I don't think it's sympathy you want, just...I don't know, support? I feel the same way, kind of. And I only had one class with him. Shit sucks."

"You do?"

"Yeah, I think so," she says. "Plus, you're not that kind of person. Like, you are clearly *distraught* over this. Way more than most of the people in this school."

"But what if I *am* that kinda person?" She gives me a look. "Have you ever felt that way though? Seriously. Have you had those exact feelings when you found out something bad?"

She hesitates. "I mean, probably. I just don't overthink them if I do."

Sighing a shaky breath, I run a hand through my hair. It's greasy from not washing it this morning.

"They're just thoughts, April. Thoughts about a friend who disappeared randomly last week. It's a really fucked up situation. And you have OCD, so of course it's gonna consume you, in weird ways that don't make sense. Have you talked to Dr. Glen about it?"

I shrug, resting my head on my folded arms on the table and turning away from Kat. I don't even want to talk about it anymore. I don't want to talk at all.

# CHAPTER 11

"What's up with you?"

Greg's standing in my doorway. I'm hunched over my laptop on my bed, notebook next me, eyes focused on my screen. "Nothing," I say.

He leans against my door frame and watches me. "You sure? You're doing that thing with your eyebrows."

I instantly pull my hand away from my face and sit up straight, meeting his eyes. "Yeah. I'm fine. Just can't figure out this math equation," I lie.

"Lemme see. Maybe I can help." Before I can shut my computer, he's already next to me, staring at my screen. Staring at my Google search of "reasons someone might go missing."

He looks at me with a mix of pity and concern, and a hint of frustration. "April, come on. Don't do that."

"Do *what*?"

"*This*." He gestures at me sitting on my bed. "The whole detective game you play."

"It's not a game, Greg. I'm just—"

"Save it for college, April, when you're studying journalism and have the actual experience to get involved."

He's talking to me slowly, careful with every word. Like I'm fragile, someone who needs to be looked after and warned. Warned about the dangers of the world, as if I haven't been overly aware of them my entire life.

"Not when you should be focusing on applications and, I don't know, getting better so that you can actually get *into* college."

I pretend not to hear what he said. I pretend he's not even

there, turning my attention back to Google.

Greg reaches over me and grabs my laptop, slamming it shut.

"What the hell, Greg?" I say. "Give it back." I reach for it, but he jumps back, holding it against his side like a textbook.

"You gotta stop," he tells me. "I'm serious, April."

"I—" My eyes start to glaze over and my nose stings. "I can't."

Greg doesn't say anything, just looks at me, his face softening. He's in jeans and a black T-shirt, and his light brown hair looks wet, like he just showered. I wonder where he's going, if I'm keeping him from somewhere important. He should just leave. He's wasting his time.

"You can," he tells me. "And you know that. You're stronger than this."

"This has nothing to do with my OCD," I say, my voice defensive.

"Yes, it does. You know it does." The fact that he's so calm, and I'm so *not*, makes me even madder.

He sits down next to me, placing the computer on the other side of him.

"Look, I know it makes you feel better to help people, or whatever, but—"

"*Don't* go there," I snap, but he continues over me.

"—you have to know where to draw the line. And getting involved in a missing person's case is far past that line. This is becoming one of your obsessions. You think I haven't noticed?"

"What are you talking about? Noticed *what*?"

"Jenny told me you showed up the other night."

I freeze.

"She messaged me on Instagram. Said you looked distraught and wanted to make sure you got home okay."

I try to process what he's telling me. *Jenny* was checking up on *me*? It should be the other way around.

"I was gonna let it go, but...you're getting wrapped up, April. You're not the police, or a detective, or even his family or close friend, for that matter. I know that he was your classmate and you want to help, but sometimes, there's nothing you can do. You have to accept that."

"I can't," I mutter.

"You can't control everything in life, April. No matter how much you want to."

*     *     *

Later that night, I'm studying in bed with my door locked when Dylan texts me a bunch of question marks. Above it is the good-morning text he sent me this morning.

*Crap.* I've been so in my head that I never answered.

Instead of messaging him back with some lame excuse, I call him. I want to hear his voice, especially since I haven't seen him in almost a week—since the day he asked me out.

I sit cross-legged on my bed and rest my phone on my leg, putting it on speaker mode.

"Hey," Dylan says, his voice muffled. It sounds like there's wind in the background.

I try on my peppiest voice. "Hiiii. I'm so sorry I didn't text you all day. Today was crazy."

"It's all good." His voice is flat.

"How was your day?"

"It was good."

"Did you have class?" I ask.

"I missed it."

"Why?"

"Overslept."

"That sucks…" I pick at my bedspread. "Can you make up the work?"

"It's not a big deal."

I bite my lip, not knowing what else to ask him, other then, "What's wrong?"

"Nothing's wrong," he says, his voice going up an octave. "Why would something be wrong?"

"I don't know. You just seem really short."

"I'm fine," he says, then waits a whole ten seconds before

adding, "I just miss you, babe."

I smile, feeling a little better hearing him say that. It's like everything melts away. All of the sadness. The secrets. The fear. I lean back against my wall and let out a long breath. "I miss you so much," I tell him.

"I wanna see you. It's been over a week."

"Tomorrow?"

"Noooo, *now*."

I look down at my pajamas. "I wish I could, but I have to study."

"But that's what you told me this weekend...Come over! You can do it here."

"You *really* think I'd be able to concentrate with you there?"

"I'll be good...Well, I'll try, at least."

As much as I want to, I can't let him see me like this. My face is still puffy from crying, and I'm not sure I can fake happiness right now. "I can't, Dyl. I'm sorry."

He's silent for a few moments. "Okay," he finally says. "How about I come over for a movie night tomorrow? I'll even let you pick. And we can order takeout or something."

There's shuffling on his end, and I can hear a few guys talking in the background. "Yeah. Yeah, sounds good. I'll text you, okay?"

He hangs up before I can answer, and anxiety instantly resurfaces, beckoning me to continue my investigation. There's no way I'm focusing on math right now.

I grab my laptop from the end of my bed and load Tristan's profile again. His page looks like any other 17-year-old male's would. In other words, it doesn't tell me much about him. The last post I see is a meme that Jenny shared on his page a month ago. It's a picture of Michael Scott from *The Office* saying, "I declare bankruptcy!" The caption reads: "When all your favorite bands are touring at once." Tristan "liked" it.

Tristan and I have a similar music taste. I know this because we're friends on Spotify, and that's because he complimented my Knuckle Puck shirt one time last year in class, and we spent half the period gushing over their new album, *Shapeshifter*.

"A lot of people don't like it, but I think it's their best one yet," I told him at the time. We had a sub that day, and we'd already finished our in-class work. I was facing him, my legs over the sidebar of the tablet desk. "*Copacetic* was awesome, but this one seems more...mature?"

"That, and it's a bit more upbeat," he said. "There's some slow ones, but overall, I just enjoy their sound better. It's a catchier album."

"For sure. I, like, *crave* these songs. Whereas, with their other albums, I didn't feel so invested, you know?"

He grinned at me, his green eyes sparkling. "Yeah, I feel that. I can't wait to hear them live."

I widened my eyes. "You're seeing Knuckle Puck? When?! Where? I'm *dying* to hear *Want Me Around* live."

He laughed. "Some venue in the city. I think it's in February. I'm meeting my friend who goes to school in New York."

The girl behind Tristan leaned forward, her long brown hair falling over her shoulders, blue eyes narrowed.

"Did you just say you're seeing *Nickleback*?" It was clear by her expression that she disapproved.

Tristan and I burst out laughing at the mixup, and the girl looked confused and annoyed at our reaction. She turned back to her blonde friend before Tristan could correct her.

Tristan turned to me, cheeks pink. "Hey, you should come with me. To the concert, I mean."

"Oh, uh..." I didn't know how to tell him that New York made me nervous. That I'd never taken a train in my life, and I wasn't eager to do so any time soon. Not even for one of my favorite bands. "I'll let you know," I said anyway.

His expression fell, and he nodded like he understood. "No worries. Just figured I'd put it out there."

I pull up Spotify on my browser and shuffle *Shapeshifter*, wishing I was back in that moment. Back in that conversation.

Maybe I would've changed my response.

And then I see it: Tristan's name on the right side of my Spotify, where it shows you what your followers are listening to. His account is active, as of ten minutes ago. And he's playing *Want Me Around.*

# CHAPTER 12

"I'm so sorry I'm late!" I say as Dylan opens the door. He turns sideways so I can come into his apartment, his face blank.

Cheers and loud voices echo in the kitchen, where a cracked white plastic table is set up for beer pong. I walk in to find six guys, including Dylan's roommate, standing around and drinking.

"Hi," I say, overwhelmed by the crowd. I'm in leggings and a sweatshirt with my glasses on, my hair tied in a loose bun on the top of my head.

"Yoooooo is this your girl?" one of the guys say. "I'm Gabe." He's about my height with tan skin and a goofy smile, and I'm caught off-guard when he gives me a one-armed hug. He smells like alcohol, but I can't help but laugh. His energy is contagious.

"Are you guys coming out with us?" another guy says as he dunks a pong ball into a red solo cup.

I'm about to respond when Dylan grabs my hand and pulls me away from the group and into his room, holding a beer in his other hand. He locks the door behind him.

"Sorry about them."

"Why are you sorry?" I ask. "They seem nice." I take a seat on his bed and slip my black Converse off. Pulling my knees into my chest, I look up at Dylan, who looks annoyed.

"What's wrong?"

"Nothing." He takes a sip of his beer and kicks a balled up sock on his floor.

"Did you want to go out with them?"

He hesitates. "Not really."

"Are you sure? Cause you kinda seem—"

"Why were you so late?"

I open my mouth, caught off guard. He stares at me, and I look down.

"I got caught up at a family thing," I say, but really, I was trying to figure out if you could somehow message someone through Spotify, or track their location on the app. I spent all night debating whether I should tell someone that I saw Tristan's account as active. But when I told Kat at lunch, she convinced me that it was probably someone else, like a friend or even his dad, using his account without realizing. That he probably let someone share it, the way people share Netflix profiles.

Still, it didn't feel right to make that assumption. So I crafted a million different messages before finally IMing Jenny on Facebook when I should've been getting ready for Dylan's. I still haven't heard back from her.

Dylan brushes his fingers through his dark hair. I can hear his friends laughing on the other side of the door, and he glances over for a moment.

"Dylan, if you want to go out, I understand. I don't wanna keep you from seeing your friends on a Friday night."

"No," he says quickly, turning back to me. "I want to see you."

"Okay." I hug my knees. *I'm such a buzzkill.*

"You don't believe me?"

"No, I do. I just feel bad."

"Well, don't. I want to spend time with you." He takes a seat next to me and places his hand on my leg. "Do you want some?" he asks, offering me his beer.

"No thanks."

He finishes it off, crumples the can, and tosses it on the floor. "What about coffee?" he asks, smirking.

I raise my eyebrows. "I thought you didn't have any here."

"You told me I had to buy some if I wanted our relationship to work."

Grinning, I lean in and kiss him. He smiles against my lips.

"I should shower," he says. "I was kicking the soccer ball around before you came. I'm pretty sweaty."

"I don't care," I say, pulling him back in. But then my phone beeps with a notification from Facebook Messenger, and immediately I think it must be Jenny. And then, I start thinking about Tristan. While hooking up with Dylan.

I lean into the kiss, trying to fight my mind, trying not to let my thoughts ruin the moment. But for a split second, Tristan's face appears in my mind, and it feels like I'm kissing him. My stomach tightens. I open my eyes to look at Dylan, to get Tristan's face out of my mind, as he moves his hand under my sweater, on the small of my back, lowering me down.

We fall back onto his sheets. They smell like laundry detergent. He must have just washed them. And now, we're making out on top of them. And he hasn't showered since playing soccer. And he's gonna sleep on these sheets after getting dirt and sweat and...*whatever else* all over them.

"Wait," I say, breaking apart. I have way too much going on in my head right now. I can't focus on anything. I need to calm down. "Um. Maybe you should shower."

Furrowing his eyebrows, he lets out a nervous laugh. "Uhhhh, okay. I guess I really am pretty gross right now."

Heat rushes to my face. "No! No, it's not that." I sit up. "It's just, you're probably full of germs. And we're on your sheets, which..." He raises an eyebrow at me. "I'm sorry, I'm just a germaphobe."

I downplay it so I sound a little less insane. This is yet another stigma I'm feeding, but sometimes it's easier to make light of the disorder. It's the only way people can even begin to understand. The only way they can relate, and possibly even empathize.

Dylan runs his hand through his hair, he's trying to settle his breathing. His cheeks are red like he's embarrassed. "It's no big deal," he tells me anyway, and gives me a peck before grabbing a towel off the floor and heading to the bathroom. All his friends are gone now, out partying like he should be. The apartment is silent, and I can hear him turn on the shower from his room.

I crawl under his covers and rest my head on one of his pillows, unlocking my phone so I can check my Facebook messages. Sure enough, Jenny responded.

**Jenny:** That was me on Tristan's account. I know it sounds stupid...I just wanted to feel like he was home again. Like we were hanging in his room listening to his music on his laptop like old times. I'm sorry to get your hopes up.

Tears stream down my face as I stare at the message for what feels like hours. This pain isn't my own, not really, but it cuts so deep I can't ignore it.

I hear Dylan turn off the shower, and I wipe my tears, but more replace them. My eyes are swollen and heavy, so I pretend to be asleep. I don't have the energy or the guts to explain this.

Dylan opens the door to his room a few minutes later. I hear him place something on his nightstand, then rustle through a few drawers before sitting on his bed and switching the TV on. I recognize *One Tree Hill* right away, but he's a few episodes ahead of where we left off on Saturday. I'd know—I binged the entire rest of the third season this week. He must've been watching it, too.

The bed suddenly vibrates, and I realize Dylan's phone is ringing. I don't move.

"Hello?" he says quietly. Pause. "'Cause my girlfriend's sleeping." More pause. "Shut up, Mandy. I'm not coming out tonight."

*Mandy*. Mandy, the blonde girl from the bar. Mandy, his "friend" who eyed him like a chew toy. Mandy, who calls him "Dyly" and is apparently asking him to hang out tonight.

"Because I'm staying in with April," Dylan continues. I hold my breath so I can listen to her response, but she's speaking too low. "I'm not ditching my girlfriend."

I can hear her laughing, and then her muffled voice says something I can't quite make out. *Great*. I'm sure she's making fun of me, taunting Dylan for being with a girl who falls asleep before 10 pm on a Friday.

I hate Mandy. I've met her once, and I already hate her.

"Alright, well I'll talk to you tomorrow or something. Have fun."

Dylan settles next to me on the bed, pulling the comforter over himself so that we're both tucked in together. His body is warm from the shower, and he smells like soap. Wrapping his arms around me, he rests his head against the back of my neck.

Something about his presence, his touch, makes me start to cry harder than before. But I can't let him see me like this, so I squeeze my eyes shut tighter and hold my body as still as possible.

The scent of coffee wafts in the area, and I realize with a lurch in my stomach that he made me a cup. It's a shame it'll have to grow cold.

# CHAPTER 13

"I don't care how nice of a guy you think he is," my dad tells me as I zip up my heeled combat boots by the front door. "If he wants to take you out, I need to meet him first."

I'm wearing a plaid skirt with knee-high socks and a chunky sweater, waiting for Dylan to pick me up for our dinner date downtown.

"Okay, dad." I walk over to the couch where he's sitting and plop down next to him, nudging his shoulder. "You could smile, you know."

He stares straight ahead at the TV, where a music history documentary is playing. "Ha-ha."

"Where's mom?" I ask him.

"Some work event in New York."

"On a Saturday?"

He shrugs. "You know how it is."

I sneer, and Dylan texts me that he's outside. I jump up and message him to come to the door.

"Is he here?" my dad asks, craning his neck to look out the window behind him.

"Yeah, he's coming up."

I open the door before he can ring the doorbell. He takes in my outfit and grins. When he tries to kiss me, I pull him in for a hug.

"Uh...my dad wants to meet you," I whisper, and I grab his hand and pull him to the living room where I now see Greg sitting. *Great.*

"Hey...So, this is Dylan. Dylan, this is my brother, Greg, and my dad."

He lets go of my hand and stuffs both of his in the pockets of his windbreaker.

"Hi," he says, smiling. "Nice to meet you guys."

"Nice to meet you, too," my dad says. "Why don't you take a seat?" He points at the loveseat, which makes a 90-degree angle with the couch my dad and Greg are on.

"Dad, we kinda have reservations downtown, so…" I say as Dylan sits down.

"So, Dylan," my dad starts, ignoring my comment. He folds his arms over his Metallica T-shirt. "How'd you meet April? You go to school together, or..?"

*Shit.*

Dylan glances at me, confused. I bite my lip. *Maybe I should've mentioned this earlier.* "Uh…No, sir," he says, turning back to my dad. "I go to Southern Connecticut State."

My dad pauses, glancing up at me before focusing back on Dylan. "You're in college?" His voice remains steady, which somehow makes me feel even more uncomfortable.

Dylan nods.

"What year?

"I'm a sophomore."

"You do realize April is still in high school."

Dylan swallows. "Yeah."

"*Dad.*" I shoot him a look. I didn't exactly expect him to love the first boyfriend I took home, but I at least hoped he'd be cordial about it. "I'm gonna be in college next year."

"And by then, he'll have been in college for two years," Greg says, as if he's so much older and wiser. He's 21 and still hasn't had a serious girlfriend.

Dylan turns to me like he doesn't know what to do. He shakes his head, probably thinking that dating someone like Mandy wouldn't warrant a family meeting with an interrogating father and overprotective brother.

"I mean, yeah, college is a completely different world than high school," Dylan starts. "But I really like April. I don't know, that's all that really matters to me."

My dad nods slowly. "Alright." He still doesn't look convinced, but to my surprise, he drops it. He starts asking about Dylan's major and whether he's involved in any clubs on campus, to which Dylan raves about his soccer team, his face lighting up the entire time.

"So, where are you two going tonight?" my dad asks once the conversation dies down.

"Maria's," I tell him.

"Oh man, I could really go for their meatball sub right now," Greg says, lying his head back on the couch cushion.

"Greg, maybe you should go with them," my dad says.

I shoot him a look.

"Oh, I'm messing with you. *Go.* I know how you get when you're hungry." My dad looks at Dylan. "It's not pretty."

Dylan laughs extra loudly.

"Your dad's cool," he says as we get into his car.

"Yeahhhh, he's alright. Sorry for all the questions."

"Nah, I get it. I actually expected him to be more strict. I mean, I *am* two years older than you."

"He trusts me," I say.

I look away from him, out of the window at the colorful mountains.

"Does that bother *you*?" I ask. "That I'm so much younger, I mean?"

At a red light, he grabs my hand tightly, and I turn back to him. He looks me in the eye.

"I don't give a shit about your age. Just as long as I'm with you." He hit the gas as the light turns green. "Does it bother *you*?"

"Not at all."

We park on the street when we get there and walk hand-in-hand to the Italian restaurant. It's dark and cold outside.

I remember the nights I spent here with my mom in middle school, window shopping during Christmastime. They'd decorate the lampposts with red bows and line the shops with string lights. We'd go into the high-end boutiques that smelled like patchouli. She'd pull dresses and tight sweaters off the racks and hold them up to me, encouraging me to try them on, but I'd beg her to bring me to the bookstore for a leather journal or a new novel.

I wish she was home to meet Dylan tonight. She probably would've calmed my dad down. She probably would've *liked* that Dylan was in college. That I was finally being a normal teenage girl.

"So...I have to tell you something," Dylan says as we sit at a booth for two. There's a white tablecloth on the table and a small candle between us.

"Okay," I say warily.

"When you were over last night, Mandy called me. She was asking me to come out and started giving me shit for staying in. She was drunk, so I just told her I was busy and hung up."

I nod and pretend I don't already know all this.

"But today, she came over..." He looks down at the table, then back up at me. Suddenly, I'm not so hungry anymore. "She told me she doesn't like that I have a girlfriend. And, I don't know, it bothered me. Not that she's upset, but that she had the nerve to say that, you know?"

"Um..." I take a sip of water in an attempt to calm myself down. "Yeah, that's messed up. Why does she care?"

"Well, that's the thing...We hooked up once, earlier this semester. Before I met you."

*Oh.* "Oh."

"But I don't like her," he adds quickly. "She's not my type at all. We were just friends who got drunk and...you know. But I guess, I don't know, now she's all territorial."

I shake my head. "Why are you telling me this?"

He opens his mouth, then closes it like he's considering what I asked. "Because I felt bad keeping it from you? I don't know. I'd want to know if someone said that to you."

*Well, lucky for him, no one would.*

Our waitress brings bread and butter to the table, and I lean back in my booth, playing with my hair and staring into space.

"April, say something."

"What do you want me to say? I don't like her." It comes out before I can sugarcoat it.

Dylan's lips curl up a bit. "That was kind of hot."

"What?"

"Nothing." He takes a piece of bread from the basket. "I just wanted to let you know. I don't want us to keep anything from each other, you know?"

"Sure."

"So...yeah. That was it. And then I told her, 'Well, too bad. I really like April.' And then she left."

I nod slowly. "Are you still gonna hang out with her?"

His guilty expression already tells me the answer. I shift in my seat, inhaling a deep breath. I feel like I just chugged a bottle of wine. I kind of wish I did.

"Is that okay?" he asks.

*Not really.* "Do I have a choice?"

"I mean...We're friends. Our friends are friends, too. When you're in college, you know, you can't really avoid people."

I don't say anything, because I guess I *wouldn't* know. Maybe my dad and Greg were right.

"Look, you're the one I want to be with, okay?" he adds. "Plus, it's not like she wants to date me or anything...She just—"

"Wants to sleep with you?" I say.

His cheeks turn red, and he stares down at his plate.

"That's great to know, Dylan. Thank you for telling me."

He must sense the sarcasm in my voice, because he reaches across the table and takes my hand.

"April, you don't need to worry, okay? I didn't have to tell you, and maybe I shouldn't have, but I *wanted* to. Because I respect you, and I don't want you to think I'd ever hide anything from you. I don't like her. She was just a drunk hookup. You're so much more than that."

*God, I'd hope so.*

# CHAPTER 14

"I mean, that's messed up, right?"

"Um, yes," Jade says. "We saw how Mandy was all over him at the bar. And now she's getting all territorial?"

Jade's holding a shopping bag on each arm as she, Lindsay, Brenda, and I walk through the mall.

Lindsay narrows her almond brown eyes. Her short black hair is pulled into a messy bun that somehow doesn't look so messy. I can see the contour on her face, the dark red blush on her cheeks.

"Yeah, that's no bueno," she says to me, pouting. "And I bet he only told you so he could use it against you if you ever get jealous."

"What do you mean?" I ask.

"He's probably thinking, 'Well, I told her about it, so she has no right to doubt me.' And then if you do, you'll look like a psycho because 'he was honest.'" She makes quotes with her fingers.

"You don't know that," Brenda says to Lindsay. She turns to me. "Maybe he's just insecure and wanted to get a reaction out of you."

"That makes sense."

I mean, I *did* ignore his texts the entire first day of our relationship, and then show up super late to his place the next day. Maybe he just wanted to know that I really *do* like him.

We all stop walking as Jade stares at a pair of boyfriend jeans in the window of *American Eagle*.

"Well, either way, he shouldn't be hanging out with her," Jade says, leading us into the store. "I mean, he legit hooked up with her a month ago. And he's still gonna hang out and party and get drunk with her? After she completely disrespected you?"

I sigh, toying with a T-shirt on the rack in front of me. "I don't know what to do. I can't tell him who he can and can't see."

"Yes, you can," Jade says.

"Orrrrr," Brenda starts. "You can just be honest with him and tell him it bothers you."

"I think he's aware. I mean, I already told him I don't like her."

"And what'd he say?" Lindsay asks.

I hesitate, my cheeks flushing. "That it was hot."

Brenda narrows her eyes. "That *what* was hot?"

"My reaction, I guess."

"That's...weird," Jade says, wrinkling her nose as she sorts through jeans on the table in front of her.

"Yeah, I thought so, too."

"I really think he was trying to make you jealous," Brenda says.

"But why?"

"Are you guys having sex?" Lindsay asks me suddenly.

"Lindsay!" Brenda exclaims.

A wave of heat rushes over me. "Uh...No, not yet." I look at Jade, who looks at Lindsay with a shared expression of pity. "Why?"

"He's in college. If he's not getting it from his girlfriend, he's getting it somewhere else."

"Oh, *stop*, Linds," Brenda says, rolling her eyes. "It's been, like, three weeks since they met. Not all guys are pigs."

Lindsay lifts her hands. "Don't shoot the messenger."

# CHAPTER 15

"Where are you going?"

I'm in the kitchen brewing coffee when my dad walks in with a book in his hand. By the tone of his voice, I can tell he's not pleased. And it might have something to do with my outfit.

Dylan asked me to go to a Halloween party with him so I could meet his friends. When I told Jade, she insisted I borrow her costume since she has theater rehearsal all weekend. So, instead of just putting tape on my glasses and tucking my T-shirt into my jeans to sport the "nerd" look, I'm a "sexy maid" in a frilly black and white short dress with a puffy tulle skirt. At least I'm still wearing my Converse.

"Uh…a Halloween thing," I tell my dad. "With Dylan."

"'A Halloween thing?'" he repeats, eyebrows raised. "What *kind* of Halloween thing? A party?"

"It's not really a *party.* It's more of a…hangout." I turn my back to him and pour myself a cup of coffee. "Want some?"

"Don't change the subject. And yes, I do."

I smile, offering him a steaming mug from across the kitchen island as he takes a seat.

"Dylan wants me to meet his friends, that's all. It's just gonna be a small group of people at his friend's house." That's the line Dylan used on me. I'm not sure how accurate it really is.

"And you have to wear *that* to meet his friends?"

"It's Halloween!" I argue.

My dad's about to respond when my mom walks in. She does a double-take at me.

"Well, look at you! You look *gorgeous*."

I raise my eyebrows at my dad. "See? Mom's okay with it."

"Not really helping my argument here, Viv," my dad says.

I laugh, rolling my eyes and pouring cream into my coffee. "Dad's upset because I'm going to a *hangout* with Dylan."

"I'm not an idiot. I'm a professor, for Christ's sake. I know what goes on at college 'hangouts.'" He makes air quotes.

"Oh, would you relax?" my mom starts. She shoots him a look, and I know exactly what she's trying to tell him with it: "*This is good for April. She needs to be a normal teenager.*"

This time, I'm thankful for her input.

\*       \*       \*

As soon as we get to the party, I regret coming. I'm already uncomfortable, crossing my arms over my chest and taking in the large crowd.

I follow Dylan, who's dressed as a soccer player, into the kitchen and we collect our cups from some guy handing them out at an old wooden dinner table. How anyone could eat in a room this dirty is beyond me. The tiled floor is covered in smeared mud from everyone's shoes, the sink is piling with crusty dishes, and the garbage can is lying on its side, overflowing with cans and fast food wrappers.

"Yooooooo." Gabe, who I recognize from Dylan's apartment a few weeks ago, approaches us with his arms wide. He's wearing a red shirt and fake mustache. "It's-a me, Mario! Except, I'm Spanish."

"What's up, dude?" Dylan says, laughing.

"Oh, you know. Hanging in the corner 'cause I have no friends other than you two."

"You just met April," Dylan tells him.

"Actually, we met last week, so I think that counts."

"Yeah, we're actually best friends," I add matter-of-factly. "It was like...friendship at first sight."

"She's the Luigi to my Mario."

Dylan shakes his head and puts his arm around both of our shoulders.

"I need a drink," he says.

We walk down to the basement, and it's clear this is more

of a "party" than a "hangout." I feel a pang of guilt, knowing my dad would be uncomfortable with this.

"Want some beer?" Dylan asks me.

"That's okay. I think I'll have some of that stuff." I point to a pitcher by the DJ stand across the room. It's filled with pink liquid.

"Uh, no, you won't. That's punch."

I stare at him, not understanding.

"It's probably laced," Gabe elaborates.

I scrunch my face. "Beer it is," I say, like I have a choice.

We wait in the keg line, or should I say *mob,* for a good ten minutes. Dylan stands behind me. Placing his hands on my waist, he kisses my cheek.

"You look so hot in this costume," he whispers in my ear.

"Awwwwwwwwww," Gabe says from behind us. "So fucking cute, I wanna kill myself."

We laugh, and I quickly separate from Dylan. When we finally reach the front of the beer line, a guy who looks too young to be in college overflows my cup with foam. I take a sip and immediately cringe at the bitter taste. Nothing worse than warm, cheap beer. But at least I'll have a drink to carry around for show.

"What's wrong, don't like the taste of Natty Light?" Gabe asks, smirking.

"This is disgusting," I tell him, making a face.

Dylan downs his cup before budging out of line, then gets a refill as I stand off to the side with Gabe. When he's done, he asks if I want to play pong, and the competitive girl within me jumps at the opportunity.

The three of us head back upstairs where a plastic table is set up.

"Me and my girl!" Dylan yells, pointing to me and talking to the guy in charge of the game. It's so official, there's even a list. The guy scribbles our names.

The room is packed and humid. I'm already dripping in sweat, so I pull my curled hair up into a ponytail and fan my face frantically with my hands. "You okay?" Dylan asks me.

"Yeah, I'm fine. Just a little hot." I smile and look around the room. I see a bunch of people from high school who I recognize but have never spoken to.

"Yeah, it's hot as fuck in here!" Gabe says, pulling at his T-shirt.

We wait there for a good ten minutes as the teams before us play. I try to look preoccupied, focusing on my phone as Dylan and Gabe watch the beer pong matches.

When I glance up, I see a blonde girl in the corner by herself. She's leaning against the wall, staring at her feet, and it looks like she's about to cry. Her cheeks are bright red and she's hunched over.

*Jenny?*

"I'll be right back," I tell Dylan, squeezing his hand before making my way through the crowd.

Jenny's sitting on the floor now, hugging her legs to her chest, her forehead resting on her knees. Her long hair falls over her shoulders like silk.

"Hey, are you okay?" I ask her, crouching down to touch her shoulder.

She looks up, her blue eyes glistening with tears, eyeliner smudged underneath. My heart drops.

"April? What are you doing here?"

"I'm with my boyfriend," I tell her. "What's wrong? Do you want to go talk?"

She nods, so I offer her my hand to help her up and lead her into the nearest bathroom, shutting the door behind us so she has the privacy to cry.

And that's exactly what she does.

She hunches over the sink, holding her face in her hands while resting her elbows on the counter. Her back shakes with sobs, and all I can think is that something must've happened to Tristan. Something bad.

"What is it?" I ask quietly, standing next to her by the door. I'm lightheaded.

She grabs what looks like a used tissue off the sink and dabs her eyes before I can get her a clean one. Sighing, she turns to face me, stumbling. I reach out to steady her.

"I should've known," she tells me.

"Should've known what?"

"That something was wrong."

I pause. "What do you mean, 'something was wrong?'"

"He was crying!"

"Whoa, whoa, whoa...Back up. Who was crying? And why?"

She sighs, leaning against the bathroom counter. "I was at school the night Tristan went missing, and he texted me at, like, 3 o'clock in the morning saying, 'It was my fault.'"

"What was your fault?" I ask, confused.

"No, *his* fault."

"Okay, what was *his* fault?"

She throws her hands up. "I don't know! I asked him what he meant, but he ignored me. So, I called him, and I could tell he was crying. He just kept apologizing."

"And you don't know what he was apologizing for?" I ask.

"No. He wouldn't tell me. So I called my dad to see what was going on, but he'd been sleeping, because, like I said, it was 3 a.m. And when he checked Tristan's room, he wasn't there. Even though his car was outside."

My eyes glaze over as I stare at my dirty Converse.

"Do you think he..." My voice trails off. I don't even know what I'm getting at. Or maybe I do, but I can't bring myself to say it.

Jenny leans over the sink again, tears streaming down her face.

"I don't know." She looks at her reflection with a pout and narrowed blue eyes. Her hair waterfalls over her shoulders. "He was so out-of-character, April."

Suddenly, there's a pounding on the bathroom door.

"Yoooooo, I gotta piss!!!" a male voice booms from the other side of the door. We both ignore it.

"Did you ask your dad if he seemed off that night? Before he texted you?" I ask.

Jenny starts to talk, but the guy bangs again. "Hurry the hell up!"

"WE'RE BUSY!" I yell back, hoping he finds somewhere else to go to the bathroom. I watch Jenny, waiting for her to continue.

"He said he seemed normal. But he did find a half-empty bottle of whiskey in Tristan's room."

I shake my head. This isn't the guy I had English class with. And it breaks my heart that maybe I didn't know him as well as I thought. That maybe, if I had taken the time to *get* to know him, I could've stopped this somehow.

Jenny sits on the closed toilet seat, crossing her legs. A bright blue rug stained with dirt and dust frames the toilet. "If he was okay, if he just, like, ran away because he was upset, I feel like he would have made sure that I knew. Or he'd be home by now." She starts crying again, and I stand there awkwardly, letting it all sink in.

I need to help Tristan. And the only way I can do that right now is by being there for Jenny.

"Can I see your phone?" I ask her, wanting to make sure I have her number so I can check in if needed.

She hands me her cell, and I put my number in and text myself from her phone.

"Oh God." Jenny says, standing up quickly. She's holding her stomach and staring at the sink like— "I think I'm gonna be sick."

She starts bending over the sink dry heaving, and I immediately feel queasy. There's another knock on the door suddenly, and I swing it open to see a small brunette.

"Where's Jenny?" she demands. I point behind me, my own stomach unsettled now, and she pushes past me and holds Jenny's hair back. "Girl, are you okay? Drink too much?" she asks calmly.

As I step out of the bathroom, I'm so dizzy that I feel like

I just downed five shots. I try to push through the crowd, but I have tunnel vision, and everything around me is a blur.

"There you are!" Dylan says, grabbing my wrist and tugging me over to him. "You left me to fend for myself. Thank God I got another partner in time."

I look over to see Mandy, who's dressed as a vampire in a tight black dress with fake white fangs and red "blood" on the corners of her mouth. She has icy blue eyes that don't even acknowledge my presence.

"I don't feel well," I tell Dylan, needing to get out of this house.

He furrows his brows. "What's wrong?"

"I just really don't feel well. Can we—"

Mandy shoots a pong ball across the table and sinks it in one of the cups.

"Nice!" Dylan cheers, then high fives her. And I can't watch this. Not now.

I turn on my heel and push through the crowd toward the door, leaving Dylan with Mandy.

I just need some air. Cold air. And I'll feel better.

But I can barely even make it two feet. It's like being at a concert and trying to fight your way to the stage. Everyone's body heat is suffocating me, and their voices mesh into one overwhelming sound that rings loudly in my ears. There are so many colors, so many costumes, so many scents, like alcohol and fruity perfume and old garbage.

*Sensory overload.*

My vision starts to fade in and out. All the noise grows muffled. My body becomes numb.

Somehow, I make it outside, as someone guides me to the side of the house. My breathing is more like gasps for air, my face wet with tears as I start to register that Gabe is next to me.

"You okay?" he asks me, his hand on my arm.

I take a few deep breaths as I lean against the metal fence, realizing I just had a panic attack in the middle of a college party.

"Oh my God, I'm so embarrassed."

"Don't be embarrassed. No one saw but me." Gabe stands next to me awkwardly, watching me with concern. "You didn't have the punch, did you?"

"What? No, I just…felt sick."

"Well, it was like a sauna in there, so I don't blame you."

I look at the house, white with dirty siding. There's a few people smoking on the wooden patio, and I can hear everyone inside from out here. It's a lot less intimidating from a distance.

"I suck at these things," I say.

"What? Parties?"

I wipe my eyes. "Basically anything with people."

He laughs, and my lips curl into a smile. "Yeah," he says. "People are the worst."

"April, there you are," Dylan says, jogging over to me. "What happened?" He notices Gabe and his face grows tense.

"She sorta had a…" Gabe starts, then looks at me. "She didn't feel well, and I saw you weren't with her, so I wanted to make sure she was alright."

"What's wrong?" Dylan asks me, ignoring Gabe.

"I told you I felt sick." It comes out a little harsh.

He stares at me for a moment. "Okay, well…do you want me to take you home?"

I don't say anything, because I don't know what I want. I'm just some stupid little girl, tagging along with the older kids, trying—and failing—to be cool enough. "Yes? No?" Dylan asks.

"If you don't mind."

"Alright…I guess I'll see you later, man," Dylan tells Gabe.

"Wait, dude, are you sober?" Gabe asks.

Dylan scoffs. "I'm fine. I had, like, two beers," he says before starting toward his car.

"Thanks again," I tell Gabe, then follow Dylan down the gravel driveway.

Thankfully, the air helped calm me down a bit, but my stomach is still in knots. Before putting the key in the ignition,

Dylan stares straight ahead as if he's contemplating something. But then he turns on the car, pulls away from the curb, and takes me home.

# CHAPTER 16

I can't sleep. I can't stop thinking about what Jenny said. Every time I close my eyes, I see Tristan crying. Drunk. Alone. Devastated.

Rolling over to grab my phone off my nightstand, I open Instagram and type in Tristan's name in the search bar. The light from my phone makes me squint.

Obviously, Tristan hasn't posted since he went missing. So I click on the tagged photos section.

The last photo was the one Zach tagged him in when he first went missing. Other than that, there's a bunch from Jenny. A few old ones from this girl he used to date sophomore year, who I had ceramics class with. Some from our classmates when we had a sub. I'm even in one of them.

I tap the photo to get a closer look. The guy taking the picture has two spiky ponytails on the top of his head, courtesy of the girls in our class. His smile is wide and goofy, and everyone behind him is squeezed into the photo—including Tristan and me, who are leaning close to each other. Tristan's arm is around me.

I remember that day. It was the same day Tristan and I were talking about music. The same day he asked me to go to the concert with him in New York. When I was too afraid to say yes, because New York City is such an overwhelming place. You could easily lose your way around, and no one would even care. No one would be able to find you, to help—

Suddenly, I have a surge of hope. New York. Of course, he'd go to the city. Especially if he has a friend to stay with there.

I sit up in bed and pull my hair into a tight bun. I click

back to Tristan's own feed, scrolling down to February of last year. And then I see it: a photo from the concert in the city. I tap the photo once, noticing he tagged someone in it, and see a user named @coltonhares.

I click on his username. He doesn't have many photos, but his most recent one was posted a few days ago and is tagged at the beach—*my* beach. Tristan told me he lived in New York. And the rest of his pictures seem to confirm that.

So, what was he doing here? Unless...

Logging onto Facebook, I type in Tristan's name. Then, I check his friend's list for a Colton Hares. And sure enough, his profile shows up. But it's private. The only picture I can see is a small selfie of him laughing on the sand with a beer. He has dark hair and pale skin.

I need to talk to this guy. I don't care how crazy he might think I am. This is too much of a coincidence, and I don't believe in coincidences.

If you message someone who doesn't follow you on Instagram, they can't see it unless they click to their message requests. I could follow him, but I'm not sure he'll follow me back, considering he doesn't know who I am. Plus, it's not like I'm some hipster model like Brenda who warrants thousands of followers.

Facebook might be more reasonable. Especially if he notices that our mutual friend is Tristan. Then, I can message him through Facebook Messenger, which hopefully he'll be able to see right away, if he has the app on his phone. Don't most people have the app on their phone?

Before I can talk myself out of it, I send him a friend request.

# CHAPTER 17

On Sunday night, Kat and I sit at her kitchen counter with mugs of hot chocolate on as her mom makes us pancakes for dinner.

"So, Jenny has no idea what he was apologizing for?" Kat asks me. I filled her in on everything Jenny told me at the party last night, but I left out the part about Colton. I still don't know what to do about that. I don't want to get anyone's hopes up if this is just me overthinking things as usual.

"Nope," I tell Kat. "No idea at all."

"That poor family," Ms. Bailey says as she flips a pancake on the griddle. Her curly red hair is in a high messy bun, the sleeves of her shirt rolled up.

"*God*, I feel so bad for Jenny," Kat says.

"And for Tristan," I add. "Jenny said he was really upset. Crying, even."

Kat bites her lip and looks down at her mug. I can pick up on nervous energy.

"Do you think he, like…" I start, hoping I don't have to finish the thought out loud.

Ms. Bailey sighs, leaning her elbows on the counter across from us. "Let's not go down that road, sweetie," she says.

"You're right. I just…feel like I'm going insane thinking about this."

"It could drive anyone insane, which is why we have to try not to dwell over it," Kat tells me.

I laugh. "I am literally a diagnosed dweller. There's no way of stopping it."

"Did I tell you about my Tinder date?" Kat asks me, clearly

attempting to steer the subject in a better direction. I let her, even though I'm still thinking about Tristan.

"Um, no!" I feign. "Who's the lucky guy or gal?" Kat hands me her phone, and I look at some girl named Sky's Tinder profile. She has long platinum hair and a model-like frame. In every picture, she's sporting ripped jeans or fishnets with long band T's and flawless makeup. "She's cute. Very emo hipster-y."

Kat grins. Her auburn curls, pulled back into a high ponytail, bounce as she does an excited dance. "We're going to see this Indie band tomorrow night at some venue by the beach."

"Nice."

"I figured it's a good spot to meet since it's a public place. Just in case she's, like, a catfish or something."

"And if she is, a group of hipsters will be able to save you?" her mom asks.

"Hey, we might not look it, but we're a tough breed."

I wonder what it's like to have a mother who's also your best friend.

Kat and her mom are only seventeen years apart. It's always been just the two of them. Kat's never met her dad, but she doesn't seem to care. With a mom like hers, who needs a deadbeat father? She makes time for mother-daughter movie nights, dinner dates, late-night gossip sessions—despite being a high school English teacher and freelance writer.

Kat turns back to her phone, scrolling through Sky's pictures, a smile tugging on the corners of her mouth. My own phone buzzes with a text.

It's a link from Dylan to some long story titled, "He Wanted A Divorce. She Had One Simple Request." I open the article, wondering why Dylan would randomly send this to me.

We haven't spoken since last night, when he dropped me at home before heading back to the party. All day, I couldn't stop wondering if he spent the night hanging with Mandy, Lindsay's words replaying in my head: *If he's not getting it from his girlfriend, he's getting it somewhere else.*

I scan my screen, reading. The story starts with the husband cheating on his wife with his coworker. He tells his wife he wants a divorce. In response, his wife has one request: that he carries her from their bedroom to the front door each morning for a month, like he did into their bridal suite on their wedding day.

The husband, though confused, agrees, and in doing so each morning, he realizes he still loves his wife. This simple act of intimacy is enough to remind him how much she matters to him.

At the end of the thirty days, he no longer wants to leave his wife. So, he breaks it off with his colleague, comes home with flowers for his wife, and finds her lying in bed, still. Too still.

Turns out, for months, she had been battling cancer. All while her husband was pursuing another woman, too busy to notice how sick his own wife was. And by the time he realized all of this, it was too late—she was dead.

I text Dylan back, wondering what he's getting at: What made you send this to me?

**Dylan:** It has a good message. I thought you'd appreciate it.

I'm still thinking of how to answer when another text pops up.

**Dylan:** I hope you know how much I care about you.

# CHAPTER 18

"And how did that make you feel?"

I'm sitting across from Dr. Glen, like I always do on Tuesday nights. Only this time is different. Instead of word-vomiting like usual, Dr. Glen has had to pry details out of me.

I shrug. I don't have the energy to explain anything to her today. Especially not my latest panic attack at my first college party.

Sometimes, my mind becomes so cluttered that I can't think straight enough to understand what, exactly, is bothering me. It just leaves this mess of a million contradicting thoughts that feel like an itch I can't scratch.

"Did you tell Dylan about your disorder?" she asks me.

"Not yet."

"Why's that?"

"I don't know. It hasn't come up, I guess."

She raises her eyebrows. "You don't think your panic attack was a good time to explain it to him?"

"Well, I'm not sure he *knew* I had a panic attack…" I think back to the party. How he stayed back with Mandy as Gabe helped me outside. My stomach sinks. "I just told him I felt sick."

Dr. Glen presses her lips together. "I see. Well, maybe that's something you can bring up this week. It's important for your partner to understand your illness, or to at least be aware of it."

"Sure," I say, but I'm not really listening. I'm too busy thinking about Mandy with Dylan. About what she said to him when she found out we were dating. How pretty she looked Saturday night. How *normal* she was, playing pong with Dylan without a care in the world. *Must be nice.*

When I get home from therapy, I'm about to walk into the kitchen to make a peanut butter sandwich for dinner when I hear my parents talking. About me.

My mom's voice tells me she's in one of her moods where everything annoys her.

"I mean, is the therapy even helping?"

"I'm sure it is," my dad says matter-of-factly.

"Well, I'm not. She spends an hour there every single week, and for what?" I hear glasses clinking, like someone's putting away the dishes. My dad, probably. "I mean, the *one night* she goes out like a normal teenager, she comes home crying after one hour. She needs to learn to get a hold of herself or she's going to lose the people in her life. You think her *college boyfriend* will want to deal with—"

"She has a *mental* disorder, Vivian. It's not something you can just turn off. You think *she* wants to deal with it every single day?"

My mom sighs. "Well, if it's that hard on her, then maybe she should see a psychiatrist instead of suffering." Her voice is softer now. "Half the planet's on Xanax. My boss said—"

"April already told us she doesn't want to go on medication. Or do you not remember having that conversation with her?"

I remember it. I remember leaving school early that day because I couldn't stop crying. I remember sitting with them on the couch that night to talk about my frequent anxiety attacks and how we might treat them. My dad weighing the pros and cons of trying medication while my mom emailed clients from her phone, only looking up when directly asked for her opinion. Which was to "take the meds and get on with life."

"You think she can keep living like this?" my mom continues. "You think she could handle going away to *college* like this?"

"You know what I think? That she's about to be an adult who can do whatever she wants to do. And you know what wouldn't hurt? Having a little more support from her own mother."

"Oh, *do not* put April's mental state on me."

I don't want to hear the rest of this. I don't want to hear another word. I slip back out the front door, completely unnoticed.

I need to get away from this house. Away from everyone in it.

# CHAPTER 19

The beach has always felt like home. Something about the ocean air calms me. It's cold outside, but I roll my windows all the way down and blast the heat to make up for it.

The town is dim and desolate. I don't see a single person, and there are only a few houses with lights on. My music is the only sound I hear, probably because it's playing at the highest possible volume.

That is, until Dylan's call stops Boston Manor's *Laika* mid-chorus. I answer with the buttons on my steering wheel. "Hello?" I mutter.

"Hey, babe. How was your day?" Dylan's voice blares through the stereo of my car. I dial down the volume.

"Fine."

Tugging the car down a side street, I park near a church, only a block from the beach.

"Are you driving?" Dylan asks, talking over other voices around him.

"I was."

"Where are you?"

"I'm at the beach."

He doesn't say anything, but the background noise seems to dissipate with each passing second until it's completely gone.

"You're at the beach?" he asks, his voice clear now. I inhale a deep breath as goosebumps spread down my arms and legs. "Are you by yourself?"

"Yeah."

"Why?"

I grip the steering wheel until my knuckles turn white. "I just wanted to get out of my house."

"What happened, babe? You're worrying me." His voice is so tender that before I can stop myself, I'm crying. But I conceal the noise so that he can't hear me. "Which beach are you at? I'm coming to meet you."

I tell him, because I really don't want to be alone. Not as much as I thought I did. What I really want is to just be distracted.

The town is a half hour from his school, but he's here in 15 minutes. He parks behind me and gets out immediately, walking up to the passenger's side of my car. He's in jeans and a hoodie, his hair damp. Settling in the seat next to me, he shuts the door and looks at me.

It's obvious I've been crying, even if he didn't witness it himself. My eyes are bright red and my lips are swollen.

"Did something happen?" Dylan asks me, studying my face. He grabs my hand and watches me, like I'm a child who needs protection. Like I'm still that same third-grader I once was.

I stare straight ahead at the beach in front of us, swallowing the lump in my throat. When I don't answer him, he says, "Let's go for a walk."

I roll up my windows and turn my car off, shivering as the air hits me. I tug on the sleeves of my jacket, then stuff my hands in my pockets.

Dylan walks with his arm around my waist as we pass an open liquor store. I stop in front of it. "I could use a drink," I tell him.

Dylan hesitates. "Okay...What do you want?"

"Anything."

He guides me into the store, which is brightly lit by fluorescent lights. The door jingles when we walk in, and my stomach does somersaults. I've never been in a liquor store before. Greg always makes me wait in the car.

Dylan brings me down the wine aisle instead of in the

back near the hard liquor. He shows me different bottles of sparkling wine. "Do you like white or red?" I shrug, and he picks white.

As we wait in line to pay, I notice the guy in front of us has a Knuckle Puck shirt on, and immediately I think of Tristan. He collects his cases of beer and turns around, and we make eye contact. He's tall and skinny with bright blue eyes and dark hair. "Nice shirt," I tell him.

He nods at me, smiling. "Awesome band," he says. When he notices Dylan next to me, his expression changes.

Dylan stiffens. "Do you know him?" he asks after the guy walks out. He hands the cashier our wine.

"No, but he has good taste in music."

Dylan pays without even being carded, and when we step back outside, I'm suddenly excited. It's strange how one person can make the world look so much brighter.

I grab Dylan's hand and tug him toward the beach. When we reach the sand, I bend down and tug off my converse, my body shivering in my light coat.

I flop down on the sand when we get closer to the water, watching the waves tease the shore. Dylan sits next to me and hands me the bottle out of the brown paper bag.

"You open it."

I go to do just that, but realize it's not a twist off.

"Wait, is this one of the kinds that pops off, like champagne?" I turn the bottle in my hands, inspecting the top of it.

He smirks. "Yup. You gotta loosen the cage a little and hold the cork down until you're ready."

I do what he says, placing my finger over the cork so it doesn't happen too soon.

"Oh my God, this is scary!" I laugh, angling it toward the ocean.

"Wait! Not yet!" Dylan fishes his phone out of his pocket. "I wanna get a picture of you...Okay. Ready. Set. Go!"

I move my finger. His flash goes off. Nothing happens.

"What did I do wrong?" I ask, pouting. I turn the bottle up

so I can look at the cage again to loosen it more.

"Don't face it toward you!" Dylan yells, pushing the bottle down so it's facing the ocean again. It pops, and wine explodes all over my pants.

"Drink it!" Dylan yells, laughing.

I tilt my head back and chug as fast as I can. The wine is sweet and bubbly, settling in my stomach like liquid pop rocks. I keep drinking as my mind wanders back to what my mom said. About getting a hold of myself. About losing Dylan. I want to forget it all.

"Okay, easy…" Dylan says, gently grabbing the bottle from me. His smile falters as I shoot him a look.

I dig my feet into the damp sand. My toes are frozen and starting to get numb, but I keep burying them deeper, deeper, deeper.

Dylan takes a few sips of the wine, occasionally glancing at me, like he's waiting for me to speak.

"*What*?"

He winces at my tone, then shakes his head and stares out at the ocean. I know I shouldn't be taking this out on him, but I can't control my attitude tonight. This is why I wanted to be alone.

I try to focus on the sound of the waves against the rocks, closing my eyes and taking deep breaths. But it's windy out, and my hair is getting the brunt of it, snapping my face like little rubber bands.

"I grew up here," Dylan says suddenly.

I look at him, confused. "Where?"

"This town. My parents live here."

"Oh."

"I know that kid from the liquor store," he continues, picking at the label on the wine bottle. The waves are loud, and he's talking so low that it's hard to hear his voice. "He went to my high school."

"Were you friends with him?"

He scoffs. "No. He was an asshole. Like everyone else

there."

"I'm sorry," I tell him, chewing on my lip.

He shakes his head, then meets my eyes. I can't read his expression, but his cheeks are flushed red. He looks younger tonight. More innocent. Not like someone who would "get it somewhere else."

He wouldn't do that. *Would he?*

I lean in and kiss him, needing his lips on mine, needing to feel grounded. He hesitates before kissing me back, and when he does, he tries to slow it down.

But the thoughts are catching up to me. Everything Lindsay said about Dylan. Everything my mom said about *me*.

I fall onto Dylan as he lies back on the sand. I tug my jacket off and toss it to the side, then tug at Dylan's shirt.

He grabs my hands away. "April, stop..."

"What? Why?" I look down at him, confused.

He shakes his head, catching his breath. "Not like this."

"What do you mean?"

Sitting up, he places his hands on my shoulders. "You're tipsy...and clearly upset about something."

"I'm *fine*."

"Well, this doesn't *feel* fine."

"*What* doesn't feel fine?" I ask, tears forming in my eyes. "Us?"

"No! I didn't mean it like that." He positions my chin toward his so that I'm facing him. I close my eyes, my face wet with tears. "Hey, stop. Don't cry, babe."

"I'm so confused. Why don't you want to be with me?"

"It's not that I don't want to, April. You're just...you're way more important than that."

"Than *what*?"

"Than what we were about to do in the middle of the beach, while I'm sober and you're not."

I pull away and glare at him. His chest moves with every breath, and his eyes are wide. My entire body is trembling, and I don't know if it's from the alcohol or the cold or the anger in my veins.

Dylan grabs my hand. "I can't just ignore the fact that you were crying before I got here, April. You won't tell me what happened."

I don't say anything. Instead, I grab the bottle of wine and finish it off. Then I get up and walk away.

# CHAPTER 20

"April, come on." Dylan grabs my hand as I stomp through the sand toward the street. "You're not driving like this."

I spin around to face him, stumbling a bit. "I'm not. I just want to go for a walk."

"You're not going for a walk by yourself right now."

As Dylan's eyes search me, I look down at my bare feet covered in sand. How did I get here?

The air is damp, and I'm shaking, chilled to the bone. I thought maybe the alcohol would numb me, but it's like my thoughts, my emotions, are even more powerful than before.

"I don't want to lose you," I tell Dylan, my voice just above a whisper.

"*What*? Why would you lose me?"

"Lindsay said that if you aren't getting it from me, you'll get it from someone else."

Dylan stares at me, face blank. I watch as his eyes narrow. "What are you trying to say?"

"I don't know."

"Are you asking if I would cheat on you?" I'm about to say no, but I realize that *yes*, that's exactly what I'm asking him. He lets go of my hand and runs his fingers through his hair. "You really think I would do that?"

"No." I shake my head quickly, then pause. My throat is tight as I try to swallow my cries. "I don't know."

"Wow. Well, that's nice to know, April. Thanks for the trust."

"No, wait!" I tug on his hand as he tries to walk away. "I didn't…" My voice gets caught in my throat. "I'm sorry! I'm just

—I'm drunk, Dylan."

I'm sobbing now, holding onto his hand as he watches me fall apart in front of him. *My mom was right. I can't keep living like this.*

"What?" Dylan asks. "What do you mean, you 'can't keep living like this?'"

Realizing I said that out loud, I place my palm on my forehead to shield my eyes. I can't look at him.

"*April.*" His voice is stern, yet laced with concern.

"I didn't mean it. What I said about you." I look him in the eyes. "I'm just being stupid. I get these thoughts in my head and they get stuck. And I can't get them out." My chest heaves as I cry. "It's not you," I choke out.

I peek up at him, my eyes nearly swollen shut. He doesn't say anything, just stares behind me at the houses along the beach. "I'm sorry," I tell him.

"Come here." He wraps him in a hug and I take in the scent of his cologne, relaxing a bit. "It's okay."

*It's okay.* As long as his arms are around me.

# CHAPTER 21

It's been a long week, so I take myself on a bookstore date Friday night. Dylan's out with his friends, Kat's at that concert with her Tinder date, and Jade's with Adam. For once, I can be alone without feeling like I should be somewhere else, with someone else, doing something else.

After grabbing a coffee, I walk my normal route straight to the mystery section. An acoustic Indie song plays as I scan the shelves for intriguing titles or attractive covers.

Across the store, I see Zach helping someone find a book. He looks tired. What I wouldn't give to see Tristan with him again, laughing together.

Tristan could make anyone feel better. He had this calming energy to him.

*Has.*

I remember one day, he walked me to the nurse after I'd made myself sick with worry. Greg had felt nauseous the night before, and I thought he had the stomach virus, so I was sure I would catch it. I stayed up until my alarm went off the next morning, listening from my room to hear if he was in the bathroom throwing up at all.

I was so tired the next day that I completely forgot we had to read an assignment for class. Of course, it was the one day we had a pop quiz. As soon as I sat down and saw the stack of papers in Ms. Bailey's hands, my heart dropped to my toes, and I became so dizzy I was certain I was coming down with whatever my brother had.

I started panicking about that, too, which made me feel like I was actually gonna throw up.

I couldn't sit still as my body shook with nerves, so I jumped up and started walking toward the door. But I must've gotten up too fast, because my eyes went black for a moment. I steadied myself on the doorway just as Tristan walked in the room.

"Are you okay?" he asked, resting a hand on my arm.

"I don't feel well," I muttered as I walked past him and into the hall. Ms. Bailey followed me out.

"April, what's wrong?"

Ms. Bailey and I had a good relationship, and not just because her daughter is my best friend. I was the only student who ever really paid attention to her, and she was the only teacher who ever really *got* my attention.

She asked me if I needed to go to the nurse's office as I leaned against a row of lockers with my eyes shut, and I thought maybe I should, since I did feel sick. Anxiety or not, the physical symptoms were real.

She wasn't convinced that I was well enough to walk myself though, so she called Tristan into the hallway.

"Could you take April to the nurse? She's a little light-headed and I want someone with her just in case."

"Of course," he said, watching me with concern.

When we were out of earshot, he asked if I forgot to do the reading, too.

"Yeah, I actually did," I told him. "But I swear that's not why I'm going to the nurse."

He laughed and walked behind me, his hand hovering near my back, like he was scared I'd fall over any second. "Are you dizzy?"

"Yeah. My brother is sick, so I probably caught it," I said, even though Greg had woken up feeling fine, reassuring me that he just ate too much. But who knows? Maybe he was fighting something, and now I had it.

"That sucks. I hope you feel better." We continued in silence for a few steps as I took deep breaths in and out, like Dr. Glen always told me to do when I was panicky. "My sister's home sick, too. Some weird sore throat thing. I'm gonna pick her up soup later."

I smiled. "That's sweet. Are you guys close?"

"Yeah. She's my best friend."

I thought about how he acted with her in the counselor's office that day sophomore year. Making sure she was alright, putting on a brave face for her. "She's lucky to have you."

He shrugged as he stared ahead at the empty hall, his dirty blonde hair falling over his eyes. "Are you and your brother close?"

"I guess. He's more protective than anything."

"That just means he cares, trust me. It's a brother's job." We walked to the first floor of my high school, where the nurse's office was. I stared at my feet in silence as we made our way down the steps, the stomp of his worn work boots echoing in the staircase. "We should hang out sometime. You know, outside of Ms. Bailey's class."

I didn't know what to say. No one at school ever really acknowledged me. Mostly because I didn't give them the chance to. I kept my head down, only spoke when I was around my friends. Or in English class.

"Yeah, sounds good." It was a lie, but I wanted to believe it.

When we hit the bottom of the staircase, I paused, dizzy again. I didn't want to go to the nurse yet. I wanted to keep talking to him. He made me feel better.

Tristan looked at me like he understood. He sat down on the last step, and I sat next to him.

"So, you do anything fun over Christmas break?" he asked me.

I shrugged. "If you count binge-reading a new mystery series as 'fun,' which I do, then yes."

Tristan grinned, his eyes sparkling, like he was somehow intrigued by me. I blushed and looked away.

"How about you?" I asked.

"Helped my dad with work, mostly." He clasped his hands

in front of him, resting his elbows on his knees. After a few moments, he added, "This is always a hard time of the year for my family."

My heart instantly sunk. "I can't even imagine."

Tristan paused, staring ahead in thought.

"She loved Christmas." I don't have to ask him who he's talking about to know it's his mom.

"She went over-the-top with it. Like, one year, she made my dad set up speakers outside and coordinate our decorations with Christmas music."

I laughed. "I remember that. Kat and I loved it. We'd sing along every time we passed your house."

He smiles, then looks down at his hands. "The holidays make me feel like she's with me, but also make me so aware that she's *not*, you know? She died right before Christmas last year, and it's like...I don't know. I almost feel like the holiday is tainted now. Or maybe I'm just crazy."

I picked at my skinny jeans, pinching my leg over and over. "You're not," I told him, meeting his eye. I knew crazy. I *was* crazy. And he was far from it. "I'm sorry, by the way. About your mom. I don't think I've ever told you that."

"Thanks, April. It's been some time, but...you know." He shrugged. "It's still there."

"You can't just get over something like that."

He nodded, and a comfortable silence fell between us. There was no one in the hallway or staircase. For once, I felt safe in my own school. "So," he said after a minute. "Are you feeling any better?"

I was. The nausea had subsided, and I was only a little shaky. "Yeah, much." But I still didn't want to go.

"Good. I was worried you might pass out."

I laughed. "So was I."

He stood up, offering me his hand. I took it. It was warm in my palm as he slowly helped me off the step.

"Thank you for walking me," I told him. It was just the two of us in the staircase. My hand was still in his. I hoped he couldn't tell how dry it was from washing it too much.

"Hey, you got me out of that pop quiz, so I should really be thanking you."

He wasn't much taller than I was, so we were eye-to-eye.

"So," he continued. "You know, that Knuckle Puck con-cert is coming up next month...There's still some tickets left, if you're interested."

I paused, wanting to say yes, but my body wouldn't let me.

"No pressure. I know you didn't seem too into it last time I asked..." His smile looked more like a grimace. "I promise this is the last time I'll bring it up."

"No, I want to go," I said, surprising myself as much as him. "I'd love to go with you."

He grinned, and I felt giddy. "Yeah?"

"Yeah." I smiled, enjoying the thought of making a new friend for once. Maybe it'd be good for me. Maybe *he'd* be good for me.

But I never gave myself the chance to find out. I went so far as letting him buy the tickets, but I never showed up for the train. And when I tried paying him back in class the next week, spewing excuses about being sick, he wouldn't accept my money. I'm not sure he accepted my apology either. No matter how much he assured me, "It's fine," I knew it wasn't.

We didn't keep in touch after class ended for the year, when summer arrived. I haven't seen him since. And now, I might never see him again.

\*     \*     \*

"April? You good?"

I stand frozen in front of Zach. I try to nod, but I'm not sure if my head actually moves.

"You look pale. Do you need water? I can get you a cup from the cafe."

I shake my head.

This is all my fault. What if Tristan needed me? What if he needed me, and I shut him down, rejected him, made him think

I didn't give a shit — all because I was afraid?

I'm such an idiot.

Zach is still staring at me.

"Sorry, I just..." My voice trails off as I wonder how to explain myself.

"What happened?" he asks.

I debate not telling him. I don't want to sound insensitive, considering he has an actual reason to miss Tristan. But his eyes are sincere, and, well, maybe I have an actual reason, too.

"I fucked up. With Tristan."

Zach stiffens. "What do you mean?" he asks.

So I tell him about the day Tristan walked me to the nurse. How he asked me to hang out. How I agreed. How I stood him up.

I let Tristan believe that I didn't care about him. About our friendship.

"Tristan's a reasonable dude. He got over it," Zach tells me once I finish talking, and it's evident he already heard this story from Tristan, which makes me feel even worse. "Don't dwell on it, April. Regret can tear you up if you let it."

He doesn't have to tell me that. I know it firsthand.

"But what if I could've stopped him?" I ask.

"April, Tristan was *not* your responsibility. You can't blame yourself for what happened, just because you didn't want to hang out with him."

"But I *did* want to, Zach."

Zach doesn't say anything for a few moments. He looks out at the store in thought before turning his attention back to me. "Then why didn't you?" he asks finally.

That's the million-dollar question. And there's only one answer: "He deserved better."

# CHAPTER 22

"*Soup*?" my dad says as he walks into the kitchen. "You're making your boyfriend *soup*? Really, April?"

I'm heating up a can of Campbell's for dinner, mixing it with a wooden spoon as Dylan sits at the counter. "But it's"—I grab the can and read—"BBQ seasoned pork soup. With natural smoke flavor!" I say in a dramatic commercial voice.

Dylan laughs, and my dad shakes his head at me. "Like mother, like daughter."

"*Ow*." I place my palm on my chest. "Please *never* say that again."

My dad shoots me a look.

"Be nice." He turns off the stove, puts his hands on my shoulders, and guides me to the counter. "Sit. Let me take care of dinner before you burn the house down."

"I appreciate your confidence in me, Dad." I take a seat in the stool next to Dylan.

"Dylan, do you like steak?" my dad asks as he opens the freezer.

"Is that even a question?" Dylan says.

"Good answer."

It's nice having just the two of them here. Mom's at some Thanksgiving work party; Greg's at his friend's house. And my two favorite guys are having dinner with me.

After defrosting the steaks, my dad preps them with seasonings, then takes out three sweet potatoes.

"Ohhhh, are you gonna make that fancy sweet potato thing?" I ask. Turning to Dylan, I explain, "He puts brown sugar and marshmallows on top. If you haven't noticed, he's who I get my sweet tooth from."

My dad starts showing Dylan how he makes the sweet potatoes, and Dylan nods the whole time, listening intently. I can't help but smile.

As they talk about when to layer the marshmallows and what temperature to cook the potatoes at, I get a notification from Facebook: Colton Hares accepted your friend request.

*Oh my God.*

"I'll be right back," I tell the guys as I race up to my room. Immediately, I open the app and scroll through Colton's profile. He hasn't really posted much, just shared some memes and videos of basketball players. But I can see more of his personal information now that I'm "friends" with him, and I realize he used to go to NYU but now goes to a community college near here.

So, I guess the storyline makes sense: he used to live in New York City, when Tristan went to the concert with him. But now he moved to Connecticut to attend community college. Which means he must be from around here in the first place.

I open my Facebook Messenger app and tap Colton's name. Before I can stop myself, I type:

Hi Colton, I'm sorry if this seems weird or random, but I realized you're friends with Tristan and I remember him talking about you in class

I backspace, then retype:

Hey, I'm April, Tristan's friend

I backspace again. Then retype again:

Hey, Colton. I know you don't know me, so I'm sorry to reach out like this, but I thought that maybe we could talk about Tristan. I'm sure by now you've heard he's missing, and I guess you're the only person he talked to outside of our town. I remember him telling me you guys went to a concert together, so I figured you might be close. At the risk of being blunt...do you know anything? Did he contact you at all? I'm just really worried about him and want to know he's okay.

My finger hovers above the send symbol. Should I really do this, or is it crazy?

Probably the latter. But if it helps me find Tristan, then so be it.

\*　　　\*　　　\*

After dinner, Dylan and I grab coffee downtown, then sit

in his car near the park and listen to music. It's late, and all the shops are closed now. No one is around us. The streetlights don't reach our car.

"I don't want to take you home yet," Dylan says as it starts to rain, a few heavy drops hitting the car one at a time.

I glance at my phone for the time. It's 11.

"My dad didn't give me a curfew."

"Well, good."

Dylan reclines his seat, yawning. I do the same as *Hear You Me* by Jimmy Eat World comes on.

"Aw man, I love this song," Dylan says.

"I know, me too."

Dylan stares up at the top of his car, hand under his head. "I like the other version better though."

"There's another version?"

"Yeah, look up 'inner ear session.'"

I search for the song and hit play when I find it. Turning up the volume, I sit up and pull my feet under me, focusing.

The sound is completely different. It's like I'm in the studio with the lead singer. It's more raw, less edited in a sense. He pronounces words differently, almost unnaturally.

"I like it," I tell Dylan when it's over. "But the ending isn't as powerful in my opinion."

"*What*? I think it's more emotional."

"I don't know...It just doesn't hit me the same way."

He rolls his eyes playfully, then grabs my arms and pulls me to him. I lean over the center console and kiss him, but his car is so small that it's hard to find room, and I end up hitting the horn with my knee while trying to climb on top of him.

My cheeks rush with heat, and Dylan cracks up, shaking with laughter beneath me.

"You're such a klutz."

I fall back onto my seat. "Shut up! Maybe if your car wasn't so small, we could actually hook up without me breaking my leg."

He smiles, his eyes dancing with mine, then lets out a little laugh.

"What? Do I have something on my face?" I ask, tugging down the car visor to check the mirror.

"No, you idiot." Grabbing my wrist and tugging me toward him, he plants a kiss on my lips. He leans his forehead against mine. "I just can't help but think how lucky I am to have you."

# CHAPTER 23

I wake up at 7 o'clock Thanksgiving morning because I'm too excited to sleep. Thanksgiving has always been my favorite holiday, not just for the food, but also because it's the kickoff to the Christmas season. And this year, with Dylan, is going to be even more special.

"You're up early," my dad says, handing me a cup of coffee.

My mom sits at the counter, flipping through a magazine. I take a seat next to her.

"I bet your brother won't be up for another few hours," my mom says to me.

"Yeah, I didn't hear him come home until, like, 2."

She smirks. "Thanksgiving Eve is always a good time."

My phone buzzes on the counter in front of me.

**Dylan:** I'm making your dad's sweet potatoes for my family today. :)

I smile as another text comes in.

**Dylan:** Happy Thanksgiving, btw. Thankful for you. <3

**Me:** Hopefully they're better than my attempt. ;) I'm thankful for you too. <3

"What are you smiling about?" my dad asks as he spreads flour on the counter for the pie dough. My stomach growls in anticipation. He makes the best pumpkin pie.

"Dylan said he's using your sweet potato recipe for dinner tonight."

My dad smiles like he's proud, and my mom looks up from her magazine.

"When did Dylan have your sweet potatoes?" she asks my dad.

"Saturday."

"Yeah, he had dinner with dad and me when you were at the Thanksgiving party," I explain.

She raises her eyebrows. "Wow, he must be really into you if he's spending his Saturday night at home with you and your *dad*."

I decide to take this as a compliment.

"You still haven't met him yet," I point out to my mom.

"I know, sweetie. Work's been crazy. But I'm sure there will be plenty of time to meet him, given how head-over-heels you two seem for each other."

We spend the rest of the morning watching the Thanksgiving Day parade together. Greg joins us barely in time to catch the ending. Then, I shower and get ready for dinner. Though it's only just the four of us as usual, I still dress up.

As my parents, Greg, and I sit down to eat, my phone rings with a call from Dylan. I get up from the table and walk into the other room.

"Hey, what's up?"

He doesn't say anything, but it sounds like he's crying.

"Dylan, what's wrong?" I ask, my heart sinking at the idea of him upset.

"Can I see you?" His voice is drained, almost a whisper. "Can I pick you up? Please."

I look back at my parents and Greg at the table. They'd understand. "Of course."

"Who was that?" my dad asks as I walk back into the kitchen.

"Dylan."

"Everything okay?"

"I'm not sure. He sounded really upset." I sit down, pushing my food away. I'm not so hungry anymore. "He's gonna come pick me up."

"You're not staying for dinner?" Greg asks.

"He can come in," my mom offers. "Why doesn't he eat with us?"

"I think something happened. He didn't seem up for talking."

"Well, why don't you make him a plate," my dad says.

"It's okay." I bring my food to the counter and scrape it into containers to pack away for tomorrow.

"You gonna be back by tonight?" my dad asks me as I wash my dish. I can tell he's disappointed I'm leaving, which makes me feel guilty. "We're decorating."

I smile at him. Every year, we put the Christmas tree up on Thanksgiving night. I wouldn't miss it for the world.

"Of course. I'll be here."

Dylan looks tired when he picks me up. His eyes are bloodshot and his face is pale, like he's sick. "What's going on?" I ask from the passenger seat.

He just shakes his head. I reach for his hand and he lets me hold it, but it's cold. I trace circles with my thumb and lean my head on his shoulder.

The weather is gray and damp, and I can't help but think back to our first date, when I told him I loved cloudy days. We've come so far since that day, nearly two months ago. I love him so much that it hurts—especially now. It kills me to see him this way.

Dylan drives us to the beach in silence. No radio. No talking. Just the sound of crumpling leaves beneath his car. He parks on a side street, keys still in the ignition. He taps his fingers on the wheel and stares out the windshield in front of him.

"Can we go for a walk?" he asks.

"Of course."

We make our way to the sand and settle by the water. I shiver in my dress, pulling my knees into my chest as a mist comes off the water.

"My parents are getting a divorce."

Dylan's voice is strained, and doesn't sound like his own. I open my mouth, not knowing what to say. "I'm so sorry" is what comes out, and I'm mad at myself for not being able to come up with something better to comfort him.

I grab his hand, and he shifts, taking a few deep breaths.

Pulling his hand away, he presses his fists into his forehead, like he's willing himself not to cry.

"It's my fault," he says.

"How could that possibly be your fault?"

He looks at me. "They argue about *me*."

"No one can break a good marriage, Dylan. My parents fight about me all the time. That doesn't mean—"

"No, you don't get it," he says, voice hard. "I'm failing two of my classes. They've been arguing about my grades since high school. But now, it's really bad, 'cause they're paying all this money for me to go to college, and I'm blowing it. My mom thinks I should transfer to community college, but my dad thinks I need to get my shit together and stick it out."

"Well, what do *you* think you should do?"

He hesitates for a second. "I don't even know, April. I don't know what I want. I'm just not happy."

I pause. "You're not?"

He shakes his head, staring out at the ocean.

My body swells with guilt. This entire time, our entire relationship, Dylan was struggling in school, struggling with his family, struggling with his mental health. And I didn't even notice.

"You're the only person who makes me feel okay," he tells me. "From the moment I met you, you put me at ease. I don't wanna—" His voice catches. "I don't wanna fuck this up."

"How would you fuck it up?"

"Because you're so...*put together*. You have a future. I don't know what I'm doing with my life."

I can't help but laugh.

"Dylan, I am *not* put together. You saw how I got a few weeks ago when we were here. I have my own—"

"You're too good for me," he continues, talking over me. "My brother told me as soon as you get into college, you'll leave me."

*Brother?* I furrow my eyebrows.

He never mentioned he had a brother. Just a younger sister.

"And yeah, he's an asshole, but honestly, he has a point. Why wouldn't you leave me?"

I stare at him, but he won't look at me.

"Why wouldn't I leave you?" I repeat. "Because I love you, Dylan."

Dylan's lips curl up the slightest bit, his eyes glistening. "You do?"

I grab his hand again, and this time, he lets me hold it.

"Yes. I do." I lean my head against him and close my eyes. "I love you."

"I love you too," he whispers, then kisses me to prove just how much.

\*     \*     \*

"What the *fuck*, April?"

I wake up to Dylan holding my phone and glaring at me. My head is pounding. My dress is slipping off my shoulder. I tug it back up.

How long were we asleep? And why does he look so mad?

I grab my phone from his hand and check the screen. There's a Facebook message. From Colton.

"Call me" with his phone number.

*Oh no. No no no.*

"Why the fuck is someone from *my* town asking you to call him?"

His *town? What?*

"What did you do, look him up on Facebook after the liquor store?" he continues. "I told you he was an asshole. I told you I didn't like him."

"Dylan, what are you talking about? I—"

"Don't act like you don't know!" he yells. "I *knew* you were into him when you complimented his stupid shirt."

It suddenly dawns on me that Colton, Tristan's Colton, is the same guy I saw buying beer here the other night. The same one that went to Dylan's high school. The same one that Dylan hates.

I jump up, my heart in my throat.

"Dylan, please, it's not like that!" I try to reach for his hand, but he pulls it back from me like I burned his skin. "I can explain. Let me explain!"

"Explain what? Why some douchebag from my high school is messaging you his phone number?"

I bring a shaking hand to my forehead.

I can't keep hiding this. I can't let him think this is something it's not.

"Dylan, there's this kid. He's been missing for the past few months, and—"

"What are you talking about?"

"This kid from my high school. He went missing the week I met you, and I've been trying to find him because I—"

"What does this have to do with Colton?"

I swallow. "I think he might be staying with him."

A tense silence lingers between us as Dylan processes what I'm telling him.

Then, he shakes his head like he can't stomach the sight of me.

"What the *fuck*, April?" His voice is loud, louder than the roaring waves in front of us.

"Dylan," I plead, my head spinning. "It's not like that. Please, please believe me. I can even show you the message before that."

I scramble to bring up the messages as Dylan stares at me, his eyes hard. The deep brown, once so soft and warm, sends chills down my arms.

He's not buying it.

My face burns and I can't seem to take a deep enough breath. I feel like I'm tied to railroad tracks and a train is flying toward me, and I can do nothing to escape my fate.

I'm a terrible person. A terrible girlfriend. I should've been honest. I should've opened up earlier. He's dealing with his parents' divorce, with school, with depression, even. And now...now, he thinks his girlfriend is cheating on him.

"I thought you were different," Dylan says. "God, and I just opened up to you like an idiot."

I want to defend myself. Tell him he's wrong. Tell him I *am* different. That I didn't do anything. But I can't even bring myself to speak.

I try one last time to pull Dylan to me, but he pushes me off. There's tears in his eyes. I did this to him. "Please," I try, but he shakes his head.

"I'm taking you home." His voice is broken.

I trail behind him as we walk to his car. The air makes my tears feel cold against my face. I don't even bother wiping them away.

I can't go home. I can't leave Dylan. I can't lose him. He's all I have.

Once in the car, Dylan steps on the gas with a heavy foot, accelerating quickly down the road, tires squealing. He stares straight ahead like he's focused on the road, but I can tell he's stuck in his head.

"My friends thought I was an idiot for wasting time on someone in high school, but I didn't even fucking care."

"Dylan, I didn't do anything." My voice is high from crying so hard. I sound desperate. "Please believe me."

But he doesn't. Why would he?

I look out the window as colors blur from my tears.

We're done. We're really done.

We started out so fast that we lost control. Now we're slamming the breaks.

But it's too late. We're shattered.

And I'm above.

Looking down at the mess we made.

# CHAPTER 24

Everything is dark.

I try to open my eyes, but I can't. My head is spinning.

I hear voices. Feel hands on me.

*Dylan?*

I blink. A blurry figure hovers above me.

*Dylan?*

I wanna scream, but I can't. I'm paralyzed. Dull colors mix together like an abstract painting. And suddenly, pain strikes my temples.

My body shudders. I breathe, sharp and desperate. Like I can't get enough air.

A warm body lies next to me, holding me.

*Dylan?*

I reach up to adjust my glasses, but they aren't there. I touch my head instead. There's liquid on my fingers. Red.

My eyes fall shut. I force them open. Shut. Open.

My ears are ringing. My body swaying. Back and forth. Back and forth.

I want to sleep. Sleep it off.

Flashing lights burn my eyes. Sirens wail. Someone covers my ears.

*Dylan?*

Everything is bright.

*     *     *

I'm going to have a heart attack.

"Where's Dylan?"

"He's okay, April," Kat assures me. "He's okay."

"Can you read me the third line?" a nurse asks.

My parents, Greg, and Kat all watch me, surrounding the hospital bed I'm lying in.

I squint at the letters in front of me, my temples throbbing. "I don't have my glasses."

"They broke in the accident. She can't see well without them," my dad explains to the nurse.

She nods, jotting something down.

"April, can you tell me what happened? What's the last thing you remember?"

My head hurts as I think back. "I was at the beach. With my boyfriend."

"Uh-huh. Then what?"

I remember the conversation about Dylan's parents. The message from Colton. The fight. But the rest feels like a dream I can't piece together.

I don't say anything.

"Okay...Can you tell me what today is?"

"Thanksgiving."

"Good." She turns to my parents. "She'll need a CT scan to ensure there isn't any serious injury, but she should be fine." She looks back at me. "April, do you feel sick at all? Nauseous?"

"No."

She nods, fixes something on the machine next to me, then walks out.

"What happened?" I ask no one in particular. Everyone stays silent. "Can someone please tell me what happened?"

"You were in an accident, sweetie," my mom says, stripped of her usual glow.

Greg sits in a chair across the room, biting his fingernails, his leg shaking up and down. He looks about ready to murder someone.

"I know that. But where is Dylan? Is he okay?" I ask again.

"He's fine," Kat tells me again. Her eyes are red and glossy. "I talked to his friend. He just hurt his knee a bit."

I sit up. "His knee? Is it bad?"

"April, would you please stop?" my dad says. His tone is

harsh, and he looks tired.

I sigh, falling back down and staring up at the ceiling. My head pounds behind my eyes.

How did I get here? How did *we* get here?

A few hours after my CT scan, which I struggled keeping still for, I'm dismissed to go home with medications and instructions.

"Everything looks good," my nurse explains. "Just keep an eye out for any of these symptoms."

She starts listing a bunch of random things, like tremors and vomiting, which makes my stomach sick just hearing it. When she leaves, Greg and my dad wait outside the room as Kat and my mom stay to help me change.

"What time is it?" I ask.

Kat checks her phone. Her hair is pulled into a messy bun, a few curls falling over her pale face. "Eleven-thirty."

"How's your head?" my mom asks, handing me the bag of clothes she packed me.

"Okay." I pull on an itchy sweater and step into my leggings. I sit back down on the bed, my body weak and achy. "Do you know where Dylan is? I wanna see him before I leave."

"Actually," Kat starts, her face rushed with pity. "He was already discharged."

I stare at her. "You mean, he went home?" She and my mom share a look. "Did he ask to see me at all? Did he come by here when I was getting the CT scan?"

They both shake their heads.

"But, why would—"

"April, not now," my mom says. "Let's just get you home, okay?"

On the ride home, I sit between Greg and Kat and Google "concussions," reading through tons of articles about how people with brain injuries shouldn't sleep, or should be woken every two hours to ensure they aren't slipping into a coma.

"Are you sure I should be going home?" I ask my parents. "Because WebMD says that—"

Greg rips my phone from me. "Stop Googling, April. Jesus Christ."

I open my mouth to speak, then stop.

Everyone stays silent. Kat rests her head on my shoulder.

"You shouldn't be on your phone," my dad says after a few minutes. He grips the steering wheel tightly. "Gotta give your head some time to recover."

"Okay, I will, but sometimes CT scans don't catch—"

"April." My mom whips around to face me, her expression hard. "The nurse would not have sent you home if you weren't ready to go home."

I sigh, covering my face with my palms.

"I can sleep over, if it makes you feel better," Kat says to me.

"You don't mind?"

She shakes her head. Then, she mouths: "We need to talk."

# CHAPTER 25

"Be straight-up with me. Were you guys drinking?" Kat looks at me like she already knows the answer. Like she's caught me red-handed.

I narrow my eyes at her.

"No...why?"

We're lying on my bed in our pajamas. It's past 2 a.m. My parents and Greg are asleep already, but I can't even think about closing my eyes right now.

"We weren't gonna bring this up to you tonight because you need to rest, but I don't think I can keep this from you."

I sit up slowly, bracing myself as my heart quickens. "What?" I ask Kat cautiously.

"Before you got to the hospital, your parents talked to a cop who apparently checked Dylan's BAC at the scene." I stare at Kat. "April, he'd been drinking."

*No.*

I shake my head and jump up from the bed, practically trembling.

"No, we were together all day," I say. "He didn't drink."

He wouldn't do that. He wouldn't drive drunk. Not with me in the car. No way.

"You need to sit," is all Kat says.

"I need to talk to him." But I can't find my phone anywhere. I rip the comforter off my bed, searching frantically.

"April, listen to me," Kat says, sitting on the edge of the bed and looking up at me. Her face is pained, as if it hurts her to tell me this. "His BAC was *just* under the typical legal limit. I think it was like 0.07 percent or something. But because he's under 21…"

Her voice trails off, and I feel like I'm going to suffocate. Like I can't breathe. Like I'm losing oxygen.

"What did my parents say? Oh my God, what did my dad do?"

"Well, he wasn't happy…to put it lightly."

"What is he gonna do? Is he gonna press charges? *Shit*, Kat, is Dylan gonna go to jail?"

"I don't know, April."

"I'm gonna throw up." I sit down at the edge of my bed, hunched over, my stomach in a tight knot.

Just this morning, I was smiling at Dylan's texts. About my dad's sweet potato recipe. About how he was thankful for me. I told him I loved him. He said it back.

Now, not even 24 hours later, our entire relationship is shattered like a million pieces of glass on the wet pavement.

I should be mad. I should hate him. I should never want to see him again. But I don't feel any of that.

Kat holds me as I fall apart, and all I can think about is how hurt Dylan was. About his parents. About his grades. His life. *Me.*

"We got into a fight, Kat. Before the accident."

"What do you mean?"

I explain everything, from Colton to Dylan's parents. I tell her about the night at the beach when I saw Colton at the liquor store, not realizing it was him. I fill her in on my obsessive investigating and how it basically ruined my relationship with the one guy I've ever loved.

"April, there is no excuse for what he did. I don't care what he was going through. I don't care what he thought you did or didn't do. He could've killed you."

My head throbs with realization. "I know."

And maybe that's why it's so hard. Because I have no choice but to move on now.

I can't go back to him. Not after this.

# CHAPTER 26

I ignore everyone all weekend. Jade's four voicemails. Zach's Facebook message. Jenny's call. Brenda's text message. I can't bring myself to speak to anyone.

It's like my life is at a standstill. I can't move forward because I don't know where to go. I don't know that I *want* to go anywhere

I feel nothing, mostly, aside from a headache. It's like I'm trapped in a fever dream, too exhausted to open my eyes and see the pain for what it is.

On Sunday, I sleep until noon and stay in bed until three. I'm watching Netflix when my dad knocks on my door. He pushes it open slowly, holding a cup of coffee and a plate with grilled cheese on it.

"How's your head?" he asks, sitting on my bed and placing the sandwich and mug on my nightstand.

I don't move from my pillow.

"Fine."

He nods, pressing his lips into a tight line and staring out the window. It's been raining all weekend. Gusts of wind whirl outside, making the house creak and windows whistle. My room is dark from the lack of sun, the only light coming from my TV.

My dad turns to me.

"So," he says.

I know where this is going, and I refuse to dance around it. "Kat told me."

"Told you what?"

I try to keep my voice steady. "That Dylan was drinking."

His face is red and drawn, and he wipes his hand over it. I can tell he hasn't slept much.

"How could you have let that happen, April?"

"*What?* What do you mean, 'let that happen?'"

"I trusted you. I trusted your judgment. I let you drink, for crying out loud! All your mother and I have ever asked of you is that you don't drink and drive, or get in the car with someone who drank."

I prop myself up on my elbow.

"Dad, it's not like I knew he was drinking!"

He gives me a look.

"How did you not know? Are you really that naive? Or do you just think *I'm* that naive?"

I blink at him.

"I guess I'm that naive, dad." I push myself up in my bed so that I'm sitting, then lean back against the wall. "It's not like he was *drunk*. If he was 21, they wouldn't have even considered it a DUI. It's just because he was—"

"Are you *seriously* making excuses for him, April?"

I pause. My dad looks at me like he doesn't recognize me. Like I'm someone else. Like I've betrayed him. And I'm tired of feeling like I have no voice in this family.

"This isn't fair, Dad. Everything I do is wrong. I try to please you by being a good daughter and following the rules. Then mom picks a fight about how I need to 'be a normal teenager' before I lose everyone in my life. So I try to please *her*, and now suddenly, I'm some naive girl who almost got herself killed. Like this is all my fault."

Tears spill out of my eyes, hot and burning my skin.

"I didn't know, Dad. Call me naive, but I promise I had no idea he drank."

My dad stares at me with an expression that I can't read, but I know what I said cut deep.

"What do you expect me to say, April?" His voice is low, like he doesn't have any energy left to fight. I lean my head back and close my eyes. "You could've died in that accident. Meanwhile, he barely got away with a scratch."

"But I didn't know, Dad. I trusted him." I swallow the lump in my throat, rush with every emotion I managed to fight off all weekend. "Don't you know how hard this is for me? I loved him."

He winces when I say that, like he can't believe that I could be so young and stupid. He sighs, turning away from me.

I can hear my mom downstairs blasting her workout pop music, and Greg down the hall playing video games. Like everything is normal. Like their futures didn't just crash before their eyes like mine did.

I'll never have a normal life like they do. I'll never wake up without panic on the horizon, never feel happiness without guilt. These past few months, I've tried to run away from that darkness within me, tried burying it so far down in hopes to stifle it. I should've known it would catch up eventually. It would resurface with a vengeance I couldn't match.

"I know this is hard on you," my dad finally says. "I just need you to understand how dangerous it is to get caught up with the wrong person."

I don't have the nerve to tell him that I still don't think Dylan is *the wrong person* for me. He's just misunderstood. And I know how that feels. My own family doesn't understand me.

"Please don't press charges," I say, my voice quivering. I'm on the verge of tears, and if I start crying now, I won't stop. I take a deep breath. "Please, Dad. I know what he did was wrong, but please don't make this more complicated than it needs to be. I don't want to think about it anymore. I just want to move on."

That's a lie. I want nothing but to run back into Dylan's arms. To talk through things. To be on the same team again.

But I can't do that, and there's no sense feeding a fantasy.

My dad hangs his head, his elbows on his knees, and squeezes the bridge of his nose between his eyes.

"I won't press charges, because I don't want you to have to go through that. But let me make this very clear." He turns to face me, looking me in the eyes. "Dylan is not welcome here again. You're almost 18, and I can't dictate how you live your life outside of this house. But I hope this was a wakeup call for you, April."

*    *    *

There's still a dull ache in my head as I get into my car on Monday morning. I put the keys in the ignition and stare ahead of me, shivering in the cold air.

Thinking about going back to school after all of this makes me sick to my stomach. How am I gonna face Jade and Brenda and Lindsay and everyone else in this town? My whole life, I've tried keeping my head down to avoid attention. Now, I'm the center of it, right up there with Tristan. Only, I'm forced to experience it firsthand.

I still haven't called Colton. Part of me feels like it would be wrong because of Dylan. Part of me is embarrassed for reaching out to him in the first place. Another part is fucking confused.

I don't even know who I am anymore. My thoughts are so conflicting that I can't identify with any of them. It's like listening to five songs from different genres at the same time, expecting to find peace, to gain clarity.

Turning on my stereo, I hook up my phone and shuffle my playlist. The sun is bright today, forcing me to squint. I'm still adjusting to my new glasses, which my mom picked out for me on Saturday. They're thick maroon frames, and they have my updated, stronger prescription I never bothered filling.

My head spins as I pull away from the curb, like it did when I got into the accident. I tremble as my eyes grow heavy.

Immediately, I tug my car to the side of the road and put it back in park. I've barely made it two houses down the street without feeling like I might pass out.

I can't drive like this. What were the doctors thinking, sending me home to "resume normal activity" within a few days? I could hurt someone.

I grab my phone and call Kat, but she doesn't answer. So, I try Jade.

"*Finally* you're talking to me!" she says when she answers. She drills me with question after question, but I cut her off.

"Can you drive me to school?"

"Of course! I'll be right over."

I back my car up the few feet I drove and park it in front of the house again. Jade pulls up five minutes later, and I open the passenger door and climb in.

"Hey," she says cautiously. Her perfume is so strong it makes me queasy. "How are you feeling? I tried calling you, like, ten times this weekend. I stopped over too, but Greg said you were sleeping. Did he tell you?"

I don't answer her. My head throbs with every word she says. Suddenly, I want out of this car, too.

I use my arms as a pillow and lean against the window, shutting my eyes as Jade goes on about how bad she feels. How it's her fault for setting Dylan and me up. How she should've known better, that something was "off" with him.

By the time we get to school, I already feel like I've endured an entire day. Grabbing my backpack off the car floor and adjusting the strap on my shoulder, I follow Jade to the back entrance of the building, ignoring all the stares I'm getting.

Jade walks me to my locker on the second floor, telling me how Adam called Dylan out for driving drunk. How they got into a fight over it.

"Jade, just stop!" I yell just as Lindsay and Brenda approach us.

Jade doesn't say anything. None of them do. They all just watch me. Everyone is frozen, staring at me. Waiting for me to go crazy. Waiting for me to do something worth gossiping about.

I'm so fucking tired of this. Of *everyone*. I slam my locker and storm down the hallway, away from them, dodging whispers and pitying expressions left and right.

I miss the one person in this school who made me feel at home.

# CHAPTER 27

"How was your holiday weekend?" Dr. Glen asks me as I walk into her office. Then she notices my dad behind me. "Oh, hello, Mr. Valentini. Is everything alright?"

"Well, not really," he says.

"I'll let you guys settle in. Would you like some water?" She heads to the mini water machine behind her, where a pile of small plastic cups are stacked.

"We're okay," my dad tells her.

I slump on the couch like normal, only this time making room for my dad. He takes a seat next to me.

It wasn't my idea for him to come in. Sure, I needed the ride. But I don't need him talking to my therapist for me. I'm 17 years old. Nearly an adult.

Dr. Glen sits in her usual chair.

"I take it this hasn't been a good week?" she asks my dad, as if I'm not in the room.

"I'm afraid not."

Before I can chime in, my dad explains everything. Dylan. The accident. How I've been quieter and more irritable than usual. How I refuse to drive anywhere. And the entire time, I stare at the clock across the room, watching as the hands tick. I count each second, reaching 243 by the time I'm acknowledged.

"Now, is this driving fear because of the accident, April?" Dr. Glen asks me.

I blink at her.

"It's not a *fear*. I got a concussion. I get dizzy when I drive now. Why would I drive when I don't feel well, and risk hurting someone?"

My dad audibly sighs, and Dr. Glen looks like she doesn't know what to say. She stares at me, doing that trick she always does to get me to speak more. It won't work this time.

"She went to the ER, and everything looked fine," my dad explains. "I even called her doctor yesterday to make sure she can drive, and he said there's no reason she can't." He turns to me, but I don't look at him. "You have no serious symptoms, April. You're not throwing up. You're not experiencing memory loss. You're not getting tremors or vertigo. This only seems to affect you when you try to drive. Which is why I think it's your anxiety."

"Everything is, isn't it?" I snap. "Do you even see me as a person, dad?"

I don't even know what I mean by that. It just slips out of me.

"Alright, let's take deep breaths here," Dr. Glen says.

"Don't be ridiculous, April," my dad says at the same time.

"Sometimes, anxiety can be very misleading," Dr. Glen goes on, raising her voice as if to tell us both to shut up. "Especially OCD, when it's on a loop like this. It can create these physical symptoms, convince us we aren't safe when we really are."

I fold my arms and lean back against the cushions, already accepting whatever exposure is to come. It's hard to be your own advocate when your disorder constantly hijacks your identity—your own mind.

"For now, let's just get you behind the wheel, alright?" She talks to me like I'm 5, and with my dad sitting next to me, that's about as old as I feel. "Just a short drive around the block this week. Start with a few minutes, adding a minute each day. You can stick to your neighborhood streets for now. Does that sound reasonable?"

"Do I have a choice?"

Dr. Glen tilts her head.

"Well, yes. It's your life. Your journey to recovery. But if you want to get better..."

"I have to do the work, I know."

I hate myself for acting so bitter, but I can't help it. I've lost all energy, all desire, to see Dr. Glen's perspective. I will never be okay. Why bother trying?

As soon as we get home, I run up to my room and slam my door. I don't want to see my mom, deal with her judgment about therapy, about refusing to drive. Or talk to Greg, who thinks tough love is the answer to everything.

I rest my head on my pillow, tug my blanket up to my chin, squeeze my eyes shut. I'm empty. Empty and alone.

I picture Dylan lying in his apartment alone, his door locked like mine, watching TV just for some light. It makes me physically ill.

I want to be there with him. After all of this, I still want to be there with him.

It's pathetic.

I open Instagram and look back at my profile, at the pictures of Dylan and me. The one from the day he asked me out. One from a movie night at his apartment. One with Gabe from the Halloween party. One with my dad making dinner.

I throw my phone at the end of my bed and grab an old towel off the floor. It's marked with mascara from the last time I cried, a portrait of heartbreak. Hiding my face in it, I muffle my sobs.

My phone buzzes by my feet, the screen lighting up the room a bit. I jump up, relentless hope convincing me it's Dylan. But of course, it's not. It's an Instagram DM from Gabe.

**Gabe:** Hey April. How are you holding up?
I would've messaged you sooner, but I thought I should give you time before I reached out.

I'm surprised at how happy I am to hear from him. For some reason, his presence was comforting. Like an old friend's.

I roll onto my back and type a response.

**Me:** I'm doing okay, thanks. It really means a lot that you reached out.

I wonder how much Dylan told Gabe about that night. If he knows about our fight. If he thinks I cheated, too. It bothers me that he might. I don't want him to think poorly of me.

**Gabe:** Of course. Dylan's my friend and all, but what he did was wrong.

**Me:** Is he okay?
**Gabe:** He'll be alright.
**Me:** What does that mean?
**Gabe:** He's okay. He's going through a lot right now, but he will be alright. He's moving back home next week.
Just take care of yourself and don't worry about him, okay?

But I can't do that. I can't stop myself from worrying. Can't get rid of this pit in my stomach.

I need to talk to Dylan.

\*　　　\*　　　\*

I feel a familiar pang of excitement, like I always do when I know I'm going to see Dylan. But this time, I have to remind myself, is different.

I begged Kat to take me to his apartment tonight. She wouldn't comply at first, telling me Dylan doesn't even deserve to hear from me. But when I started breaking down during lunch period, she dropped the protective friend act.

"If this is what you need to do to move on, then fine," she said as I cried to her in the cafeteria bathroom. "But I don't agree with it one bit."

It's only been a week since I last saw Dylan, yet it feels like it's been months. It's Friday, and half of me hopes he's not home, that he's out with his friends so I can get some closure, know that he's okay without actually having to face him. But the other half is so desperate to see him, I'd probably wait on his doorstep until he got home.

I'm shivering as I knock on his door while Kat waits in the car. When I hear shuffling on the other end, I'm certain I'm going to faint. It reminds me of our first date, how anxious I was to see him. I miss that innocence we had.

Dylan opens the door wearing gray sweatpants and a black T-shirt. His eyes go wide when he sees it's me.

"What are you doing here?" he asks, stunned.

"I have to talk to you."

"April, I can't…"

"Look, I'm not trying to get back with you, Dylan. I just need to explain myself. Please, just let me talk for, like, five seconds."

Glancing back into his apartment, he steps into the cold air and shuts the door behind him. The fact that he won't let me in is like a punch to the gut.

"I'm sorry," I say.

"I should be saying sorry to you, April."

"I have OCD," I tell him before I can stop myself. "And it's not what you think. It's not just hating germs or being organized or whatever. It's...it's really consuming sometimes."

He stares at me like he might cry.

"I know."

"What? You do? Did Jade tell you or something?"

"No, I didn't know you had it. I meant, I know what OCD is. My little sister has it." He looks at me with sympathy I don't deserve. "It's pretty bad. She can't even make it through a full day of school."

I close my eyes, tears streaming down my face. *His poor sister.* I was her once.

*I still am.*

Dylan reaches for my hand. I let him take it.

"April, it's okay."

"No, no it's not. I should've told you," I say. He would've understood. From the start, I could have prevented all of this. "I should've told you everything."

"I wish you did."

"Dylan, I didn't cheat. I wouldn't—"

"I know," he whispers. "I know you wouldn't."

We stand hand-in-hand, our faces close. Dylan shuts his eyes like it pains him, and I do the same, because I can't look at him without wanting to rewind this entire month. To do it all over again, but differently. The right way.

"Dylan? Is the pizza here?"

I freeze at a familiar voice.

Dylan opens his eyes and looks at me with deep remorse, and my body wants to sink into the ground.

Because in the doorway stands Mandy, her light hair tied

in a knot on her head, loose, curly strands framing her golden skin. She's wearing his sweatshirt. The same one I used to wear.

I open my mouth, but I don't know what to say. I look at Dylan. At his red cheeks. His downcast eyes.

I drop his hand and walk away from him. And this time, I don't look back.

# CHAPTER 28

A Severe Thunderstorm Warning alert blares on my TV. It's humid and unusually warm for a late November night. I lie still on my covers, wearing an oversized Boston Manor T-shirt. From my bed, I peer outside my window, searching the clouds for lightning. Waiting for the first strike.

When I was little, my dad and I used to climb in his truck and go "storm chasing," driving around the neighborhood in the pouring rain. It made me feel brave. But really, we were in one of the safest places to be in a thunderstorm, I later learned.

I miss my innocence. I miss being someone I was proud of, even if I was oblivious. I miss the way it felt to be ignorant. To be carefree and happy.

Thunder starts rumbling outside, low at first, then growing angrier. I shut my TV off and let the lightning brighten my room.

I wish I was with Dylan, wish his arms were around me while we listened to the rain. But now he's with Mandy, and I'm all alone, like before we met.

Things were easier then. I didn't feel much, aside from the usual guilt and anxiety, but at least I had nothing to mourn. Now, I can hardly breathe without a sharp pain in my chest.

Cloud-to-ground bolts of lightning flash, one immediately following the other. Suddenly, I have the urge to go outside. To be in the middle of it all.

I get out of bed and tug on shorts, then quietly walk downstairs, slipping out the front door.

From the porch, the rain sounds like marbles falling from the sky. Despite the frequent lightning, I sprint to my car and hop in, soaked.

I don't put my key in the ignition. I don't shuffle my Spotify playlist. Aside from music, rain is the only other sound that calms my thoughts. So, I recline my seat and take it all in. The pelting of the drops against my windshield. The grumbling of the thunder.

I can't help but think about Tristan, where he is right now. If he's safe. If he has shelter of some sort.

I've wanted to check up on him since the day Colton messaged me back. Since Thanksgiving. But the thought of doing so, after the fight and the accident, made me feel like I was betraying Dylan. Like I was confirming his suspicions.

But what haunts me the most is the idea that Colton doesn't know anything. And if that's the case, then I've just about lost all my faith.

Either way, I know I have to find out.

I bring up Colton's Facebook message. The one from the day of the accident. The one that triggered Dylan's and my fight.

I select the phone number he sent me. And this time, I call it.

"Hello?"

Hearing Colton's voice makes me sick to my stomach, because I'm not sure I can handle what he's going to tell me.

I take a deep breath, trying to slow my heart rate.

"Hey, Colton. It's April. Um, Tristan's friend?"

There's a pause, and I hold my breath as I wait.

"Uh...hold on," he mutters, his voice lower. A few seconds later, he says, "Hey, sorry about that."

"It's okay. I'm sorry, actually, to call so late. I just...thought we could talk." A few moments pass, and he doesn't say anything. "Do you know anything? About Tristan, I mean?"

He hesitates. "I'm sorry, I don't."

A crack of thunder shakes my car, making me jump.

"I don't understand," I say. "Why did you tell me to call you? If you don't know anything?"

I'm crying now, my fight-or-flight response compelling me to get out of the car and run. But I have nowhere to go. No one to run to.

"I'm sorry," he says, and I can tell he means it. "I didn't want to ignore your message. I thought we could talk about it, share what we know..."

"What *do* you know?"

He sighs into the phone. "That he's safe. Wherever he is."

"What makes you say that? It's been *months*."

"Because I..." He pauses. "It's Tristan. We have to trust he's alright."

But I can't do that. Not when all the evidence is telling me otherwise. I'd be an idiot to stay hopeful right now. After everything that's happened in my own life. After the discussion with Jenny.

"I'm sorry if I got your hopes up," Colton says, his voice laced with regret. "I really am."

I hang up on him.

Through my windshield, the street looks warped from the rain. Colors bleed into each other. My head pounds behind my eyes. And I want out. Out of it all.

I rip my door open and step out of my car, the rain instantly drenching me. But I'm drowning in my thoughts instead, and I just want them to stop.

I stand in the middle of the street and stare ahead at the road, at the quaint houses with porch lights on. I look at mine. It's no different.

*I don't belong here.*

My hair is wet and knotted, but I let it fall over my face, let the rain soak my shirt. My bare feet ache on the ground, and I shiver as I walk down the road. Then run. Then walk. Then run. Then hunch over, my sides aching, head throbbing.

A bright bolt of lightning makes me jump, but I don't care. It's real and it's there, and maybe I'm in danger, but maybe that's okay. I'm not safe, but I never really felt I was anyway.

I sit on the sidewalk and breathe. Giddiness overcomes

me as I inhale deeply, exhale slowly. I could run away, if I wanted to. Is that what Tristan did? I don't blame him.

I could run away and leave everyone, everything, behind. *They'd be better off without me anyway.*

Two headlights approach me, and my stomach drops. I don't know how far I ran, but I know I'm still on my street.

The car slowly pulls up next to me, and I start to panic, but my legs won't move.

I fucked up. I should've stayed in bed. I shouldn't be here. *But I don't want to be anywhere else either.*

"April, what the fuck?"

Greg gets out of his car and stares at me, and I've never felt such strong relief and dread at the same time.

"It's raining," I tell him, trying to point out that he's getting soaked.

"Are you drunk?" he asks me.

"No."

"Get in the car."

"No."

"*April.*" He doesn't move closer to me, but part of me wants him to. Part of me wants someone to care. I know someone cares. I know many people do. But I can't feel it. I want to feel it.

I bury my face in my hands and cry, loud and hysterical. I don't know what's happening to me, but I'm scared.

Greg doesn't say anything else. He slams his door, sits next to me, and puts his arm around me. And we sit there in the downpour, silent, before finally going back home.

# CHAPTER 29

I can't make it to Friday. It's already Thursday night, but I can't handle another day of school. Can't keep showing up, forcing smiles, feigning interest. I just don't have it in me.

I'm shivering under my covers, my head pounding, and I'm pretty sure I have a fever. I *hope* I do. Then I'll have an excuse to stay in bed all day tomorrow. To see no one.

I grab the thermometer out of its typical place in my nightstand drawer and stick it under my tongue. It reads 98.5. I throw it against the wall.

I might not be ill, not by medical standards. But that doesn't mean I'm not suffering.

A few hours later, I finally cry myself to sleep.

\* \* \*

*Everything is dark.*

*"April, it's okay. You're okay. I'm here. You're gonna be okay. I'm not leaving you."*

*I blink to clear my eyes as they focus, just barely, on the boy kneeling next to me. I'm lying on the wet ground feeling ill, so ill.*

*"An ambulance is on its way. You're gonna be okay, I promise."*

*The boy lies down with me. He strokes my hair. "I'm here. I got you."*

*I want to talk to him, ask him who he is. How he knows me. But I'm so dizzy, I feel like I'm spinning.*

*"Dude, don't let her fall asleep!" another voice calls in the distance, muffled.*

*But I want to sleep. I need to sleep.*

*"April, stay with me." The boy's voice is desperate. I try to look at him again. I can't see his face well. But he's scared. I'm scared.*

*"Please. I need you to be okay."*

*"Who are you?" I manage.*

*He brushes wet hair out of my face.*

*"April...it's me."*

*     *     *

I jolt awake. My entire shirt is soaked in sweat.

I grab my phone from beneath my pillow, frantic. It's midnight. I need to talk to Kat.

**Me:** Are you awake?

My heart pounds in my ears, each beat like a smack to the temple, as I watch Kat type back to me.

**Kat:** Yeah, what's up? You ok?

**Me:** You said you saw Dylan's friend at the hospital after the accident. What was his name?

**Kat:** Idk, why?

**Me:** What did he look like?

**Kat:** Tall, pale, dark hair...

I quickly load Facebook on my phone, type in Colton's name, then download his profile picture. I send it to Kat with question marks.

**Kat:** Yes, that's him! Why? Do you know him?

I ignore her text and reload Colton's Facebook again. He works at a car dealership near the beach.

I need to talk to him, but calling won't work. I need to do this in person.

*     *     *

"Hi, I'm supposed to come in and meet with someone named Colton today," I say into my phone. "I was just wondering what time he's working. He gave me his card last weekend, but I misplaced it."

I make my voice as high-pitched and innocent as possible, trying to hide my anxiety.

"Sure thing! One moment," the receptionist says in a peppy tone. I wait, picking at my eyebrows for a distraction. "Oh, here it is! He's in from 9 to 5 today."

"Great, thank you!"

When I hang up, I instantly feel guilty. I hate lying to

people. I especially hate the fact that I told my dad I was too sick for school today.

But this is more important. *Tristan* is more important.

At least I have a purpose again, and that motivates me to get out of bed today. I tug on my high-waisted jeans and a cropped sweater, slip on my sneakers, grab my coat, and head out the door.

My hands shake as I grip my steering wheel. I have such a nervous stomach that I couldn't even drink my morning coffee. It's 11 a.m. now, since I waited until Greg woke up and went to class before leaving.

I plug my phone into the aux and play Turnover, a band that always seems to calm me down. I need all the moral support I can get, considering I haven't driven more than three feet since my accident. That, coupled with my lack of sleep and pounding head, is not grounds for a good driver.

As I pull away from the curb, I'm extra careful to look out for pedestrians, just in case. I continue down the road at a snail's speed, slamming my breaks every few seconds.

*I can't do this. There's no way.*

Hot tears well in my eyes, blurring the road ahead as I sit at a stop sign. I grip the wheel, my knuckles turning white. I'm stronger than this. I know I am. I *have* to be.

I step on the gas and accelerate slowly as I make the turn. A few moments later, a car pulls up behind mine, tailgating me. I have to speed up. So I do. But I go exactly the speed limit. Which really pisses off the guy behind me.

When I turn onto a busier road, I hit a bump. Ripping my car to the side of the road, I put it in park and jump out, frantic. My body trembles as I duck under my car, checking for dents or blood, or any possible indication that I hit someone. But there's nothing. I look back down the road as cars pass, and I see nothing in the road either.

*It's just your OCD,* I tell myself. *Just your mind playing tricks. Like always.*

It takes everything in me to get back in my car. I take a

deep breath and let the thoughts be there. Let the pain and the torment taunt me. Let myself feel like the absolute worst person to walk the earth. Like some murderer involved in a hit-and-run.

I must loop back ten times before finally making it to Colton's work. What should have been a half-hour drive took fifty minutes.

After parking far in the back, I get out of my car and stare at the large building. My body feels weak, like I'm gonna pass out on the sidewalk. I'm so nervous. The sun is bright, the air misty, filled with scents of the ocean. I inhale a deep breath and walk inside.

There are so many people here. It's loud and hectic and smells like a mix of a million different perfumes.

"Can I help you?"

I whip around and see a middle-aged man smiling at me. He's wearing a button-up shirt with a tie, neatly tucked into his dress pants. "Oh, uh...I'm supposed to be meeting someone here. Colton? Colton Hares?"

He nods, then points me to his right. From where I'm standing, I can see a tall guy showing an older couple a car I don't know the name of. My heart speeds up.

"Thanks," I tell the man before making my way over.

My legs might give out any second, but I let them take me to where I need to be. As I get closer to him, Colton glances up at me while talking to the couple, and his face drains of color. He must recognize me, somehow.

"Uh, can you excuse me for a second?" he says to the couple, and they nod and circle the vehicle they were checking out as Colton walks over to me.

"You lied," I tell him before he can say anything. "I know you know where Tristan is."

He looks around us like he's scared someone will hear our conversation.

"I don't know what you're talking about. I don't—"

"You were at the accident," I say, raising my voice so he

knows I will make a scene if I have to. If that means pulling the truth out of him. "And so was Tristan."

Colton's expression changes, and he runs a hand through his dark hair.

"Follow me." He leads me to a hallway across the room, then into an office. Shutting the door, he turns to face me. "I was at the accident, yes. But I don't know why you think Tristan was there. He wasn't—"

"Colton, you're lying," I say, but I don't even know this for sure. Maybe he isn't lying. Maybe my dream was just wishful thinking, and not a real memory resurfacing. "You have to be."

My eyes start to sting as panic jolts through me. Colton looks at me with deep blue eyes.

"Fuck," he whispers, running his hand over his face. "Don't cry. I can't handle when girls cry."

"I need to know he's okay.".

"He is, April. He's okay." He looks at me with regret. "You were right. He was at the accident with me."

I came here expecting to hear those words, but they still pack so much relief that I don't know what to do with it. I swallow a lump in my throat.

"Where is he?"

He glances down at his feet. "I don't know."

"You do know."

"I did know, but after the accident, he went somewhere else, just in case someone saw him...I don't know where."

I stare at him. *He's bluffing.*

"Bullshit," I say. Colton avoids eye contact. "Fine. But someone needs to tell his family. They're frantic, thinking he's —"

"No! You can't do that."

I pause, narrowing my eyes at him. "Why not?"

"Because it's..." He shakes his head. "It's complicated. His situation. It's not what you think."

"You don't know what I think."

"You don't understand."

"So explain it to me," I say.

"I—I can't. I can't do that to him. This is his own issue."

"Colton. Is he staying with you? Do you know where he is?"

Taking a deep breath, Colton meets my eyes.

"Yes."

"Yes? Yes, what? Yes, he's staying with you?"

"Yes, he's staying with me." Colton leans back against his desk, hands resting on either side of himself, and watches me process everything.

"I need to see him," I say after a few moments.

"You can't—"

"Let me see him, or I'm going to the police."

I surprise myself with those words. I'm not one to blackmail someone. I mean, isn't that illegal? But I need to talk to Tristan. If I can't, if it ends here, I don't know what I'll do.

He's obviously in trouble. And I need to help him.

Colton's expression turns from panic to frustration, then finally, to sympathy.

"When?"

"Today," I say, my voice stern. "Now."

He nods, and I can tell he's sorting out the plan in his head.

"Stay here. Let me just finish up this sale, and I'll tell my boss I have an emergency."

"Thank you. Seriously." I hope he knows I mean it, despite my ambushing him at work. Sometimes, you gotta do what you gotta do.

Ten minutes pass before Colton returns. We walk out to the parking lot, and I get in my car, following him back to his apartment. Thankfully, it's only a few blocks away, and I manage to keep my anxiety low enough for the time being.

As we walk up the steps to his apartment, my heart races. I can't believe I'm doing this. I can't believe I'm here. I can't believe *Tristan* is here.

Colton unlocks the door, and I wonder if he was able to warn Tristan I'm with him.

"Does he know I'm coming?" I ask.

Colton shakes his head as he opens the door.

"Hey, you're home early."

It's strange, hearing Tristan's voice for the first time since he went missing. These past few months, I thought the worst. I thought he was alone, depressed, maybe even dead. I can't believe he's here. I can't believe he's okay.

I swallow a lump in my throat and step inside. When he sees me, Tristan freezes, and I'm close to fainting.

"*April?*"

# CHAPTER 30

Tristan stares at me. "What are you—"

Before he can finish his question, I step toward him and throw my arms around him, surprising myself as much as him. He inhales slowly and wraps his arms around me, and I instantly relax.

I pull away after a few moments, wiping my eyes with my sleeve. He just looks at me, like maybe he knows how worried I've been. How much his absence has plagued me.

"I'm sorry, dude. She's pretty persistent..." Colton says, and I feel myself blush. "I'll let you guys talk."

Colton walks down the hall, away from us, while Tristan just stands there, stunned, his green eyes wide. He shakes his head, then grabs my hand and tugs me into a bedroom next to us. I sit next to him on a twin-sized bed, shaking my leg up and down, up and down. The room is small and simple. A few bags rest in the corner, clothes and toiletries spilling out of them.

I have so much to say, so much to *ask*, but I don't even know where to start.

"Let me guess," Tristan says. "You remembered the accident?"

The sound of his voice instantly transports me back to last year, to our conversations. Life was so simple then. I didn't realize it at the time, but now all I wish is to go back.

Tristan turns to look at me, but I keep my gaze down at my feet.

"Yeah," I tell him. "But not right away."

"I figured you wouldn't. You kept asking who I was...I tried to go in the ambulance with you, but they wouldn't let me. So Colton made me go home before someone realized who I was."

I don't say anything.

"How are you feeling?" he asks me, then his expression turns hard. "You're not still with that guy, are you?"

I sneer, tucking a strand of hair behind my ear and thinking back to last night. To Dylan with Mandy. My stomach lurches.

"April, you know you deserve better than that."

I shake my head, then look at him.

"Don't do that."

"Do what?"

"Try to make this about me. That's not why I'm here."

He nods slowly, looking away. After a few moments, he says, "It's a really long and complicated story."

I glare at him.

"Tristan, I just drove half an hour to some guy I don't even know's work, cornered him to get information, then followed him to his house to *listen* to your story. For all I know, I could've showed up on some serial killer's doorstep."

He raises his eyebrows, smirking.

"Sorry, I've been watching *The Ted Bundy Tapes*," I tell him. "You never know."

"How did you even know who Colton was?" Tristan asks. "And that I was staying with him?"

I smirk. "It's a really long and complicated story."

He laughs, then nudges me with his shoulder. "Not fair."

We sit in silence for a few moments, and I can hear that Colton's watching *Star Wars* in the other room. I didn't peg him as the sci-fi type, but for some reason, it makes me feel a little more comfortable being here.

I still can't believe I'm here.

"Colton told me you messaged him."

I blink at Tristan. "Wait...you knew?"

"Well, yeah. I just didn't know how *you* knew. Or why you cared."

"Why I cared?" I repeat.

He shrugs, studying me for a moment. Shame washes over me like a riptide, tugging me underwater.

"I mean, I don't know," he says. "You stood me up last year. And then we just...stopped talking."

"*You* stopped talking to *me*," I point out.

"No, I didn't, April." There's an edge to his tone. He sighs, lowering his voice. "I didn't care that you bailed...I cared that you got so uncomfortable around me after, you could barely look me in the eye. Like we were never...I don't know, *anything*. Not even friends. And that...that *sucked*."

I don't say anything.

"Look, I'm not mad," he adds. "It's cool that you didn't wanna hang. But why did you act like I was some stranger after? You'd run out of class before I could even talk to you, you changed partners whenever we had a group project..."

I swallow the lump in my throat.

"I thought that's what you wanted. I thought you were mad at me. You acted weird, too, Tristan."

"I acted weird because you acted weird! April, why would I even be mad? Because you got sick and couldn't come to the concert?"

I look down at my feet.

"I wasn't sick."

"Yeah, I figured...But even so. I'd never be mad at you for not wanting to go out with me. I'm not that guy. And you of all people should know that."

"Well, I *did*." I meet his eyes. "I did want to go out with you."

Tristan tilts his head at me slightly. His dirty blonde hair curls at his ear, and I can't help but notice it's longer than it was last year.

"I have issues, Tristan," I continue. "But it was nothing against you."

"What do you mean?"

I take a deep breath and let it out slowly, hands gripping

my knees. "I freaked out 'cause I was scared."

"*Scared*? Why were you scared?"

"I don't know. 'Cause you're *you*."

"What does that mean?" he asks.

I shake my head at him.

"You were my best friend. And maybe that's pathetic, because we never even hung out outside of school, but I don't know, Tristan. You were. And I just felt like it was easier, you know, to keep our relationship—*friendship*—at a distance. I thought if we hung out, things would get weird, because *I'm* weird, and that we'd lose...whatever it is we had." I blink, and a tear streams down my cheeks. "I have issues."

Tristan's face softens. "You don't have issues, April," he says.

"You don't understand!" I yell, surprised by my own voice.

Tristan leans back on his hands, staring straight ahead in thought. Then, he looks at me, *really* looks at me, his eyes searching my face like they might find an answer. To what? I'm not sure. But I'm forced to look away.

We listen to the sound of Colton's movie, the air around us tense. Part of me wishes I could get up and walk out, jump back into my car and drive directly home so I could hide under the covers for the rest of my life.

But the other part? Doesn't ever want to walk away from Tristan again.

"I didn't run away."

Tristan's words don't sink in right away. I look at him, my mind trying to process what he just told me.

"My dad kicked me out," he says.

I open my mouth, but nothing comes out. Questions whirl around in my head, begging to be answered. But he continues before I can ask anything.

"Do you know how my mom passed away?"

"Yeah," I manage.

"No, I mean...do you know *how*?"

I don't want to say it out loud. "An...accident, right?"

"She ran a red light and was struck by a truck. Her brakes gave out." He looks me in the eyes. "The brakes that *I* repaired for her a few days before."

*No.*

I cover my mouth with my hand, chills racing down my arms and legs. Tears fill my eyes immediately.

"Tristan, you can't blame yourself," I say instinctively. "That was just an—"

"Accident? It wasn't, though. I mean, I was rushing it, April. My dad taught me the week before, and I got cocky and breezed through it because it's such a simple process. But I missed one stupid minor step, because I wasn't paying attention, and now my mom is dead."

I don't know what to say. I don't know what I *can* say.

"No one knows but my dad," he continues. "And as much as he tries not to, he resents me. I don't blame him for it, I really don't. But I just couldn't deal with it anymore.

"That night I left, he got mad, *really* mad. So then I got mad, and...things escalated, and he told me to leave."

"But..." I shake my head, trying to piece all this information together. "But Jenny said she called your dad that night, and he acted like he had no idea you were even gone. He said he checked your room and you weren't there, but there was an empty bottle of whiskey or something."

He raises his eyebrows, then lets out a sarcastic laugh.

"Nice."

"So...that's *not* what happened?"

"Not at all. I wasn't the one who was drunk."

I hesitate. "Your dad was?"

He nods slowly. "He gets like that sometimes. Like I said, I don't blame him. He looks at me and sees the reason his wife is dead."

"Tristan, this is—" I search for the right words, but I'm not sure there are any. "This isn't okay."

He dismisses me with a shrug.

I look down at my hands, pushing and pulling my ring up and down my pointer finger.

"I don't get it. Why didn't you at least continue going to school, even though you're staying with Colton out here?"

"I honestly had every intention to do that." He hesitates. "But then...my dad went and filed a missing persons' report, as if he wasn't the one who kicked me out in the first place. And I guess part of me wanted him to worry about where I was," he says, his voice small. "I was just so mad. Everything escalated so quickly. I didn't even have time to grab my shit that night because my dad was getting violent with me. He broke my phone after I texted Jenny, because he thought I told her he was drunk and a mess, when really I was just trying to apologize to her for everything."

My chest aches for him.

"Why *didn't* you tell Jenny?" I ask.

"She and my dad, they're so close. They've always been. I couldn't tell her he kicked me out. I couldn't tell her *why* he kicked me out."

I narrow my eyes at him. "Why? Because she might take your side? She might help you?"

He shrugs. "I don't know what you want me to say, April. My dad is all Jenny has. *She* is all *he* has. I already took my mom from them..."

"Tristan, what about you? Who do *you* have?"

"That's not the point."

"You're acting like Jenny doesn't care you're gone, but you're wrong. She is a complete *wreck* without you, Tristan."

Tristan winces. I don't mean to hurt him. I really don't. But he needs to realize just what he's doing.

He holds his head in his hands, his elbows propped up on his knees. His face turns red, like he's suffocating, buried deep in the turmoil. And I want to comfort him. I want to put my arm around him and hold him tightly against me, the way I should have the day he found out his mom passed away. But, as usual, I'm frozen, held captive by my thoughts.

"I don't expect you to understand," he tells me, his voice muffled. He looks back up at me. "But you can't say anything, April. I don't want anyone to know about this. That's why I told Colton not to answer you. I don't need you getting involved in this, okay? I'm fine. Seriously. You don't need to worry about me."

I shake my head.

"Where do you go from here, Tristan? What are you gonna do, stay here forever? Hide away forever? Let your dad get away with kicking you out, blaming you for running away...?"

"I'm almost 18," he says matter-of-factly. "Then, I can leave here, get a job, get my own place..."

"What about school? College? What about Jenny and Zach and Colton, even? Do you know how much trouble he could get in for harboring a runaway who's a *minor*?"

"I don't know, April," he says, his voice rising. He rubs his face with his palms before looking at me. "I don't know. I'm trying to figure this all out, okay?"

I take his hand and curl mine around his without thinking. "You don't have to do it alone."

He hesitates, and for a moment, I think he might ask me to stay. But then he pulls his hand away wistfully. And I swallow my pride, because this isn't about me.

A gust of wind blows against the window, and the sky is starting to grow cloudy now. I should leave. I can't make him talk to me. Can't drag him with me.

I grab my keys out of my jacket pocket and look at him, hoping he'll object, the way I wish he did when I bailed on that concert. But he just looks back at me, his eyes bloodshot.

"I hope you understand," he tells me.

I do. So, I walk away.

# CHAPTER 31

Two panic attacks and over an hour later, I finally make it home. My parents are still at work, but Greg's car is parked out front.

*Not good.*

"Where were you?" Greg asks, standing in his doorway. I jump at his voice as I try to sneak into my room. "Thought you were sick."

"Uh, yeah. I just went to pick up some medicine."

"What'd you get?"

"You know, just some Advil and cough drops."

He leans against his doorframe, arms folded across his chest.

"Huh, that's weird. 'Cause you were gone for over three hours."

I freeze. I open my mouth to spew a quick excuse, but Greg cuts me off.

"My second class got cancelled. Been here all afternoon...You can't talk your way outta this one, April. Where were you?"

I sigh, not in the mood to talk to anyone right now.

"Nowhere." I keep my eyes down and try to walk to my room, but he quickly moves ahead of me and blocks the doorway.

"Really? That's why both you and your car were gone all afternoon?"

"I was just...*out*, okay?"

He gives me a look. "Out *where*?"

"It's none of your business!"

"It *is* my business, if you're lying to dad and skipping school and sneaking around with Dylan behind—"

"What are you *talking* about? Dylan wants nothing to do with me. I wasn't with him."

"Then where *were* you?"

I stare at him. He looks exhausted, dark circles under his eyes like he hasn't slept in days. I want to ask if he feels alright, but I don't know how to talk to him lately. It seems like every conversation I have with my family is one-sided. I'm always the one getting yelled at or preached to. The one who needs looking after, who can't cope on her own.

For once, I wish I could assume someone else's issues and shed mine for a while. Be the person who is offering help, not the girl desperately in need of it.

"I went to find Tristan, okay?" I say, my voice shaking. "I thought I knew where he was, but I was wrong. So I drove back home. Happy?"

At least half of it is true.

Greg just blinks at me.

"*Happy*?" He runs his hand through his hair, face red. "Are you kidding me, April? I thought you said you'd stop with that. Jesus Christ, you'd think everything with Dylan would've been a wakeup call."

I can see tears in his eyes. I've never seen my brother cry. Not when he fell off his bike at age 7 and needed stitches. Not when his best friend and only real love turned him down. Not even when Mom had a breast cancer scare.

"I don't know what to do with you, April," he says. "First, the accident. Then the other night during the thunderstorm. Now this? I don't know how to handle you anymore."

"No one's asking you to, Greg."

He looks at me like I just slapped him across the face.

"You're my little sister."

I swallow a lump in my throat. He stares at me, and I look away. All I want right now is to collapse into his arms, let him protect me like he used to in middle school, cry to him and hope he can do something, anything, to take this pain away.

But he can't. And frankly, that's not his responsibility.

I try to remember how it felt when Greg and I were close. Like Tristan and Jenny were. When we were little, Greg used to make a rope out of T-shirts, tying one end to my door knob and the other to the bathroom door knob next to my room. That way, every time I tried to open my door to get out, it wouldn't budge. He thought it was the funniest prank in the world, and so did I, for a while.

Until the OCD kicked in. The claustrophobia and fear of being trapped. The inability to be a little sister with a sense of humor anymore.

And now, instead of locking me in, he's locking me out. Afraid of leaving me alone. Afraid of what might happen when he isn't watching.

*    *    *

I spend the night scrolling through Instagram in my bed, watching people live their lives, all smiles and "good vibes." It makes me feel more alone than ever.

I click back to my page and notice it doesn't look much different. In every photo, it seems like I'm having the time of my life, carefree and overjoyed—when really, I've been miserable. Behind each picture is a terrified, sad girl who doesn't even know who she is.

I'm tired of wearing this facade.

I sit up in bed and don't bother wiping the tears out of my eyes. Using my front camera, I take a picture of myself for my Instagram story, puffy eyes, bleeding mascara, and all. On it, I write: People aren't always as happy as they seem.

I don't know what compels me to share it. Maybe I really do just want attention. Is that so wrong?

Or maybe I just want to stop living a lie. Maybe I'm tired of pretending I'm okay when I'm not. I am not okay.

I. Am. *Not.* Okay.

I wish I had an excuse for the way that I am. A concrete reason why I can't stop falling apart. But I can't explain my turmoil without being misunderstood. Can't cope without feeling like a fraud.

Resting my head on my pillow, I shut my eyes tight as warm tears well in my eyes. Everything hurts. Physically just as much as mentally. I want it all to go away. I want this gnawing in my gut to fade. I want my head to stop throbbing, my bones to stop aching. I want these thoughts to leave me alone.

I want to fall asleep. Wake up with a different mind. Or maybe not at all.

I dig my fingernails into my palms.

*Take it back.*

But I can't.

*     *     *

A few hours later, my phone vibrates aggressively, jolting me awake in a panic. Shivering, I sit up in the pitch black and retrieve it from the mess of sheets and blankets.

"Hello?" I ask without checking the screen. Kat's been calling me all night, and if I keep ignoring her, she'll drive here and *make* me talk.

"Hey, April."

I recognize the voice. But it's not Kat's.

"Colton? What's up? Is everything okay?"

"Yeah, everything's fine. I'm out right now, so I figured we have time to talk without Tristan hearing."

"About what?" I ask, staring into the darkness. My eyes are adjusted enough to make out the mess my room is, just how I left it. Contents from my leather messenger bag spilling onto the floor. Books and notepads piled next to my bed. Old coffee mugs claiming my nightstand.

And there's a small Christmas tree in the corner that my dad set up for me when I was out this morning, but I unplugged it.

"About Tristan..." Colton says. "Look, I was trying to protect him. That's why I kept lying to you. I'm sorry about that. But now that you know...Well, he said he told you everything? About his dad?"

"Yeah, he did. It's—"

"Bullshit, I know. It's been killing me being the only one who knows. I don't know how to help him."

Colton sighs, creating static in my ear. He sounds like he's about to have a panic attack, his voice frantic, words rushed.

"He doesn't want to tell the police or anything, which I can understand. They'll put him with other family, and the closest family members he has are in Virginia. Aside from his sister, but she's at school, and you already know he doesn't want to add more shit to her plate. Plus, he'll be 18 in a few months. So, I guess it makes sense that he's just gonna stay with me for now, until college. But, I don't know. People think he's *missing*, you know? His own sister. His friends."

"Yeah, I do know," I say. My heart races, feeding off Colton's panic. "They're probably thinking the worst. I know I was."

"I keep telling him that. But he says them knowing the truth *is* the worst."

"Worse than him being dead? I don't think so."

"I know, I know." Colton pauses. "I just don't know how to handle this. I *can't* handle this."

"Look, I know how he feels right now," I admit, twirling a strand of my hair around my finger. "Of course, not to the same extent. But I've been in that headspace, thinking I'm to blame or whatever. That I don't deserve help."

Colton doesn't say anything, but he doesn't need to. Just saying it out loud is a relief. Admitting it not only to myself, but to someone else.

"I could tell he felt that way when I talked to him," I add, refocusing my thoughts. "I don't want him to feel that way."

"I don't want *anyone* to feel that way," Colton tells me. And somehow, I know he means me, too.

I lie back on my pillows, staring up at the ceiling. Maybe I've been going about this the wrong way. Maybe it's okay to be upset. Maybe, instead of dwelling on my own agony, I can use it to get others through theirs. I mean, that's what an investigative journalist would do, right? Help people?

"Let me help you," I tell Colton.

"How?"

"By being a friend through this." *Something I should've been a long time ago.* "Can I come over tomorrow? To talk to him again?"

Colton pauses, and I hold my breath, hoping he accepts my offer, realizing this is as much for me as it is for Tristan.

"Yeah, fuck it. Come over."

# CHAPTER 32

"I'm going downtown with some friends," I tell my dad as I head out in the morning. Thankfully, Greg didn't tell him about my skipping school yesterday, or about finding me in the street the other night, so he has no reason not to believe me.

"You driving?" he asks, sipping his cup of coffee alone at the counter.

"Yup."

He smiles at me. "I'm proud of you, April. Really tackling your fears lately."

"Thanks…" I pour coffee into a to-go mug, hiding my face from his. "Where's Mom?"

"Brunch with her friends."

*Of course.*

"Well, I'll text you if plans change," I tell him before slipping out the front door. Any more conversation with him and the guilt will bury me alive.

I decide to break up my drive into two parts: first, I drive to Target, since it's halfway to Coltons', and I need to pick up some things; then, from there, I drive to his place.

Again, it takes me much longer than it should, but I don't have any major panic attacks.

*Progress.*

Before I can even knock on the door, Colton lets me in. He's wearing dress pants and a black button-up.

"Hey," he says in a low voice. He looks relieved.

I smile. "Hi."

"He's in the living room." Colton moves to let me in, then starts walking out the door.

"Wait, where are you going?" I whisper-yell so Tristan doesn't hear.

"I have work."

I squint at him. "Wearing that?"

"I work two jobs. Serving tables today for fancy brunch-goers."

"Oh." I look down the narrow hallway that leads to the back of the apartment, where Tristan is. Panic jolts through me. "I thought we were in this together!" I whine.

"We are! I'm doing my part...feeding and housing the kid." Colton laughs. "You'll be fine. Just talk to him."

Colton shuts the door behind him, leaving me alone with Tristan in the apartment. As I step toward the den, my legs wobble beneath me.

Tristan's lying on the couch watching *The Office* when I walk in, legs hanging over the end of the loveseat. He's in joggers and a T-shirt, completely oblivious to my presence.

I stand against the doorframe and watch him. My mind seems frozen, like it can't comprehend what's happening. Tristan is here. I know that. I've known that for a few days now. Yet, I still can't believe, after all this time, he's right here. In front of me. And I can't deny the rush of excitement it brings.

This time, I won't look the other way.

"Tristan," I say to get his attention.

Tristan whips his head around. For a brief second, his eyes light up. But just as quickly, his face falls. I wish that didn't hurt so bad.

"Can we talk?" I manage, holding up a plastic shopping bag from Target. "I have something for you."

His expression hardens. "April, I thought we—"

"*Please,*" I cut him off, desperate to gain his trust. "Just hear me out."

Tristan stares at me, his eyes a dark shade of green, and I can tell he's torn, which is the last thing I want right now. To add more stress to his life.

He sits up and moves to one side of the couch, and I take

it as an invitation to sit with him. So, I do. And I can feel his anxiety like my own.

"I'm not here to drag you home or anything," I tell him.

I'm facing him, my back against the armrest and knees pulled to my chest, as he slumps against the opposite side of the small couch.

He looks down at the bag I placed on the floor.

"What's that?" he asks me.

I reach in, taking out the contents. "This," I say, holding up a phone, "is for you."

He looks at the phone in my hand, then back up at me, his face scrunched. "I'm confused."

I adjust myself so that I'm sitting on my feet, legs bent under me. "It's a prepaid phone. Basically, you can call or text me without being tracked. So, now we can talk whenever without having to worry. I bought two, just in case."

Taking the phone from me, he turns it over, inspecting it with furrowed eyebrows. "Why?"

"What do you mean 'why?' I just told you."

He meets my eyes, and I'm not sure how to read his expression.

"No, I mean, *why* are you doing this for me?"

"Because I want to." My voice is small.

He hands it back to me. "I can't take this from you."

"Why not?"

"Because..." He runs his hand through his hair. "You shouldn't even be here. I mean, shit, April, it's your senior year of high school. You should be out with your friends or worrying about college or something. Not worrying about me."

My heart sinks. If only he knew how much I wanted that. To have a life. To be able to spend time with friends without having to bite my tongue or hide my compulsions. To have the strength to go off to college and leave my worries behind.

Is this what he thinks of me? That I'm just some loser with nothing better to do? That I'm just involving myself in his drama to escape the void that is my life?

*Is he right about all that?*

"Are you crying?" he asks me. I shake my head, but he leans forward and grabs my hands away from my face, and there's no more hiding my crazy.

"Shit, I'm sorry, April," he says. "I didn't mean to make you upset. I just don't want you getting involved. Especially with my dad, you know? It's not—I don't want that."

He talks quickly as he pulls me in for a hug. I feel warm and safe in his arms, and I don't want him to let go, don't want him to look at me when I'm like this. "I'm sorry," he continues. "I'm an asshole. I didn't mean to make you cry."

"No, you're not." I talk into his chest, my voice muffled and high. I sniffle, willing myself to get it together. I'm here for a reason. To help Tristan. Not to make this about me. I always make everything about me. "It's not your fault. I'm just going through some stuff."

He pulls away and looks at me, hand on my shoulder. "Can we talk about it?"

I wipe my eyes. "It's complicated."

"You're talking to a guy who ran away from home and is now living with an emo 19-year-old two towns over." I laugh, and Tristan smiles. He drags his hand down my arm, then lightly squeezes my wrist. He doesn't let go. I don't *want* him to let go. "I don't think you have to worry about 'complicated' with me."

"I just want to help you, that's all," I tell him.

An awkward silence fills the air, and his fingers are still gently gripping my wrist. He pulls it away and grabs the phone resting on the couch next to him and stares at it. "Okay," he says, turning the phone over in his hand. "Well, it's not an iPhone...but I guess it'll do."

I can't help but snort, and he grins at me. "Cute," he says, and my cheeks blush. "Jokes aside..." He looks me in the eye. "I appreciate this so much."

I shrug. "You don't have to thank me."

"No, I do. I mean, you took the time to find me...and you came back to help me, even when I told you not to."

"I also blackmailed Colton," I say, smirking.

He narrows his eyes at me, lips curled up.

"Wait, what?"

I shake my head. "Don't worry about it."

On the TV, Michael Scott makes a "That's what she said!" joke, and in another life, Tristan and I would laugh. And it would feel so normal, sitting next to him, watching his favorite show. Maybe that's how it would've been if I hadn't turned him down, hadn't blown him off last year. That could've been our reality. Simple and pure.

Instead, there's a painful disconnect between us, like a million words unsaid. And I think maybe it's time I give them a voice.

I inhale a long, slow breath, glancing back at the TV so I don't have to look at him.

"Freshman year," I say. "Do you remember that party?"

"Of course I do. I didn't think *you* remembered."

"Well, I did. And I never got to thank you." I turn and meet his eye. "So...*thank you*."

He pauses for a moment, then gets up and walks into the other room. I don't know what to think. Did I say something wrong?

But when he comes back, he's holding something between his fingers. He hands it to me.

It's a small coin with a picture of a lighthouse that reads: "May you always find your way back home."

"Oh my God," I say, barely believing my eyes. I look up at Tristan standing above me. "My dad got me this. I thought I lost it."

Tristan scratches the back of his head.

"I found it on the driveway after you left that night, and I just knew it was yours. I wanted to give it back, but I didn't know how. I didn't want to bring up that night if you didn't want to talk about it, so...I held onto it, just in case."

I roll the coin over in my hand before handing it back to him.

"You have it."

"What? Why?"

"I want you to have it."

"But your dad—"

"Bought me a new one when I cried to him about losing this one."

It's true. He found a replacement and had it shipped from Etsy within two days.

"Keep it," I tell him. "It would mean a lot to me."

He takes the coin, and our fingers brush.

"It means a lot to me too, April. More than you know."

# CHAPTER 33

The last place I've wanted to be these past few weeks was at school.

Thankfully, today is Friday, and next week is a short week because Christmas break starts on Wednesday. Otherwise, I'm not sure I could stand another minute of superficial conversations about who's throwing the best New Year's party this year, or lessons on number theory. I've been trying to drown it all out with Tristan's and my shared Spotify playlist, "Some Place Like Home." He created a new account under a pseudonym consisting of random letters and numbers, using Colton's computer.

The highlight of every day is listening to the next song he drops in there, or finding my own to add. I plan on spending all night shuffling the playlist and reading my new book.

As I'm grabbing books from my locker at the end of the day, Jade approaches me. "Hey."

"Hey," I say cautiously. I haven't seen her since our fight.

"How have you been?"

"Good, I guess."

She leans against the row of lockers next to mine, folding her arms and snapping her gum.

"Really? 'Cause your Insta post on Friday didn't seem like it."

I was hoping she hadn't seen that.

"It was nothing."

"Obviously not, but oh-kay."

My phone buzzes in my hand, distracting me from Jade and her drama.

**Tristan:** Added a new song to our playlist. Check it out. :)

I can't help but smile.

"Hell-oooh?" Jade asks as I stare at his message. I look back up at her focus as she stands there, watching me. "So, are you ever gonna apologize?" she asks me.

I shake my head, confused.

"Apologize for what?"

"For snapping at me the other day!"

I narrow my eyes at her, anger bubbling inside me, and she's so relaxed, conscience as clear as her icy blue eyes. I wonder what that's like. Every mistake, every regret, haunts me like a demon seeking possession.

Guilt twists my stomach. Sighing, I grip my locker door and meet her eye.

"I'm sorry."

Jade rolls her eyes. "Yeah, really seems like it, April. I guess that's what I get, huh? For letting you walk all over me all the time."

*What?*

"Everyone wonders why I'm so loyal to you, when you clearly could care less about me," she goes on. "*I'm* the one who asks you to hang out. *I'm* the one who includes you in my plans. *I'm* the one who gets you out of bed on a Friday night when you're depressed."

My eyes start to prick with tears, and I hate that I instantly cry in these moments, when I'm angry and confused and ashamed.

"Who's '*everyone?*'" I manage.

"I don't know. Lindsay. Brenda. Adam. People from drama club."

I shake my head. This is what people think about me? That I'm a shitty friend who walks all over other people?

I want to laugh in her face. I want to tell her off. I want to hide.

My head spins, like it always does before a panic attack, and that can't happen. Not here. Not now.

"I'll see you later, okay?" I close my locker and walk away, turning my attention back to my phone, to Tristan's text. I need a distraction before I lose my shit in the middle of the hallway like last time.

**Me:** Will check later.

**Tristan:** Everything ok? Got this weird gut feeling just now…

His text comes in just as I send mine.

**Me:** No, actually. Just got into a fight with Jade.

**Tristan:** Oh no, why???

**Me:** Apparently I'm a horrible friend.

**Tristan:** Lol, I mean…I don't know Jade like you do, but I can assure you it's the other way around.

**Me:** I don't know. That's what everyone thinks, apparently. That I'm a shit friend.

**Tristan:** Well, I don't think that.

"Did no one ever tell you not to text and walk? Especially in a school parking lot."

I look up and see Kat grinning at me, gripping the straps of her Fjallraven Kanken backpack, her hair a curly mess. She falls into step next to me, and I quickly close my messages with Tristan and shove my phone in my back pocket.

"Sorry," I mutter. My heart is pounding in my ears as if I've been accused of murder, awaiting my sentence.

We make our way to her car, which is parked way in the back. She's been driving me to school most days.

"What's up? Who were you talking to?"

"No one." When we reach her car, I open up the passenger door and toss my bag on the floor before getting in.

A million thoughts and emotions buzz in my mind and body, and I'm not sure which to trust. I need to sort this out.

"Kat, do you think I'm a bad friend?"

"Ummmm no…why?"

"Jade and I just got into a fight."

She gives me a look. "Don't tell me she accused *you* of being a bad friend."

"She said everyone thinks that she lets me walk all over her."

"Everyone? You mean, her stuck up friends who would agree with anything she says?"

I shrug. "I don't know...What if she has a point? I mean, do you feel like you're the only one in our friendship who makes an effort?"

Kat pauses like she's considering the question. Then, she sticks her keys in the ignition and backs out of her spot, saying nothing. My heart quickens.

"Kat?" I ask, needing to know the answer.

"I mean...look," she starts as she drives toward the exit, and my stomach instantly lurches. "I'm not gonna lie, you get preoccupied sometimes, and it can make you a bit distant. But that's not your fault. It doesn't make you a bad friend."

I feel like throwing up.

"Yes, it does!" Suddenly, I'm mad. At Jade. At myself. At Kat even, who's just being honest with me. "You really think I don't try? Like, I'm not there for you?"

"No, April! You're always there for me." At a red light, she stops to look at me. "That's not what I meant at all. I'm just saying, if I'm being honest, you can get fixated on other things that distract you for a while. But I get it. Jade just...doesn't. She doesn't even try to. If anyone's a bad friend, it's her."

"That's what Tristan said."

Kat tilts her head at me. "Huh?"

"Uh, that's what Tristan said last year," I quickly say. "He said he didn't know why I hung out with Jade."

"Oh. Well, yeah. I can't say I disagree. But, you know, childhood friends hold merit I guess."

I sigh. "I feel like shit, Kat."

"Stop. You're not a bad friend, April."

"Yes, I am. I only focus on myself." I sink down in my seat, folding my arms over my chest.

"No, you focus on whatever your OCD wants you to focus on," Kat says. "That's not your fault."

"But I should be able to control that. I should be stronger than this. *God*, this is why Dylan left me!"

"*April*. What you fixate on does not make you a bad person...You literally fixate on helping other people. It's okay.

Really. I don't get offended or anything."

"But Jade does. And apparently, everyone else sees it too." I consider the people at my school, how shallow I think they all are. What do they think about *me*? Maybe *I'm* the issue.

All along, I thought I was the genuine one. The person who cared about everyone else. The girl who wanted to help people. But now...now, it just feels like the opposite.

"Oh God, do I have an ego problem?" I ask aloud.

"You're letting her get in your head," Kat tells me.

"But it's true. I only focus on myself. Even *you* said so." It comes out more bitter than intended.

Kat doesn't say anything for the rest of the ride home, and I stare out the window at the bare trees. The clouds are a threatening gray, and I wish it wasn't cold enough for snow. We're only supposed to get a few inches, but still. I'm already trapped in my head; I don't want to be trapped in my house, too.

When I get home, I immediately lock myself in my room and collapse onto my bed, pulling out my phone.

**Tristan:** You okay?
**Me:** I guess.
I just feel like the worst person.
**Tristan:** April, you're not a bad person. Look what you did for me.

I lie on my bed and stare up at the ceiling, drained and confused. I don't even know who I am. I don't even *like* who I am.

Another text comes in.

**Tristan:** Also, if it takes me an hour to respond, it's probably because I have to tap the same button three times to get the right letter.

I can't help but laugh as I type my reply.

**Me:** Wow, whoever bought you that phone is a shitty friend.
**Tristan:** Nah, she's pretty awesome. :)
Now go listen to the song I added. You won't regret it.

I load Spotify on my phone and select our playlist, then scroll down to the bottom. A song called "IT'S ALL FADING TO BLACK" by XXXTENTACION, who I've never heard of before, ft. Blink 182. The last part sells it for me. I tap the play button and close my eyes, letting the music fill my ears.

When Mark Hoppus's voice plays, I instantly get chills

down to my toes.

> *Now I'm just a ghost in my own life,*
> *so make the most of this goodbye.*
> *Do you still dream about me late at night?*
> *Or are you out there livin' better times?*

**Me:** Wow.
**Tristan:** Good, right?
**Me:** I love it.
**Tristan:** Not usually into rap, but he's an exception.

I replay the song and breathe, letting the music calm me down. Sometimes, it's the only thing that works.

**Me:** Thank you.
**Tristan:** For what?
**Me:** Everything.

# CHAPTER 34

"Did you seriously buy three boxes of pizza for three people?" Colton asks as he lets me in on Saturday. He's wearing a large black sweatshirt with the Emo Nite logo on it, and it makes him look skinnier than he already is.

"Well, I don't know how much you guys eat!" Although, judging by his sunken cheeks, I'm not sure it's as much as I thought.

Colton shakes his head.

"How much do I owe you?" he asks, taking money out of his wallet and sorting through bills as I place the pizzas on the kitchen counter.

"Don't worry about it."

He gives me a look, then grabs the receipt off the counter before handing me the right amount.

"You're annoying," I tell him.

"I know. That's why I have no friends."

I laugh, then open the box of pepperoni and take a slice.

"Where's Tristan?"

"In the shower."

"I should probably wait for him before eating, but I don't want to." I take a bite of pizza, and Colton smiles.

"I'm glad you've been hanging here and talking to him. He's been a lot happier."

I finish chewing before answering. "You don't mind me coming here, right? Tristan told me you wouldn't, but, you know. I don't want to intrude."

"Nah, not at all. I don't know if you've noticed, but I don't really do much. So, I don't mind having some company for once."

"What do you mean?"

"I don't really go out or anything. I wasn't joking when I said I don't have friends. I have crippling social anxiety," he says with a laugh, but I can tell he doesn't actually think it's funny. "I dropped out of college because of it. New York isn't exactly the best place for people like me."

I think about the first time I saw Colton at the liquor store. How confident he looked. I mean, Dylan was even threatened by him.

"Wow, but you seem so...*cool*."

He practically spits out his food.

"*Cool?* You're funny."

"Seriously though! I never would've known. You put on a good facade."

Colton shrugs. "Well, I guess we all have something going on that other people can't see."

"That's for damn sure."

Placing his pizza down on his plate, Colton focuses his attention on me.

"What's your 'something?'"

I can tell he genuinely cares, which is oddly refreshing and makes me feel comfortable enough to open up.

"Obsessive-compulsive disorder." Saying its full name sometimes makes it seem more than just a quirky fear of germs. "It's...complicated. And not what everyone thinks. Kinda makes it hard to feel normal."

He snorts. "What even *is* 'normal?' They put so many labels on shit today...I think we're all just a sum of whatever the fuck we've been through."

I consider his statement. *Have I ever even been through anything traumatic?*

"Nah, but I get it," Colton continues as I sort through my memories like my mind is an encyclopedia. "It sucks. I don't really relate with anyone my age. Or anyone at all, really."

"It's hard to really connect with anyone," I tell him.

"Honestly, having Tristan here has actually really helped me," he tells me, walking over to the table and sitting down. I follow him. "He doesn't get it, obviously, but he's still a good friend to talk to. Plus, it's nice to have the company. Makes me feel less isolated."

"Did you live alone? Before Tristan?"

He nods. "My mom's a single mom, and my dad's a cheating prick who started another family and forgot all about his original one...I have an older brother, but he's married. So, when I moved to college, my mom moved out and downgraded to a smaller place so she could quit one of her four jobs."

I raise my eyebrows. "*Four*? Damn."

"Yeah. She's a hard worker. Helped pay for my brother's college. Was gonna help with mine too, but that kinda backfired. I go to community college online now." There's a hint of shame in his expression. "But anyway, I couldn't move back in with her. I didn't wanna add more stress, you know? So, basically, I work for that car dealership Monday through Friday, and serve on the weekends."

"Wow," I say. "I give you a lot of credit."

"Yeah, that's how I can afford it. I also had a shit ton of savings in my account 'cause I was always an anxious kid who saved every penny I got for every birthday and holiday."

I smile, picturing little Colton stuffing change into his piggy bank.

"Well, hey, it paid off...literally."

He snorts, then shrugs. "For now. I just hope I figure my life out eventually."

"No one ever really has their life figured out."

"It smells amazing in here," Tristan says as he walks into the kitchen. His hair is wet, and he's wearing workout shorts and a T-shirt that's obviously Colton's, seeing as it's two sizes too tight. I look away before he notices me blushing.

"God damn, April. *Three* pies?"

Colton gives me a look, as if to say, "*Told you!*"

"Alright, I don't need your negativity, guys," I joke. "You'll thank me when you have leftovers."

Tristan takes a seat next to me, biting into a slice. "What do you wanna do tonight?" he asks me, mouth full.

"Nothing exciting, considering we can't leave the apartment," I joke. I wouldn't want to leave the apartment even if we could.

Colton gets up and walks to the counter, grabbing another piece.

"Sorry my place isn't entertaining enough for you."

I look over at him. "Yeah, well, you could've at least bought a pool table or something."

Tristan laughs as Colton places another slice on my plate for me. "At least I'm a good host," Colton says.

I grin. "That you are."

"I gotta do some homework, so I'll be in my room," Colton tells us, carrying his plate of pizza into the hall. He stops in front of his door for a second, then smiles at me. I know he's thanking me for our conversation. I smile back.

"We should eat on the balcony," Tristan tells me. His cheeks are still red from his shower.

I give him a look. "It's freezing!"

"Soooo? You could borrow my sweatshirt." He pushes his lip out, and suddenly I don't really care if it's 20 degrees out. Sitting on a small balcony two floors up is about as close as Tristan has been to the outside world in months. Aside from my accident.

"We don't have to," he adds.

I smile at him. "No, let's do it."

He grins, then jumps up and runs to jogs to his room. A few moments later, he comes back out with a hoodie and tosses it to me. I tug it over my head. It's warm, and it smells like Tristan, a mild yet sweet cologne.

We go out on the balcony, which is attached to the living room/kitchen, and a gust of wind makes me shiver. But I can't deny how nice it feels to have some fresh air. Especially near the ocean.

There's no chairs or furniture, so Tristan and I sit on the ground and lean against the sliding glass door, staring out at the neighborhood. Colton's apartment doesn't face the beach, but there's still a decent view of the streets below. I'm sure the sunset is beautiful from up here.

"Are you feeling any better?" Tristan asks me softly.

I turn to him. "Huh?"

"You know, about yesterday. That fight with Jade."

"Oh, right." *He remembered?*

"I guess. I haven't talked to her since." I balance my paper plate on my knees. "I feel like, I don't know. Maybe Jade was right. Maybe I really do walk all over people."

"April, this is Jade we're talking about. I don't even know the girl, and I know for a fact that she's…" His voice trails off.

I smirk. "What?"

He meets my eye, an amused look on his face.

"My mom always told me if you don't have anything nice to say, don't say anything at all."

Laughing, I bump my shoulder with his. "Jade's okay. She and I, we're just different."

"Yeah, but so are you and Kat. Aren't you two also close?"

"Yeah, Kat's definitely my closest friend."

"Does she try to change you?"

"Kat?" I think about the time I got drunk with Dylan. Kat told me it was 'out-of-character' and was worried about me. "No way. She's not like that at all."

"Exactly," Tristan says. "But Jade obviously is."

"What makes you say that?"

He places his plate on the ground next to him and turns to face me. "When she forced you to play spin the bottle on your birthday and let you leave the party alone?"

I look down at my food, suddenly not hungry.

"Yeah, that sucked. But to her, she's just trying to get me out of my comfort zone." I put my plate on the ground too, but stay facing forward, talking out toward the street instead of looking at Tristan. "My mom is the same way with me."

"There's a difference between giving someone a gentle push and forcing them to do something because you want them to. I think Jade is doing the latter."

"Yeah…I think you're right. My mom does that, too. It's a shitty feeling." I look at him, at his glistening eyes. Our faces are close. "Knowing you need to change, need to be someone else, in order for someone to love you."

Tears well in my eyes, as they always do in these moments. Quickly, I dab them away with the sleeve of Tristan's sweatshirt. "Sorry," I say with a laugh.

"Don't be sorry." Tristan looks like he wants to comfort me, but isn't sure if I'd want him to. I lean into him slightly, and he puts his arm around me.

"I feel the same way with my dad," he continues, his voice soft and soothing. "Before my mom died, even. I always felt like I wasn't good enough for him. I was never really into the same things as him. He wanted me to take over his business with him one day, but I wanted to pursue music, which he thought was nothing more than a hobby. And, I mean, I get it. He just wants what's best for me, I guess. Like I'm sure your mom does. But at the same time, I can't help but think, maybe he was projecting his own desires on me, you know?"

"Yeah, that's how my mom is. She basically thinks anxiety is something you can just 'get over,' that I should just take meds so I can be normal and do normal things, like go to parties and on dates."

Tristan sighs, tracing circles on my shoulder with his thumb.

"See, that's not fair," he says, his voice low. "I know she's your mom, and I'm sure she just wants what's best, but…Try not to let her sway you too much."

"I think that was my issue all along. It's like, I don't know who I am. So I let other people tell me. But then I end up doing something so out-of-character that I just end up feeling even worse about myself."

"Out-of-character how?" he asks me.

"Like...when I was with Dylan, I drove here, to the beach, I mean, because I overheard my mom talking about how I need to get a hold of myself or whatever. She said I'd lose Dylan and my friends, basically, if I kept worrying so much and letting it hold me back. So anyway, I left my house when I heard her telling my dad that, and Dylan met me here, and I asked him to buy me alcohol, and I got a little too drunk..."

I take a deep breath, thinking about the memory, reliving the pain like I'm still in that moment.

"My friends told me if Dylan wasn't getting it from me, then he would get it from someone else. So, I almost lost my virginity while wasted on the beach. And that's not me. At all. But I just kept thinking, 'They're right. My mom and Jade and Lindsay. They're all right: I'm gonna lose Dylan.' And it felt like he was all I had. So I did what I thought he wanted."

Tristan doesn't say anything for a few moments, and I question whether I should've shared that with him. He's just so easy to talk to, so understanding and insightful. It's hard not to wear my heart on my sleeve when I'm around him.

He pulls his arm away and runs his hand through his hair, hanging his head. Then, he looks straight out into the night.

"Did he let you?"

I shake my head quickly. "No no no, he stopped me. He said I was more important than that."

"Well, you are."

"I know. And I should've known then. I just..." I shake my head, not knowing what to say.

"You don't have to explain it," he tells me, meeting my eye. "As long as you know now."

I extend my legs out in front of me, shivering a bit.

"I really missed you, April," Tristan says. "I wish I could've been there for you these past few months."

"And I wish I could've been there for you these past few *years*." I sigh, then rest my head on his shoulder. "You have no idea how much I've missed you."

# CHAPTER 35

"What do you guys wanna order for dinner?" Colton asks Tristan and me.

I'm sitting at his table, texting Kat, who's on her way to Maine with her mom to visit her grandparents.

Tristan invited me over to celebrate my Christmas break starting, and since I'm still not talking to Jade, and Kat is out-of-state, I didn't exactly have a reason to say no.

But I didn't exactly *want* to say no either.

"I mean, we could cook for once," Tristan says, opening the fridge and staring at the few groceries inside.

Colton makes a face. "Cook? Who wants to cook?"

"Not me," I say.

Tristan looks back at us, eyebrow raised. "Do you guys not know how?"

"Hey, I know how to cook!" I say, feigning offense.

"Me too," Colton says, but I can tell he's stifling a laugh.

Tristan closes the fridge and gives Colton a look. "Oh yeah? What have you ever cooked before?"

"I make great pasta."

"Oooooh, and I make great sauce," I say. "It comes in a jar, but I have to warm it up and everything."

"Guess we're ordering out," Tristan says, rolling his eyes but smiling. "Can we go somewhere with a drive-thru though? I kind of wanna go for a drive."

Colton stares at Tristan like he's conflicted.

"I don't know, dude…" I can see Tristan's face fall from across the room. Colton sighs. "Alright, fine. But you better wear a hoodie or something. I don't need you getting caught and me getting in trouble for harboring a fugitive."

I snort. "'Harboring a fugitive?'"

"What? It's a real thing!"

"Ooooo, can we get Chick-fil-A?" I ask as Tristan runs to his room.

He comes back wearing a sweatshirt, the hood tightened so much that only his eyes show. I burst out laughing.

Shaking his head, Colton leads us out to his car. "April's got shotgun, in case you gotta duck."

"You're so paranoid, dude," Tristan says.

We pile in, me in the front, Tristan in the back. "Can I be DJ?" I ask.

Colton jokingly makes a face.

"April actually has great taste in music," Tristan tells him.

"Yeah, my mixtape is straight fire," I joke.

Colton glares at me. "I will kick you out of this car if you ever say that again."

Laughing, I buckle my seatbelt and grab the aux cord, plugging it into my phone. I load Spotify and shuffle my playlist, and *Hear You Me* comes on. Immediately, I change it.

"Hey, that was a good song!" Colton says.

My cheeks grow warm. "It's too slow." *Here, Now, Forever* by Carousel Kings comes on, and I turn up the volume to try to drown out my thoughts. But all I can see is Dylan arguing with me about which version of the *Hear You Me* is better. Dylan pulling me in for a kiss in his car. Dylan laughing at me when I accidentally hit the horn. Dylan telling me he how lucky he is to have me.

I listen to the lyrics playing now, my chest aching. It seems every song brings me back to Dylan.

*Floating all alone, living in my head.*
*Wish I wouldn't be sinking with regret.*
*Wonder how you feel living without my love in you,*
*Far from you.*

Tristan pokes his head between me and Colton. "April, who is this? They're good."

I turn to him and notice his hood is still tied tightly around his head, and I can't help but laugh.

"I can't take you seriously right now," I say, pulling his hood down. Messy curls fall over his eyes. Before I can stop myself, I tousle his hair with my hand.

Tristan raises his eyebrows and smirks at me. I quickly pull my hand back and face forward.

"They're called Carousel Kings," I say. "They have some great songs."

We listen in silence.

"Damn, those lyrics," Colton says.

"I know, right?" I say, slumping in my seat. "Like a punch to the gut."

When we park, Colton goes inside in case someone recognizes Tristan in the drive-thru. I stay in the car, scrolling through my Instagram, through old pictures of Dylan and me. I stop at the photo of us at the park the day after he asked me out.

It's strange, thinking back to that moment. I was so happy, talking about my future like it was certain, seeing Dylan as this exciting possibility at being normal. And now—now, I realize just how much of a fantasy it was.

"He's an idiot," Tristan says from the backseat.

I turn around to face him. "What?"

"Dylan. He's an idiot."

"Oh." I look back down at my phone, at the two of us on the park bench, and I feel the need to defend the boy in the picture. "He was a good boyfriend for a while."

"He drove drunk with you in the car…"

"I'm aware of that."

"And that doesn't bother you?"

I glare at him. "What do you think?"

"I think he's an asshole."

"Well, he wasn't." Not entirely, at least.

Tristan scoffs. "He knew he was tipsy and drove anyway. He made that choice. Knowing it could hurt you. Or worse."

"Okay, Tristan, I get it. He obviously didn't give a shit

about me."

Tristan's expression softens. "That's not—"

"Why do you even care?" I snap.

He gives me a look that says, *really?*

I shake my head, anger and confusion clouding my thinking.

"I'm sorry," I say. "I know you're just defending me."

"Yeah, and you're just defending some asshole who treated you like crap."

"I'm not defending him! I'm just saying...You don't know him like I do." I shake my head. "*Did.*"

"I don't *want* to know him," Tristan says. "And I don't *need* to know him to know that what he did was unforgivable."

"Who says I'm forgiving him?"

"Your excuses for him are pretty telling."

"Okay, how did we even start fighting about this?" I ask, my voice rising.

Tristan leans forward and places his hand on my arm.

"We're not fighting. At least, I'm not. I'm just saying, he's an idiot and an asshole. Case closed."

I turn away from him and stare out the windshield into the night, watching friends stumble into the restaurant, laughing like it's just that easy. They remind me of Jade and Lindsay and Brenda, who all think I'm horrible, just like Tristan probably thinks now.

Maybe I really *am* the issue.

"I'm sorry," Tristan tells me. "I shouldn't have said anything. That was stupid of me. I just care about you a lot, April, and I can't imagine losing you. And to think your own boyfriend, the one guy who's supposed to keep you safe and make you happy..." He trails off, stopping himself before he can go any further. "Sorry, sorry. It just pisses me off, that's all."

I can't help but laugh. "It's okay."

"Seeing you that day, holding you after the accident...It was terrifying, April."

"I'm sure it was, and I wish you didn't have to see me like

that," I tell him honestly.

"Well, no, I'm glad I was there. It just made me realize how much you mean to me. I mean, I already knew, but you know. It's like, 'Shit, if I lost this person, I don't know what I'd do...'"

I look him in the eyes like they're magnets to mine. I want to tell him everything I went through these past months, not knowing where he was or if he was okay. I want him to know that losing him would destroy me too, because it nearly did this year. But I can't seem to find the words.

"You're not going to lose me," I say instead.

*　　*　　*

"Have you guys ever seen *Extremely Wicked, Shockingly Evil and Vile*?"

Colton blinks at me from across the living room. He's lying on the couch on his back, feet propped up on the armrest. "What the fuck is that?"

I laugh. "It's a movie based on *The Ted Bundy Tapes*."

"Nope, don't like that," Colton says.

"I've actually been meaning to watch it," Tristan says from next to me. We're sitting on the loveseat together, surrounded by our bags of food.

Colton glares at him. "Outnumbered in my own home? You guys are the worst."

"Lily Collins is in it," I tell Colton.

He pauses. "Fine. But only for Lily."

We finish our food just a few minutes into the movie, leaving the bags and containers on the sofa table in front of us. I shiver from the cold, and Tristan reaches next to him and hands me a blanket.

"Here, we can share," I say, tossing it over him. But it's not all that big, and I have to move a little closer so it covers both of us. My foot accidentally bumps his, and he playfully kicks me back.

My phone buzzes with a message from Kat telling me she finally made it to Maine, and that it's freezing and she'd much rather be home eating nuggets with me. I laugh to myself and tell her I just had Chick-fil-A. I don't mention I had it with Tristan. Or that I only got waffle fries in case of food poisoning.

"Yoooooooooo, this dude is fucking crazy!" Colton's voice makes me look up from my phone. I see Zac Efron as Ted Bundy escaping from prison through a small hole in the ceiling.

"*Insane*, right?" I say. "Zac's an amazing actor in this."

"So is Lily," Tristan adds.

I nod in agreement. "They'd actually make a really cute couple. In real life, obviously not in the movie."

"What's wrong? Don't like serial killers?" Tristan jokes.

I smirk. "Well, if they look like *that...*"

"Dude, that's the problem." Colton holds up his phone from the other couch, and I can barely make out the Google Image search of Ted Bundy. "He looks completely normal. Like, if I saw him walking down the street, I wouldn't think anything of him except that he's a fucking stud."

Tristan and I exchange an amused look as Colton goes back to scrolling through photos, rubbing his temples as if it's stressing him out.

"We don't have to watch this if it's making you nervous," I tell him.

He looks up at me, an embarrassed smile on his face. "I'm fine."

When a gory scene of a decapitated woman comes on, I instinctively tug the blanket over my head and hide undercovers, even though I've already seen the movie three times.

"This is too fucking much," I hear Colton say, then feel Tristan shake with laughter.

"You good under there?" Tristan asks me, holding the blanket up so that he can see me.

"Better than Colton."

"Yo!" Colton yells. "I'm watching this for *you*!"

Tristan grins. We're under the blanket together, like two kids sharing secrets in the dark. I look at him, and his expression turns serious. His eyes are a warm shade of green, somehow glistening in the darkness.

"You have the nicest eyes."

I freeze.

*Did I really just say that?*

Tristan stares at me, his expression unreadable. He bites his lip to keep from grinning, then tucks a strand of hair off my face.

He leans his face closer to mine, and our lips are so close, they're almost touching. He presses his forehead against mine, and I close my eyes, trying to stop my body from feeling. There's too much buzzing in my mind for me to think straight.

"What the *fuck!*" Colton says.

Tristan's breaks out into a smile, his forehead still against mine. I press my lips together, blushing, and pull away from him, tugging the blanket down.

Colton is oblivious to us as he watches the movie in horror, his hand forming a tight fist against his mouth. Under the blanket, Tristan finds my hand and intertwines our fingers as if holding hands is just something we do. Warmth surges through my entire body, despite how freezing this apartment is. I feel like standing up and dragging Tristan into his room with me, shutting and locking the door behind us, collapsing onto his bed...

*Oh, God, this is bad.*

I should pull away.

*Why am I not pulling away?*

\*     \*     \*

Someone is coughing.

Groggy, I lift my head off Tristan's shoulder, who's slumped against the cushions, asleep and still holding my hand. His chest moves up and down with each breath. I get up, careful not to wake him.

The only light comes from the TV, which is stuck on Netflix's "Are you still watching?" page. As I walk toward the kitchen, I hear the coughing again.

Colton's outside on the balcony, his back to me. I push the sliding door open and step into the cold air.

"Hey," I say.

Colton glances at me, pulling a cigarette out of his mouth and blowing smoke into the air.

"Hey." His eyes are bloodshot with dark bags under them.

"I didn't know you smoked."

He doesn't say anything. His hand grips the railing, his knuckles white. He coughs again.

"You okay?" I ask him.

"Fine."

"You don't seem fine."

He looks at me, then smiles, leaning into the railing.

"Be careful," I tell him.

"I'm fine, don't worry. I only smoke when I'm stressed."

"No, not that. You're..." I gesture to the railing. "If that gives out, you're screwed."

Colton raises his eyebrows at me, then backs away from the railing and stares out into the night. There are few lights on in the houses below, and the ocean roars in the distance.

"That movie kinda freaked me out."

"I know, it's a little gory."

"Nah, it's just..." He pauses, taking a drag then slowly letting it out. "I don't know. Makes me think too much."

"I always think too much." A gust of wind makes me shiver in my thin sweatshirt. I fold my arms over my chest. "Like, when I first watched that movie, it made me scared that I'd, I don't know...*snap*." Colton turns to me, eyes wide. "Not like that," I quickly assure him. "I just—"

"No, April, me too. That's exactly what I was thinking. That he was so normal, and what if I somehow...I don't know, how does someone just get compelled to act like that? What if that happens to me and I lose control?"

"Exactly." I smile, which feels inappropriate during a conversation about serial killers, but I guess misery—or, in this case, insanity—loves company.

I walk forward and place my hands on the railing, making sure I don't lean too much weight on it. It's cold and damp beneath my palms.

"Wanna hear something funny?"

Colton smirks. "Always."

"When the movie first came out, I was terrified to watch it because of that fear. It's actually a type of OCD...or theme, or whatever. It's called harm-OCD, and you basically obsess about hurting people. Not *wanting* to hurt people, but being afraid that you might, if that makes sense." I pause. I've always been too ashamed to talk about this. But knowing it might help someone else, someone like Colton, makes me want to speak up. "So, my therapist made me watch the movie for exposure. First time I watched it, I cried for four hours straight."

Colton shakes his head. "Wow. I didn't realize OCD could be so intense."

"Yeah, it's very misunderstood."

"I almost wonder if I have it."

"I mean, you can have the same thoughts without having the disorder. I feel like they're common worries, just...people with OCD obsess a little more. Well, *a lot* more, actually."

He clears his throat. "How so?"

"Well, I can spend hours trying to find reassurance that I'm not a bad person, or that those thoughts aren't true. Like, I'll Google my thoughts or confess them to someone to gauge their reaction. Stuff like that. And it becomes this endless cycle where eventually you just have to accept your fears. Like the fact that, who knows, maybe I'll snap and become a murderer..."

"*Damn.* That sounds horrible."

I shrug. The moon casts light onto the edge of the balcony, where Colton is standing. There are dark circles under his eyes, and his body looks so thin in his baggy clothes.

I must look concerned, because his expression falls, and he glances down like he's embarrassed. "I'm fine."

"Huh?"

"I know what you're thinking."

"What am I thinking?"

He takes a drag of his cigarette. "That I look sick. That I

need to eat more. Blah blah blah. I hear it from my mom all the time."

I open my mouth to tell him he's wrong, I wasn't thinking that. But that'd be a lie.

"We all have something," I say, quoting him from the other night.

He looks at me and offers a tight-lipped smile.

"But you're not alone, you know...if you ever wanna talk about it."

"Thanks, doc." He blows out smoke, so much that I can't see his face.

"I didn't mean it like—"

"I know, I'm messing," he says. "I appreciate that, April. You're a good person."

I let out a laugh. "I don't know about that."

"I'm serious. I mean, what you're doing for Tristan is awesome. When you started talking to him and coming around more...I don't know, it's like he's a different person."

I feel a pang of guilt at the thought of Tristan. All I can think about is how we were just holding hands during the movie, and what that means, and if it should even mean anything at all. I mean, *God*, I just got out of a relationship with a boy I loved. My first serious relationship, at that.

And Tristan, he's one of my closest friends. He can't be a rebound. I can't just lead him on.

Colton leans against the corner of the balcony, this time against the wall rather than the railing. He rubs the back of his neck.

"Is it selfish that I don't want Tristan to go home?" he asks me.

I open my mouth to answer, but he starts talking again.

"I mean, I want everything to work out for him, obviously, and I wish he could go home and be at peace with his family, and that his dad would stop being a dick...But at the same time, I almost feel like my own selfishness is why I offered my place to him. Of course, I wanted to help. But more than that, I just didn't want to be alone."

My eyes start to sting as I watch Colton process his thoughts, confessing them like some evil criminal, when really, he's the polar opposite of that.

It hurts that someone else endures this type of pain, even if it makes me feel less alone at the same time.

"There's nothing wrong with that, Colton. You're human. And what you're doing is so kind. Just because it's a mutually beneficial agreement doesn't mean you're selfish."

Colton raises his eyebrows, then laughs.

"What?" I ask.

"Who says 'mutually beneficial agreement' in a casual conversation?"

I shoot him a look, but can't help but crack a smile. "Shut up."

"You're right, though. Sometimes, I think I'm just so scared of becoming my dad, that I question my intentions with everything."

"Well, I don't know your dad, but I can assure you you're nothing like him."

"He's *the worst*," Colton says in his Michael-Scott voice. Humor seems to be his coping mechanism of choice. "I guess that's something Tristan and I can relate with. Shitty dads."

I sigh. "I hate that his dad is doing this to him."

"Me too. I just wish he'd tell his sister or someone."

"Same. She's a complete wreck."

"I feel guilty, like I'm the one keeping it from her or something. I've never even met the girl."

"Honestly, I do, too. 'Cause she broke down to me at a party when he first went 'missing.' I told her I'd let her know if I heard anything...This is just so much more complicated than I expected."

"Ha," Colton says. "Isn't everything?"

Colton takes out his phone and starts messing with it, his screen illuminating his face. I pull mine out of my pocket and see a two-hour old message from Kat: Classic grandma line: "You'll regret that tattoo when you're my age!"

I laugh as I text a response of upside-down face emojis, and notice it's already past midnight.

"I should probably go," I tell Colton.

"Yeah, I was gonna say, it's getting pretty late. Is Tristan sleeping?"

"Yeah, he was out cold." I open the door and step into the warm apartment, feeling oddly at-home. I don't want to drive back to my house. I might be getting more comfortable behind the wheel, but it's pitch-black outside.

Colton follows me inside and shuts the door behind him, and I walk over to the couch where Tristan is still sound asleep.

"Hey," I whisper, touching his shoulder. His eyes flutter open slowly. "I'm gonna get going."

He grabs my wrist gently, a tired grin on his face.

"Don't leave."

"It's late...I have to drive home."

"Okay." He lets go of me and leans his elbows on his knees, rubbing his eyes. "Lemme walk you out."

My heart starts to quicken.

"Uh—you don't have to do that."

"'Night, guys," Colton says, disappearing into his room and shutting the door behind him.

Tristan walks me to the front door, yawning.

"You don't have to come out, really," I tell him. "I'll be fine."

"I know you'll be fine," he says, but he opens the door for me, following me anyway as I step outside.

"But what if someone sees you?" I scratch at my arm and step down the stairs, Tristan behind me.

"They won't" is all he says.

I turn my face away from him and quicken my pace. I shouldn't have held Tristan's hand. I shouldn't have fallen asleep with my head on his shoulder.

"Hey," Tristan says, placing his hand on my arm, stopping me in my tracks. I stare down at my feet, silent.

"*April*," he tries. "What's wrong? You're being weird."

"No, I'm not."

"You are."

I swallow hard as tears form in my eyes. I wish he couldn't read me so damn well.

"April, come on. I'm your best friend. You can talk to me."

"It's not—I'm not being weird," I say.

"Was it what happened before? During the movie."

I don't answer.

"You're thinking too much," he tells me.

"That's what I do."

"Okay, well, how can I help?"

My eyes find his again, and they really are the nicest I've ever seen. We're standing so close, I can see little specks of yellow.

I inhale a shaky breath, and suddenly, I'm back to that night freshman year, under the streetlight on the driveway. I was supposed to kiss him that night. Part of me wanted to, when he followed me outside and made sure I was alright. Not because he was cute, even though he was, but because I felt safe with him. There was this energy about him, this calming energy that made me believe—for once—that everything would be alright.

But something held me back. With Tristan, something always holds me back.

*What would happen if I didn't let it?*

Before I know it, I'm leaning in to kiss Tristan. His lips are warm and soft, and they fit perfectly with mine. He places one hand on the nape of my neck and the other on my lower back, pulling me against him. It's like we're fading into a fantasy, and our surroundings are just fillers.

It feels right. *So* right.

*But it's not. It can't be.*

I tear away from him. "I shouldn't have done that," I tell him, heart hammering in my chest. Tristan looks at me with a mix of longing and confusion. "I'm sorry. I shouldn't have...I have to go."

"April, wait." He grabs my wrist as I turn away from him. "You don't have to leave. Let's talk about this."

"No, I can't. I have to—"

"Don't do that! Don't just walk away."

I stare at him, and I want to kiss him again, but that's not okay. That's not what he needs. *I'm* not who he needs.

"April, I like you," he says. "I've liked you since freshman year. And I'm sorry if that freaks you out, but you—"

"Don't say that," I whisper.

"You clearly feel it too, or you wouldn't have just kissed me."

"*Stop*. Please, Tristan, just…" I squeeze my eyes shut, tears streaming down my face. "I need to leave."

"*Why?* What are you so afraid of? Come on, April, this is *us* we're talking about. We have a connection, and you know it."

I look at him through my tears, and his eyes are wide. I want to say, *Myself. I'm afraid of myself.* But my voice is caught in my throat, and I can't focus on a single thought.

I can't do this. I can't be that girl for him. The one who can give all of herself to him. The one who can be present enough to make him a priority—to make him happy. He *deserves* to be happy.

"I know this isn't the best time, I just…" He shakes his head, his eyes red. "I want to be with you, April. And I know we can figure this out. We can figure this out together. That's what we do. Like that class project where I helped you make a video so you didn't have to talk in front of the class. Or this whole shitty situation, you buying me some cheap ass flip phone so we could talk without me getting caught and visiting me whenever you can, even though Colton might be a serial killer like Ted Bundy."

I want to laugh at that, but I can't bring myself to.

"We're good together, April."

He doesn't get it. I'm losing control. I'm losing myself. I can't lose him, too.

He feels like home, but I feel like a tornado deemed to destroy. So, I leave before it's too late.

# CHAPTER 36

Christmas Eve used to be my favorite holiday, even more so than Christmas itself. The anticipation was intoxicating. I'd stay up until midnight watching holiday movies with my parents and Greg, eating too many cookies by the fire.

But once Christmas day came around, I would wake empty. My expectations were always too high, and I knew the happiness wouldn't last. Nothing lasts. So why bother getting caught up in the spirit of it all?

This year, I'm not even the slightest bit excited. While I'd usually be up early sipping coffee and wrapping presents with my dad, I slept until noon and haven't even gone downstairs yet.

I pull my hair into a messy bun and steps downstairs to the kitchen, dreading human contact. From the living room, I hear my parents and Greg speaking softly, as if they don't want anyone to hear what they're saying. I stop short of the doorframe and listen.

"She's usually able to pull herself out of a slump," I hear my dad say.

"Dad, I'm telling you, that night in the storm...I don't know what she was about to do, but it scared me."

My head spins. I can't believe Greg told my parents. *How could he do this to me?*

"She's getting bad," he continues. "I mean, she lied to you and skipped school. That's not April. I know this was a last resort, but I don't think we really have a choice."

"She really needs this program," my mom adds.

I step into the kitchen, my eyes darting between the three of them, heart pounding in my ears. Greg and my dad are sitting on the counter stools, and my mom is standing, leaning her elbows on the counter.

"What program?" I ask, staring directly at my mom. They all turn toward me like they've been caught red-handed, guilty and hesitant.

My mom glances down at her cup of coffee. Greg looks at my dad, who says, "Honey, come sit." He gets up and offers his seat, then walks around the counter to stand next to my mom. But I don't move.

"It's an inpatient program." My mom starts talking like she's delivering a presentation at work, shoulders back and voice steady. And I'm just an employee expected to nod my head.

"I think it will be good for you, April."

I glare at her. "You're kidding, right?" No one says anything. They don't even look at me. I can't help but laugh, because this has to be a joke. "I'm not going to residential therapy."

My dad inhales a long breath, grabbing the ends of the counter for support.

"We're just thinking out loud, April. We didn't make any decisions yet."

"Well, it's not your decision to make!" I yell. "I'm almost 18!"

"Actually, it is, considering you live under our roof," my mom snaps. "And you are not 18 until early spring."

I open my mouth, but I'm stunned into silence. *I'm a stranger in my own house.*

"April, we just want you to get the best treatment," my dad says softly. "If that means going to an inpatient facility, maybe you should give it a chance."

I can't believe he's agreeing with my mom. He knows how long it took me to trust Dr. Glen. He knows I'm a senior in high school with one more term left. He knows I'm planning to go away to college next year. This will mess everything up if I leave.

"Sweetie, believe me. This is the last thing I want for you," my mom says, but her tone is condescending, and I know deep down she's mocking me. "I wish your biggest concern right now was which college to go to or who to go to prom with. But that's not the case. You're not—"

"*Normal?*" I cut her off. "I'm not normal? I'm not the daughter you always wanted?"

"*April!*" My dad's voice booms against the cabinets, echoing as it strikes my temples. I know I've gone too far, but I don't care.

He's taking her side. He's no longer on my team. *Is anyone?*

I look to Greg, who avoids eye contact as he mixes his coffee with a spoon.

"I thought I could trust you, Greg."

His eyes are bloodshot when he looks at me.

"April, I didn't know what else to do."

"Don't blame your brother," my dad tells me.

"The center is in Houston," my mom says, raising her voice as if to tell all of us to shut up and listen. "You'd start up in January. We already spoke with your school."

"You talked to my *school*? Behind my back? You didn't even consult me!" My eyes begin to sting with tears, but I don't want to cry. I want to scream at the top of my lungs. "I have a plan, mom! To graduate high school and go to Boston to study journalism. You know this. And you're taking that away from me! The one thing that makes me happy, the one thing that makes me think maybe I have a future...something worth living for. And you're—you're just taking it from me!"

"The facility offers academics in addition to therapy. You'll still graduate in June," my mom tells me.

Greg looks at me like he's mourning something. His sister's sanity, maybe.

"April, have you even applied to schools yet?"

I stare at him, swallowing hard.

"I was going to, over break," I say in a small voice. "The deadline isn't until January 3rd."

They all look at me, and I know what they're thinking.

That I've lost it. That I'm too far gone.

I wish I didn't agree.

"I can't do this right now." I back away from them and walk back to my room as my mom protests. From the stairs, I hear my dad tell her to give me some space.

After tearing through my entire room, I finally find my keys on the floor and race out the front door, needing to escape this asylum. I get in my car and slam the door, taking deep breaths.

I'm about to stick my key in the ignition as I get an incoming call from Tristan. Wiping my eyes as if he could see through the phone, I slide the screen to accept the call.

"Hello?" I ask in a fake voice—not quite happy, but not hysterical either.

"Hey, look, I just wanted to apologize for last night...It's killing me the way we left things off."

"You didn't do anything wrong, Tristan. It was all me."

*It's always me.*

"No, it wasn't. I shouldn't have pushed you. I feel like an asshole..."

"You're not an asshole," I tell him, my voice quivering as tears stream down my cheeks.

Tristan pauses. "Are you okay?"

I sniffle. "Yeah, I'm fine," I say, but my body betrays me as it succumbs to sobs.

I wish I could pretend I was okay, like everyone else in the world. *Why am I so weak?*

"April, talk to me," Tristan says gently, but it only makes me cry harder. "Fuck, I hate hearing you like this...Are you with your family? Or Kat?"

"No, my family is the issue right now," I explain. "And Kat's in Maine."

"Why don't you come over? I promise, we can pretend nothing happened last night. It was stupid. You're my friend first."

I take a shaky breath and start my car. "Okay."

When we hang up, I count to six and will myself to put it in drive. But my hands are still shaking from the argument with my parents, and my eyes are swollen from crying.

*If you drive right now, you'll hurt someone.*

I grab my phone and dial the only person who might possibly drive me anywhere right now. She answers after one ring.

"Hello?"

"Jade," I start, but I don't know what to say.

"What's up?" her voice is cold.

If she thought I was 'walking all over her' earlier, she's really gonna think that now.

"I need a ride..."

She pauses. "Okay...where to?"

I obviously can't answer that. At least, not honestly. "To the beach."

"The beach? It's Christmas Eve, not to mention freezing outside."

"Jade, please." I start to cry again, desperate for an escape, knowing I can't get there by myself. "I can't drive because of my concussion," I lie.

"Okay, okay, fine. I'll be right over. Just gimme a few."

When she pulls up, I get in the car quickly, hoping my parents won't storm out and make me come back inside to talk.

"Remind me why you're making me drive you to the beach right now?" Jade asks, then takes in my appearance. "Wait, were you crying?"

"It's a long story." I pull up Colton's address on my phone and start the navigation. "Can you drive me here?"

She squints at the screen, then looks at me with a mix of pity and judgment.

"April..."

My face burns. "I know it's Dylan's town, but that's not where I'm going."

"Then where *are* you going?"

"I can't tell you." My tone is harsh, and I feel bad, but I don't have time for this. I reach for the door handle.

"You don't have to take me. I'll figure it out."

"No, April, stop!" she says, grabbing my arm. "I'll take you."

We drive in silence, and I'm grateful she doesn't bring up our fight. She glances at the GPS every few seconds, and within a half hour, we make it there.

"This it?" she asks, looking up at the apartment building with furrowed eyebrows.

"Yeah." I pause. "Please don't tell anyone where I am."

"Okay…" I can tell she wants to know what we're doing here. What *I'm* doing here. "You know you can talk to me, right?"

I shake my head. "You wouldn't get it," I tell her.

"You've never let me try." She watches me, waiting for my response.

"Thank you for driving me," I say, my tone indicating the end of our conversation. I turn to get out of the car.

"Wait," Jade says quickly. I look back at her, guilt tugging at me when I see her expression. "Should I be worried about you?"

"No."

"April…this feels wrong. Dropping you here. I don't even know who you're seeing. And you're clearly upset."

I fight the urge to cry again.

"I'm fine." I get out and walk away without turning back.

# CHAPTER 37

I fiddle with my hands, sniffling, as Tristan watches me, reminding me of Dr. Glen. He waits patiently until I'm ready to speak, unbothered by the silence.

Colton's with his mom celebrating Christmas Eve, just the two of them.

"My parents are making me go to residential therapy."

There's two cups of hot coffee in front of us, steaming. I stare at their soft caramel color, avoiding eye contact with Tristan. I don't want to see his reaction. I don't want to hear his thoughts. *She's weak. She's dramatic. She's crazy.*

He doesn't say anything.

"It's in Houston," I continue. "I'd have to miss the rest of my senior year. I'd have to stay there for God knows how long."

I start crying again, because apparently, that's all I know how to do lately. Cry and complain and worry. And mess with everyone's lives.

"Can I ask why they want to send you?" His voice is soft and curious.

I cradle my mug, sliding my thumb across the top of it, and keep my eyes down, letting the tears fall.

"My OCD's been pretty bad." I swallow a lump in my throat. "Really bad."

"How so?" Tristan asks. I look up at him, and instead of judgement on his face, I recognize concern.

"Honestly, it's been bad my whole life. But it got worse when you went missing. I started getting these disturbing thoughts, and they freaked me out. I thought that maybe I caused something bad to happen to you."

Tristan tilts his head. "What do you mean?"

"OCD is...I don't know, Tristan. It's so hard to explain."

"Why don't you try?"

So I do just that. I tell him everything. From the moment I found out about his disappearance to the night I finally realized he was staying with Colton. Every fleeting thought and fear, even the horrible ones, like wanting bad things to happen.

I tell him how I started obsessing over finding him, to the extent where I couldn't focus on school or even my relationship with Dylan. I tell him about my panic attack at the Halloween party after talking to Jenny, and how I nearly made myself sick because I saw *her* get sick. About going to see Dylan after the accident, and finding him with Mandy. About the night during the thunderstorm, how Greg had to carry me into the car because I was crying and shaking so hard. About how I can barely drive without thinking I hurt someone.

"I don't even know who I am lately," I say. "I skip school. I lie to my dad. I get involved with guys who aren't good for me, apparently. I have to rely on people for stupid little things, like driving places. I haven't even applied to college yet." I shake my head. "I *hate* who I've become."

"Well, I happen to really like who you are," Tristan tells me. "April, you're going through a lot. I wish you'd be easier on yourself. It hurts to know you're hurting like this..."

I wipe my eyes, but more tears fall. Tristan reaches over and gently brushes them with his thumb. "Why don't we watch a Christmas movie or something? Get your mind off things."

"Okay."

Tristan sets the couch up with blankets and pillows from his bed, and I check my phone, which is filled with messages from my parents and Greg, as expected. I text my dad that I'm out with Jade.

We settle on the couch, and Tristan tosses me a sweatshirt as my dad texts me back.

Ok. Please don't be late...We love you.

I lock my phone without responding. The shame outweighs the guilt, so much that I can't even bring myself to say "I love you" back. I can't even face my own dad right now.

"They're just worried about you," Tristan says softly. "They just care."

"I know."

"I'm not trying to make you feel bad or anything," he adds quickly. "You have every right to be upset. I just...I know how it feels for someone you love *not* to be worried about you. I don't want you to feel like that."

I look at him, our faces close.

"*I* was worried about you."

He closes his eyes. "I know you were," he says.

I shiver, chills spreading down my arms. I pull Tristan's sweatshirt over my head, and it gets stuck on my earring. We both laugh as he helps me untangle myself. He brushes my hair behind my ear, then pulls back wistfully.

He shifts away from me slightly.

"Look, April...I'm really sorry about the other night. That was—"

"Stop," I cut him off. "*I'm* sorry. It was *my* fault."

"No, it wasn't. You have a lot going on...I shouldn't have pressured you like that."

"Tristan, *I* was the one who kissed *you*."

"I know, but still."

"But *nothing*. It was selfish of me to do that."

When I swallow, my throat burns. My chest is tight as I take a deep breath and try to get my thoughts straight.

"I just..." My eyes well with tears for the millionth time today. "I don't want to lose you."

Tristan furrows his eyebrows at me. "Why would you lose me?"

I shake my head. "I don't know. Like I said, I keep fucking up, and...and I don't want to fuck *us* up. Our friendship, you know? It's too important to me."

Silence lingers between us as Tristan stares straight ahead into space. After a few moments, he playfully bumps his shoulder against mine. "I get it. It's okay."

Tristan puts *Elf* on, and we watch in silence, sharing a blanket like last night. But this time, we don't hold hands.

"By the way, you're not gonna lose me," Tristan says. "No matter what. I'm always gonna be here for you."

# CHAPTER 38

"Yo, guys."

I wake up to Colton standing over me, my head on Tristan's shoulder.

Only when my phone starts vibrating aggressively on the couch do I realize it's past midnight on Christmas morning.

"*Shit!*" I whisper, jolting up as I stare at my phone, my dad's number covering the screen.

"Your phone's been going off for a while," Colton says.

I answer the call, but before I can even say hello, my dad starts yelling.

"April, where are you?! I've been calling you for hours! I called Jade, and she said you're in Dylan's hometown? Do you even—"

"Dad, I'm so sorry. I can explain!" I say, my voice raspy from my burning throat.

"Do you know how this feels, April? After the accident you were in and the things you have done lately! Do you understand how this feels as your father?"

"I'm okay, I promise. I'm sorry, I'm with—" I look at Tristan, who's slowly waking up. "I'm with a friend. A good friend. I'm okay."

"Who? Who are you with? Because if it's Dylan, I swear to God, April, I'll come over there and—"

"I'm not with Dylan!" I cut him off. "I'll be home soon, okay? Just trust me. Please."

He goes silent for a moment.

"You've given me no reason to trust you, April."

"I know, dad. And I'm sorry. But...please. I'm okay. I'll explain everything. I promise."

"Just get home."

When we hang up, I jump up and grab my purse off the floor. I tug on my converse and step down the hallway. Dizziness hits me like three shots of tequila, and I grab the doorframe to steady myself.

Colton and Tristan follow me.

"What's going on?" Colton asks.

"My dad is pissed," is all I say, looking around frantically. "I don't have my car."

"I'll drive you home," Colton says.

"I'll come with you guys," Tristan adds. "I'll explain everything to your parents."

"*What?*" Colton and I echo.

He shrugs.

"Tristan, you can't do that," I tell him. "You know they'll tell the cops or your dad or whatever. You'll—"

"I need to go home," Tristan says. "Wherever that is. I need to figure it out. And I need to talk to my sister."

I stare at him, letting his words sink in. His hair is a mess of curls, and his eyes look heavy. But he's standing tall, and I know now that he's ready. Ready to face the truth, to stop running.

"You're sure, dude?" Colton asks, but Tristan is already grabbing his things.

A few short minutes later, the three of us stumble down the steps of Colton's apartment. I move so quickly that I slam into someone walking upstairs.

"*April?*"

I don't have to look at him to know it's Dylan. And, *shit*, I wish I didn't have to look at him at all. Because he looks exactly the same as the night I met him.

Tall and thin. Dark hair. Light brown eyes. Red cheeks and pink lips.

He stands frozen on the steps, and I notice Gabe behind him, carrying a bag of fast food.

"What are you doing here?" I manage.

"I *live* here." He narrows his eyes at me. "What are *you* doing here?"

I open my mouth, but I don't know what to say. What are the odds that his family lives in the same complex at Colton?

Gabe watches us with a sympathetic expression as Dylan looks from me to Tristan and Colton, both of whom are standing behind me, silent. His face flashes with anger.

"Nice," he says, nodding his head. "I was right, wasn't I?"

His voice is harsh, taunting, like it was during our fight before the accident. Gabe tries to nudge him forward and says, "Dude, come on."

"No, fuck that," Dylan says. His eyes don't leave mine. "I knew it."

Tristan steps in front of me. "You better back away from her."

"Who the fuck do you think you are?" Colton says at the same time.

"Guys, I can handle myself," I tell them, frustrated at this entire situation. I'm tired of people seeing me as weak. I don't need protecting.

I look Dylan in the eyes, and a rush of memories flood me. I bite back my tears as he stares at me with such disgust that I feel the urge a shower.

I want to tell him he's wrong, this isn't what it looks like. I didn't cheat on him and never would have. I didn't move on in just a short week, the way he did with Mandy.

But after everything, after all he put me through, he doesn't deserve to hear that.

Instead, I lock my eyes with his and say, "I don't have to explain myself to you anymore."

As I brush past him, I hear Colton says, "Boom, roasted!" and see Gabe bite back a smile while pushing Dylan up the steps.

Tristan, Colton, and I walk to Colton's car, silent. I climb into the backseat, surprised when Tristan joins me instead of sitting in the front. I stare out the window and take deep breaths, in and out. I feel like I'm in a dream.

"You alright?" Tristan asks me.

"I'm good," I say.

"I hate that kid," Colton says as he starts the car. "And what the fuck did he mean when he said he 'knew it?'"

My cheeks flush. "Do you remember when I saw you in the liquor store and complimented your shirt? When I was with Dylan?"

"The liquor store?" Colton pauses for a moment, thinking. "Oh. *Oh*. That was *you*?"

"Yeah. I didn't realize it was you either, until Dylan and I got into a huge fight about it…"

"Wait…" Tristan says, confused. "Fight about what?"

"Well, after I saw Colton, Dylan told me he didn't like him, and then I—"

"*What?*" Colton asks. "I never even talked to the kid until the accident! I literally talked to no one in high school."

"Well, I don't know, it seemed like he hated everyone who went to your high school. But on Thanksgiving, when you messaged me with your phone number, he didn't know it was about Tristan. Because I never told him about it. So he thought I somehow found out who you were and wanted to get with you, I guess."

The guys don't say anything. We're still sitting in the parking lot, the car humming softly.

"Wait, is that when you got into the accident?" Tristan asks.

"Yeah."

"*Fuck*," Colton whispers.

"What?" I ask him.

"I feel like it's my fault."

"How is that your fault?"

"If anything, it's *my* fault," Tristan says, his voice low.

"This was no one's fault," I say, angry that they'd even think that. "I shouldn't have kept anything from Dylan. And he shouldn't have made assumptions."

"He also shouldn't have driven drunk..." Colton adds. "Fucking asshole."

"And now he has the balls to say something to you tonight?" Tristan says.

I shake my head, sighing. "Whatever. Let's just go."

I buckle my seatbelt, and we drive without speaking to each other, Colton's iPod playing some Indie band I don't recognize. I stare out the window and mentally prepare myself for facing my parents. I don't know what I'm going to say to them. I'm still furious.

But at least Tristan will be with me.

If I'm nervous, Tristan must be a wreck over what he's about to do. I look at him from across the backseat. He's on the left side, by the window, and I'm on the right. His face is turned away from me, but his hand rests at his side. I take it in mine.

# CHAPTER 39

Greg bursts through the front door before Tristan and I reach the walkway. Even in the darkness, in just the faint shadows of the porch light, I can see the frustration on his face.

"Do you know how worried we've been?" he says to me. "Dad almost called the fucking cops, April."

When he notices Tristan, his expression changes from anger to shock. He looks between Tristan and me, mouth hanging open.

"I can explain everything," Tristan tells him, standing next to me, so close I can feel the warmth of his body in the cold air.

Greg shakes his head like he's trying to regain composure. He looks at me.

"You need to talk to mom and dad." He turns away and starts walking back to the house, expecting us to follow. We do.

As we walk through the door, my mom rushes over to me, but she stops in her tracks when she spots Tristan.

My dad walks up behind my mom. His face is tense, like the air around us.

"Who's this?" he asks me.

"Dad, this is Tristan. He's—"

"Tristan?" my mom asks. "Why does that sound familiar?"

"Because he's been a 'missing person' for the past three months," Greg says.

I take a long, deep breath. "Look, I was just—"

"Being a good friend," Tristan finishes for me. "I can explain everything. This is all my fault."

"No, it's not," I tell him.

"No, April. Let me talk." He looks at my dad. "None of this is her fault. The lying and all that. She's been with me, making sure I'm okay, keeping my secret for me. And I shouldn't have let her do that. That's on me."

"I didn't exactly give you a choice," I say.

"Do your parents know you're here?" my dad asks him.

I cringe at the word "parents."

Tristan shakes his head. "No. My dad...he kicked me out."

Everyone goes quiet. I hold my breath and listen to the Christmas music playing in the kitchen.

*I'll be home for Christmas.*

*You can plan on me.*

I look at Tristan. There's a scar on his cheek. How have I not noticed it before? It's subtle, right under his left eye. Did his dad do that to him?

How will he feel, being home for Christmas? Back with his dad? Not good, I'm sure. What kind of home makes you so afraid? So out-of-place?

I turn to my parents and Greg. Their eyes are filled with empathy, faces drained of color. I think back to what Tristan said earlier.

*They just care.*

My eyes sting. I have it good.

"I don't get it," Greg says to Tristan, his voice soft. "Everyone thinks you're missing."

"Yeah, because his dad is a—"

"*April.*" My dad stops me from finishing the sentence. He knows me too well.

Tristan's jaw twitches as he stares at his feet.

"My sister was worried when I left. I didn't bring my phone...My dad broke it, actually. But I couldn't tell her what happened anyway. I knew she wouldn't forgive my dad for what he did to me." He pauses. "It's complicated. My mom passed away a few years ago, and my dad...He's not the same, and it's partially my fault. No, *fully* my fault."

I'm about to tell him he's wrong, it's not his fault. None of it is. He needs to stop taking the blame. But he keeps talking, explaining everything, from his mom's accident to his dad's alcoholism, something I've never heard him admit out loud. And by the time he's done, he's shaking.

"Why don't you sit down?" my dad says to him, putting his arm around Tristan's shoulders and leading him to the couch.

I walk to the living room and take a seat next to Tristan as Greg disappears into the kitchen. He comes back with a steaming cup of coffee, handing it to Tristan.

We're all sitting around like rubberneckers, watching him, with the stupid Christmas music still playing in the background. My dad sits on the other couch, arms folded, and Greg and my mom stand awkwardly in front of Tristan and me.

"So, what's your plan?" my dad asks Tristan.

Tristan inhales slowly, staring into space.

"I'm gonna go talk to him tonight."

My dad raises his eyebrows. "Your dad?"

"Yeah."

"You don't think you should go to the police?" my mom asks him.

"I don't know…" He pauses, then shakes his head. "He's my dad. I just can't do it."

"Well, he's not exactly fit to be a father right now," my dad says.

Tristan takes a sip of his coffee, his hands shaking so hard it spills over the edge of the mug and drips onto his lap. If it burns him, he doesn't lead on.

My dad shifts on the couch. "Where have you been staying?"

"With a friend."

"He's really nice," I add. "He's actually outside, in the car...He's gonna go with Tristan so he's not alone."

"I see," my dad says. He unfolds his arms and leans forward, looking at Tristan. "Well, you ready to go?"

"Right, yeah." Tristan leans forward and places his mug on the coffee table. "I should get going. Thank you for—"

"Go get your friend," my dad says. "I'm driving."

Tristan blinks at him. His lips part, but he doesn't say anything.

My dad gets up from the couch.

"You heard me. I'll pull the car out of the garage and meet you outside," he says before grabbing his keys off the table and leaving the room.

We're all stunned into silence. I look at Tristan and shrug. A tear falls from his eye, and he quickly brushes it away, nervously laughing.

"I'll uh...get Colton then." He glances up at my mom and Greg. "Thank you. Thanks for uh...the coffee, and all of this."

My mom smiles and Greg pats Tristan on the back before heading into the kitchen to leave us alone. I get up and offer Tristan my hand to help him up. We walk to the door slowly. Tristan looks like a zombie, his eyes blank, body stiff.

"I didn't mean to make this about me," Tristan says in a low voice. "I just didn't want you to take the fall for me."

"Stop. I'm so glad you opened up to them." I pull him in for a hug. "Everything's gonna be okay, Tristan."

"I know," he whispers. "For both of us."

*I'll be home for Christmas,*
*If only in my dreams.*

# CHAPTER 40

I can't sleep. My stomach is in knots, wondering if Tristan is okay. How it's going. What his dad's reaction was. If Jenny knows yet, and if so, what she thought when she heard about everything. Does she hate me for keeping it from her?

My head throbs.

I hear my dad come inside, and my heart starts pounding. I jump out of bed and race downstairs.

"How'd it go?" I ask, nearly bumping into him in the hallway.

He presses his lips into a tight line.

"Not great, honey."

My heart sinks.

"What? Why? What happened?"

"His dad was wasted, that's what happened. Completely irrational."

"So...What did he say? Was he even happy to see Tristan?"

My dad shakes his head. "First thing he said was, 'I thought I told you to stay out of my way.'"

I swallow hard. "What the *fuck*?"

"He'll be alright, April. Colton's a good guy. Tristan's gonna stay with him for a while, turn himself in tomorrow and explain everything. See his sister."

I shake my head. "This is bullshit."

"You're right. It is. But he has people who care about him." He raises his eyebrows. "Like you."

I wipe away a tear from the corner of my eye.

"I'm proud of you, April," my dad says. "You know that?"

"You shouldn't be."

"Well, I am." He pauses. "But if you ever lie to me like that again, I'm kicking you out. Got it?"

"*Dad*. Too soon."

He laughs. "Tristan and Colton told me everything on the way over. About you cornering Colton at his job? I mean, *Jesus*, April."

"Not my proudest moment," I admit.

"You're lucky how this turned out. You gotta be more careful…"

"I know, Dad."

His face softens, and he smiles.

"Your thoughts might feel overwhelming at times, April, but they don't define you. You're gonna help a lot of people with that heart of yours."

*   *   *

I climb into bed and text Tristan a heart. He texts me back right away.

**Tristan:** Hi.
**Me:** Hi. You ok?
**T:** Did your dad tell you what happened?
**Me:** Yeah. I'm so sorry, Tristan. You don't deserve this.
**T:** It's ok.
**Me:** It's not.
**T:** It will be.
**Me:** I wish I could help.
**T:** You've helped more than you know.

Tristan sends me another text with a link to a song on Spotify. It's an acoustic version of a song called *No One's Gonna Need You More* by The Dangerous Summer. I've never heard of them before, but I trust Tristan's music taste.

I hit play and lie back on my pillow, closing my eyes and taking in the lyrics.

A line strikes a chord in my heart. I text it to him.

**Me:** "Every lonely heart can use an honest song they can sing along to."
**T:** "You're the home I've been dying to make."

I hit the repeat button and let the song replay over and over, until I finally fall asleep.

# CHAPTER 41

"Get the fuck in here and tell me *everything*."

Kat tugs me inside and pulls me into her kitchen as I bite back a smile. It's been less than a week, but I really missed my best friend.

Ms. Bailey is leaning her elbows on the counter when we walk in, her hair pulled into a messy bun. There's a plate of Christmas cookies in front of her, tin foil peeled back, and a pile of crumbs.

"Caught me red-handed," she says, mouthful.

I laugh. "Merry Christmas, Ms. Bailey," I say as she pulls me in for a hug.

Kat takes a seat in one of the stools and smacks the counter.

"April! Stop ignoring the elephant in the room!"

"I'm literally just saying hi to your mom…"

Ms. Bailey rolls her eyes and pushes the plate of cookies toward her daughter.

"She's just hangry," she says.

"I'm not *hangry*, mom," Kat says, taking a cookie anyway. "I just want to know how my best friend found our *missing class-mate,* and why she kept it from me! You know, I would be super mad at you right now if I wasn't so proud…But I will be *pissed* if you don't start talking!"

"Maybe shut up so she can actually tell us," Ms. Bailey jokes. Kat makes a face at her.

I laugh, tucking my hair behind my ears. I called Kat as soon as she texted me she was home and told her a summary of what went down while she was gone. She insisted I come over and explain every last detail in person. I don't even know where to start.

"Okay, so...You know that kid who was at the accident with Dylan?" I ask Kat.

She narrows her eyes at me. "Yeah..."

"That's Tristan's friend. Colton."

She blinks at me, then shakes her head.

"Wait, is that why you asked me about him? How did you know they were friends?"

I wave my hand as if to dismiss the question.

"Long story...But anyway, Tristan was there too."

"Where?" Ms. Bailey asks.

"At the accident."

"Whoa whoa whoa." Kat's eyes are wide as she puts out her hand to stop me from talking. "*What?*"

"I know...I was so out of it, I didn't even realize it was him. I just remembered someone holding me and making sure I was okay. But then I had a dream that it was Tristan, and I'd already had suspicions he was staying with Colton. So when you told me Colton was there, I knew it couldn't have been a coincidence."

Kat and her mom go silent. I inhale, then exhale a long breath. My hands are shaking.

"Wow, you really should be a detective," Kat says. "So... What'd you do, message Colton?"

"Yeah, which didn't work at first because he was covering for Tristan...So, then I showed up at his job and demanded he let me see him."

Kat smirks. "My fucking girl."

I tell them more about Tristan's situation, about his dad and how he didn't want anyone to know—how his dad is still not letting him come home.

"He's under 18...Can his dad even do that?" Kat asks.

"He needs to speak with the police," Ms. Bailey says at the same time.

"He did, today actually."

When I called Tristan this morning to check in and wish

him a Merry Christmas, he told me he was with Jenny, who wasn't taking the news well. She was angry, and rightfully so.

"I barely even got to talk," Tristan told me with a laugh. "She told them everything, including the stuff about my mom...She even managed to get Colton off the hook for housing a runaway."

"I'm not sure what's going to happen to his dad now, but I'm sure it won't be easy on either of them," I say. "Losing two parents in the span of two years? I can't imagine the pain."

Ms. Bailey shakes her head, sighing before covering the plate of cookies. She wipes the counter with a sponge as Kat and I stare ahead in silence.

"So, where's he staying now?" Kat asks. "I mean, he's still a minor. Doesn't he need to live with family or something?"

"With Jenny," I tell Kat. "She's getting an off-campus apartment next semester. She already told her school her situation, and they offered to help get her settled. It's not too far of a drive from Haddon High, so it works out for Tristan, too."

"Speaking of school..." Ms. Bailey says as she rinses off some dishes in the sink, sweatshirt sleeves pushed up to her elbows. "He's probably gonna have to make up for the last half during the summer."

My heart drops. *Poor Tristan.* This was all out of his control, and now he's gonna have to spend all summer before college in class?

"Yeah, and I bet he didn't get to apply to any colleges yet," Kat says.

I look down, my face burning. He's not the only one.
*But what's my excuse?*

*     *     *

"So...Tristan kissed me," I tell Kat as we settle in her room to watch *Friends*. We're sitting on the floor, a box of pizza in front of us. "Or, I kissed him, I should say."

Kat freezes, bottle of wine in her hand, which she fished from underneath her bed. She gapes at me, speechless.

"I know, I know," I say. "I've been *dying* to tell you."

"Oh my *God*! Are you guys, like…"

"No! No. We're not. We both have way too much going on right now…And I mean, I just got out of a relationship."

She twists her lips to the side.

"Well…Was it good?"

My face heats up, and I turn my head so she can't see.

"It was fine."

"He's always liked you."

I think back to what he said after I kissed him. *"I've liked you since freshman year."*

My stomach twists as I grab the bottle of wine next to Kat and swallow a few gulps.

"Just don't mess with his head," Kat tells me. "He has enough going on already…"

I glare at her. "I know that. And so do I. Which is why it was a stupid mistake."

She raises her hands in surrender, then rips off a slice of pizza from the pie.

"I have to tell you something," I say, desperate to change the subject.

Kat narrows her eyes at me.

"You didn't have sex with him, too, did you? Not that I'd judge!" she adds quickly.

"What? No, Kat!" I down a few more sips of wine, my heart banging against my chest. "I found out my parents want to send me to Houston, to this intensive residential therapy."

She widens her eyes. "Whoa. *What*?"

"I know."

She shakes her head, like she's trying to conduct herself.

"*Houston?* There's gotta be something closer…"

I pause. "Are you saying you think I need residential therapy?"

"No! I mean…I don't know. Maybe?" She presses her lips together, waiting for me to react. I don't know how. "You're just going through a lot, and obviously your current therapy isn't really helping. Or it doesn't seem to be…Right?"

I can't help but laugh. I'm so pathetic.

"Come on, I didn't mean it like that."

"I know," I reassure her.

"But seriously. *Houston?* That's insane."

My phone starts buzzing with a call. Kat raises her eyebrows at me when she sees Tristan's name on the screen. Ignoring her, I answer. Anything to escape this conversation.

"Hey," I say.

"Hey. How was your day?" Tristan asks me.

"It was good. I'm with Kat right now."

"Oh nice. I'm assuming she knows…"

"Yeah, I told her. I hope that's okay."

"No, yeah," he says quickly. "Of course. I mean, everyone will find out eventually." He pauses, and I pick at my jeans as I wait for him to say more. "Listen, I was wondering…We're all going to Colton's for New Year's Eve. If you don't have plans, maybe you would wanna come? It's just gonna be us, and Jenny and Zach. Kat can come too, obviously."

I wrack my brain, instinctively wondering what Jade has planned for us this year. We've spent every New Years' Eve together since middle school.

"Yeah," I say anyway. "Yeah, I'd love that."

"Same!" Kat says.

Tristan laughs. "Cool."

"Cool," I repeat.

"Cool!" Kat yells.

# CHAPTER 42

"What are you wearing?" I ask Kat as I brush on some smoky eyeshadow at her vanity. Her floor is covered in piles of clothing, and an Oso Oso record spins from her record player.

"Good question," she says as she sorts through hangers in her closet. "What'd you bring?"

"I packed fancy and casual," I tell her, accustomed to dressing up for New Year's Eves with Jade. I haven't heard from her since Christmas Eve, but her Instagram story tells me she's at some ritzy hotel in the city with Brenda and Lindsay. Even my dressiest outfit wouldn't be fitting for that endeavor.

"Hm," Kat says. She stands back and stares at the clothes in her closet, eyes narrowed, cupping her chin. "There's only a few of us, right?"

"Yeah, I think it's just Tristan, Zach, Jenny, and Colton."

She smirks. "Is Colton cute? I can't remember. I think he was. I know he was tall, at least."

I laugh. "Yeah, he's cute. Hey, by the way, whatever happened with that girl Sky?"

"She ghosted me after we hooked up at the concert. Thanks for the reminder."

Kat grabs a tight black dress off a hanger, then strips out of her pajamas and steps into it.

"This, with my Docs," she says, posing for me. The dress accents her figure in all the right places. "Boom."

She looks gorgeous, her red hair straightened, nearly reaching her hips. With winged eyeliner and dark purple lipstick, she makes me look like a cheap bottle of sparkling wine next to some high-end champagne Jade is probably sipping in

New York right now.

"Do that whole, half-up-half-down, scrunchy thing to your hair," Kat tells me as I stare in the mirror, feeling like a child who got into her mother's makeup.

*I look ridiculous.*

"You look amazing," Kat says as if she can read my thoughts. She puts her hands on my shoulders, meeting my eyes in the mirror. "Tristan will agree. Trust me."

I blush, tugging my hair up like she recommended, securing the black scrunchy, then finish applying mascara. I decide to wear a short plaid skirt with a tight cropped turtleneck, and my high-top Converse.

"Are you sure I look okay?"

"Yes, April. You look beautiful."

My phone buzzes with a text. "Tristan's here."

"You girls are staying at your friends' house tonight, right?" Ms. Bailey asks us as we step out of Kat's room and make our way to the front door. "You know, there's a lot of drunks on the road on New Year's Eve…"

My stomach clenches.

"Yes, Mother," Kat sings.

"And you're not drinking, right?"

Kat smirks. "Right."

Ms. Bailey isn't stupid. I know that she knows we'll likely be drinking.

"Just be safe, and call me if anything changes, alright? I can pick you up, no-questions-asked, at any hour. Got it?"

"Got it, Mamacita!" Kat gives her a quick hug. "Love you."

"I love you, too. You girls look beautiful." She smiles at me. "Have fun."

It's only 8 o'clock and already pitch-black outside. I shiver in the cold, my bare legs hating me for being so reckless.

"Hey, guys," Tristan says when we open the door.

I haven't seen him in a week, and I realize Kat hasn't seen him since before he was missing.

"Tristan, I'm gonna cry," Kat says as she slides into the

backseat next to Jenny. I sit next to her, diagonal from Tristan.

"How're you doing, dude?" Kat asks, leaning between the driver's and passenger's seats.

Tristan blushes. "I'm good, I'm good."

"You guys look *gorgeous*," Jenny tells us, her blonde hair curled and bouncy. She's in a velvet romper and over-the-knee black boots.

"So do you, girl!" Kat says before I can thank Jenny.

Zach's in the driver's seat, quiet as he pulls away from the curb.

"Hey, thanks for driving us," I tell him.

"Yeah, no problem."

I catch Tristan looking at me and feel my cheeks flush as we make eye contact. He smiles, his green eyes sparkling, then looks down at his phone.

As Zach and Tristan talk about fishing, and Jenny and Kat talk about Kat's upcoming Tinder date next week, I stare out the window at the bare trees and damp ground. I hope Zach's a safe driver.

*Chill out,* I will myself.

"Oh, can I DJ?" Kat asks suddenly, already grabbing the aux cord from Tristan. She shuffles Turnover.

"Put on *Sasha*," I joke, knowing it will piss her off. It's an old song that sounds like it's sung by a completely different band. Much more punk than alternative.

She glares at me. "I swear to God, April, if you tell me one more time that they were better before their Magnolia album, I'm going to *lose my shit*."

I laugh, amused at how defensive she gets over her favorite band. Tristan turns around to face us.

"I don't know, Kat...I think I'm siding with April on this one."

She rolls her eyes. "Of course you are."

"*Time* is another great hit," Tristan continues, fueling Kat's fire.

"I am about two seconds away from jumping out of this

car."

"Please don't," Zach says.

Jenny makes a confused face.

"I am very lost."

We all laugh and fill Jenny in as Zach continues driving in silence, well within the speed limit.

*       *       *

"'Sup, guys," Colton says as he opens the door for us. He's in yet another large band shirt and jeans, and steps aside to let us in.

"Hey," I say, smiling. He already smells like beer.

"There's, uh...shit in the kitchen, if anyone wants it," Colton tells us.

Zach and Kat introduce themselves to Colton, then Jenny pulls him aside as we all head into the apartment. I'm sure she'll want to thank him for everything he's done for her little brother. I'm also sure Colton's shaking in his Adidas, overwhelmed by the amount of humans in his home.

There are cases of beer and a few pizzas on the counter, waiting to be consumed. I smile at the lit candle on the sofa table in the living room.

"This is a nice place," Kat says, scanning the apartment as if contemplating moving in.

"Yeah, it has a balcony, too," I tell her.

"Ugh. And *right* by the beach! I'm so jealous."

Zach's quiet as he opens a beer and takes a seat on the couch. Tristan sits next to him with a plate of pizza.

"Do I sense some tension between those two?" Kat whispers to me, glancing at the guys.

Before I can answer, Jenny walks into the room, Colton trailing behind her with a red face. I catch his eye and mouth, "You okay?"

He nods, offering a little smile.

"You guys wanna take a shot or something? I brought some vodka," Jenny says to me and Kat, holding up a bottle.

I look at Kat, who grins and grabs the bottle from Jenny's

hand. I laugh.

"Sure, why not?"

"I bought plastic shot glass things," Colton says, opening a cabinet and pulling out a small stack of mini red solo cups. He hands them to me.

"Thanks, Colton!" Kat sings.

Kat pours vodka into three of the shot glasses, then turns to the guys.

"Anyone else want a shot?"

"Of what?" Tristan asks from the couch.

"Vodka."

He makes a face, and Zach says, "I'm good."

Colton shrugs as he places a piece of pizza on a paper plate.

"I'll have one."

Jenny pours one more shot, and the four of us mutter "cheers" before downing them.

"Yummy," Jenny says as Kat and I wince and cough, then skips over to the living room and settles on the other side of Zach. She rests her head on his shoulder, her long blonde hair falling cascading over him, and for the first time all night, he smiles.

*Did not see that coming.*

"They're cute," Kat says, cracking open a can of beer.

I smile. "Yeah, they are."

"*So*, Colton," Kat says, turning to him. I swear, she feels personally attacked when someone cowers in the corner at a party, always seeking out the shyest people and striking up conversations with them. That's probably why she's still friends with me.

"You're quite the hero, aren't you?"

Colton blushes, leaning back against the counter, knuckles white from gripping the edge.

"What do you mean?"

"Well, not only did you save my best friend from a car accident caused by her shitty ex-boyfriend, but you also housed my other good pal when his own asshole father wouldn't."

"*Kat,*" I say, gesturing to Tristan and Jenny with my eyes.

"Oh, *relax.* I think they know their dad sucks."

"Well, you don't have to say it," I whisper-yell.

Colton glances between the two of us. "It was really nothing," he says.

"Um, it was way more than 'nothing.' You literally saved both their lives."

"That's a bit dramatic," I say. "I had a very mild concussion."

Kat gives me a look.

"But I do agree, Colton, you're pretty heroic," I quickly add.

He presses his lips into a tight line. "I...do not know how to take compliments," he says with a nervous laugh.

Kat opens another beer and hands it to Colton. "Take a drink instead."

He shakes his head, clearly amused.

"You, too!" Kat nudges me as Tristan walks up to us. "Loosen the hell up. You look like you're at a funeral."

"Jesus, you're blunt," Tristan tells Kat.

Kat bats her eyelashes at him, and I laugh.

I lean into Tristan. "I think she's scaring Colton," I whisper.

He nods. "She's definitely scaring him."

"Ay!" Colton snaps his fingers at us. "Quit your whispering."

"Seriously though, who wants another shot?" Tristan asks.

"I do!" Jenny yells from the couch.

"Zach?"

"Yeah, I'll have one."

Tristan pours shots all around, and before we know it, we're all laughing together, chatting and joking around as if we're a group of childhood friends. The look of relief and happiness on Tristan's face makes my heart swell. Even Colton seems less tense as he talks to Zach about his job at the car dealership.

"I have to pee," I announce to no one in particular, knowing I'm about to "break the seal" as Jade would say. I float to the bathroom, or at least that's how it feels, my body light and relaxed as a feather.

As I dry my hands, I can feel myself sway slightly. I strike a pose in the mirror, then laugh at nothing.

When I open the door, I nearly bump into someone.

"Whoaaaa," Tristan says, a lazy grin on his face. He puts his hand on my shoulder to steady me. "You good?"

I beam. "I'm great."

He doesn't move his hand from my shoulder, and I don't move my legs to walk away from him.

"Are *you* good?" I ask him.

"Yeah. Yeah, I'm good."

"Good."

He shakes his head and drops his hand from my shoulder. I want to grab it.

I do grab it. Then drop it immediately, my face growing warm.

Tristan tilts his head at me, green eyes glistening.

"You're druuuunk."

I bite my lip to keep from smiling.

"So are you!"

"I know," he says with pride. When he smiles, my legs get all weak and wobbly. Or maybe it's alcohol. Either way, I never want him to stop.

*Smiling,* that is.

"Hey, I want to show you something," I tell him, walking around him and leading him into his old bedroom. He follows.

I collapse onto his bed—or Colton's, technically—like it's my own. Tristan sits down next to me as I lie on my back, scrolling through our Spotify playlist to find the song I know he'll love. I heard it this morning in the car when I was shuffling my playlist radio, and it immediately reminded me of Tristan, but I wanted to wait to show him in person.

I tap the song, and it starts playing out of my iPhone speakers.

Tristan adjusts so that he's lying on his side, facing me. He's so close, I can feel the warmth of his body.

"Who's this?" he asks.

"Summer Wars. They're really good. But you have to listen to the lyrics…"

*Had a dream that felt so real,*
*I could see you like you never left.*
*Had you for fifteen short years,*
*but it's been a whole decade since.*
*I should go outside more.*
*I should see my father.*
*All this guilt in the back of my mind,*
*not enough to bother.*

"It's about his mom," I tell Tristan. "She passed away."

He nods slowly, his eyes downcast. My heart drops to my toes.

"Yeah…I'm sorry, maybe I shouldn't have showed you this at a party." I scramble on my phone to stop the song, but Tristan places his hand on mine.

"I want to listen," he tells me.

So he does, his fingers still grazing mine. We lie in silence, letting the music sink in. At one point, he pulls his hand away to wipe a tear from his eye. I inch closer to him, resting my head on his shoulder. He leans his head on mine.

"When I'm upset, it helps me to listen to songs that relate to my own life," I tell him. "So I don't feel so alone. Maybe that's selfish, finding comfort in someone else's pain, but…I don't know. I guess it's just nice to know that other people understand."

Tristan shifts, and I lift my head to look at him.

"Thanks for showing me," he says.

"I'm sorry if I killed tonight's mood. I really know how to bring people down, huh?" I try to laugh it off, but I can't ignore the sinking feeling in my stomach, the guilt anchoring me to the bed.

"You've never brought me down," Tristan says.

He looks at me with glossy eyes, and I inch my face closer to his. I want him to know it's okay. I want him to kiss me.

Taking the hint, he leans in slowly, but hesitates at the last second, his lips just centimeters from mine. His breath is warm against my skin. I want to breathe him.

Finally, he brushes his lips against mine. They're soft and warm, and I close my eyes, spinning, in the best way.

The song changes, but I don't care. I don't ever want this moment to end. Because this is exactly what I want. And for once, it's not this obsessional need, this desperate escape, but more of a safe haven. A sense of home I've never had.

I run my fingers through his hair, my heart dancing, happy, finally happy.

He rolls me onto my back and brushes my hair out of my face. I can feel his smile against mine as he lowers himself onto me.

My body trembles as he places his hand just above my knee. I think back to the beach with Dylan, how I wanted to forget it all, lose myself in him. I don't feel that way with Tristan. I feel so much like myself, so present in my own body. *Too* present.

"Are you crying?"

It takes me a moment to register the tears streaming down my face. Tristan pulls back quickly.

"April, what happened? Did I do something wrong?"

I hide my face with the palms of my hands. I try to answer his question, shaking my head back and forth, but I can't form words. *I* don't even know what happened. It's like my body is invaded by a force of energy so strong I can't fight it. I turn away from him, lying on my side, my shoulders shaking as I sob.

"*Shit,*" Tristan whispers.

Kat and Jenny's voices echo in the other room, singing to whatever artist is playing at the New Year's Eve celebration on TV. *Why can't I be normal like them?*

All I want is to climb into my own bed, where no one can hurt me. Where I can't hurt anyone. Isolate myself from the world.

"I don't know what's wrong with me," I say, my voice high.

"Nothing is wrong with you…" Tristan says soothingly.

"I told you something was wrong with me!" I yell at him. "I warned you."

Judging by the force of my cries, I'm sure he knows I'm right.

"You're worrying me," he says. I sit up, practically choking, breathing in short gasps. He places his hand on my shoulder, but I jerk away. "I'm gonna go get Kat, okay?"

The bed shifts as he gets up, and the sound of my friends in the living room seeps into the room when he opens the door. They're getting along just fine without me. They don't need me. In fact, they'd probably be better off, no matter how much I wish I could take part in the fun they're having. Sharing inside jokes with Colton. Getting to know Zach and Jenny better. Taking pictures with Kat. Counting down the seconds to the new year by Tristan's side.

Who am I kidding? I don't belong with them. I don't belong anywhere.

# CHAPTER 43

"What's going on?" Kat asks as she walks into the dimly lit room. She sits on the edge of the bed, her red hair falling over her shoulders.

I sit up, my body aching, eyes blurry from wet mascara.

"I want to call Dylan," I tell her.

"*What*? Why would you do that?"

"Because. I don't know. What if he needs me?"

"Okay, how drunk are you?"

"I'm not drunk," I lie. "I just want to help him."

She looks at me disapprovingly. "April, you...*just* hooked up with Tristan."

*He told her?*

"I know, but..." I inhale a shaky breath, the room spinning around me. "I'm dizzy," I say. A plea for help. Get me out of this body.

"You're working yourself up," Kat says softly. "Come on. Take some deep breaths. You're okay."

I lie on my back, staring at the ceiling, wishing the darkness would swallow me whole.

I'm such an idiot. I hurt everyone around me. I claim that all I want to do is help people, but in reality, I do the opposite. I'm selfish.

"I don't deserve you," I tell Kat.

"What are you talking about?"

"I don't deserve anyone," I say, my voice raising. "You or Tristan or...*anyone.*"

Sitting up, I try to catch my breath between choked sobs. I stare out at the room, instinctively reaching up to adjust my glasses, forgetting I'm wearing contacts. I'm surprised I haven't cried them out already.

"You told me I shouldn't help Dylan, right?" I ask. "You think Dylan doesn't deserve me. Everyone tells me that. But I'm no better than him. I have issues, just like he does. He doesn't deserve someone to be there? Well, then what do you think about *me*?"

Kat widens her eyes at me.

"April, that's not—"

"No, it's true. And you know that."

"No, it's not. Listen to me!" Kat's pale cheeks are rosy, a blotchy rash spreading across her face. "I never said Dylan doesn't deserve help. I don't know what he's going through, but quite frankly, I don't give a shit. Because he almost killed my best friend and didn't even have the audacity to call her after. And he *isn't* my best friend. *You* are. *You*, the kindest, most caring person I know, who—"

"You're wrong!" I yell. "I'm not that girl, Kat! Stop telling me I'm so great when you know that I'm not. All you do is enable me. You and Tristan and anyone else who wastes their time hanging out with me."

She looks at me like she might cry, and I know I hurt her, but I don't know how to stop.

If I were her, I'd get up and leave. But she doesn't do that. She never does. And that just makes me angrier.

"Just leave me alone," I mutter, burying my face into a pillow.

"You're a good person, April," Kat says sternly. "And maybe Dylan is, too. Maybe, deep down, very very *very* deep down...he's not as shitty as I think he is. But you can't drag yourself down to fix him. You shouldn't have to."

I wipe my tears with my fingers, dragging them hard across the face.

"Someone has to."

"But not you."

"No one can fix me, either."

"You don't need to be fixed." Kat inches toward me as I squeeze my eyes shut, tears painting my cheeks in black streaks. She just sits there, next to me. "There's nothing wrong with you."

"Yes, there is," I insist. *I just wish I knew what.*

The TV blares from the other room.

*10, 9, 8...*

"You're missing the countdown," I tell Kat.

*7, 6, 5...*

"I don't care," she says.

*4, 3, 2...*

She puts her arm around me and leans her head against mine.

*1...*

I let myself cry out the last of my tears.

# CHAPTER 44

Kat calls her mom to pick us up from Colton's so I can fall apart in peace in my best friend's bed. When we get home, she takes a shower and I head to the kitchen for some water, my head still fuzzy from the alcohol.

Ms. Bailey is fixing a drink when I walk in, her thick red hair pulled back in a French braid. She's in flannel pajama bottoms and a thermal shirt, fuzzy slippers on her feet.

"I made hot cocoa," she tells me as I grab a cup and fill it with water from the fridge. "Though I'm not sure how well that mixes with vodka." She pushes a large mug across the counter to me as I settle on a stool.

I blush. "I'm sorry we drank...and that you had to pick us up."

"Hey, like I said before: no questions asked."

I blow on the hot chocolate, avoiding eye contact with my favorite teacher. My dad always tells me that his students assume he's oblivious to their lives outside of his class. It's like they think all professors are from some alternate universe, unaware of how the teenage population lives.

I know Ms. Bailey gets it. In fact, she probably gets it better than anyone, seeing as she traded her college experience for raising a daughter by herself while taking classes online. But I still feel that familiar gnawing in my stomach.

*Guilt.*

I take a sip of the rich, creamy drink, hoping it will ease the discomfort a bit. "Everything goes well with hot chocolate," I say.

Ms. Bailey smiles. "That's right."

My hands shake as I place the mug back down on the counter. I take a deep breath. It's times like these I wish I had a mom like Kat's. Someone who listens, really listens, and doesn't judge or try to change me.

"Ms. Bailey..." I start, wanting to talk about tonight, about everything that happened between me and Tristan. My panic attack. My conversation with Kat. But I don't even know where to start. "Everything is a mess."

"How so?"

"Well, *I'm* a mess, for one."

"Oh, April." She leans forward across from me, her elbows on the counter and chin in her hands. "You are *not* a mess. You're just a teenager."

"A teenager with heavy emotional baggage," I correct her.

When she smiles, her eyes sparkle, and I can see why Kat is always so positive about everything. With a mom like hers, someone who makes you feel like everything is going to be okay, who wouldn't see the bright side?

"We all have some," she tells me.

"I'm supposed to be going away to college in autumn..." I start. "I guess I thought I'd have my life together by now, but I don't. I feel like I just—I keep falling backwards." I pinch my leg, over and over, to keep myself from crying again. "I haven't even applied to schools yet. The deadline is in two days, and there's no way I..." I pause, shaking my head. "I don't think I'm ready. As much as I wish I was. Something's holding me back."

Ms. Bailey considers this for a moment.

"April, do you think I planned on getting pregnant at 17?"

I shake my head slowly.

"No. No, I didn't. I thought my life was over when I took that pregnancy test. Now, I can't imagine my life without Kat in it."

"I can't imagine *my* life without Kat in it," I say with a laugh.

She winks. "She's pretty awesome, isn't she?"

"The awesomest."

"What I'm trying to say is, without that detour, I wouldn't be who I am today. I wouldn't have an amazing daughter with an amazing best friend." She reaches over and touches my arm. "I wouldn't be teaching amazing students. I'd probably be at some miserable office job, making tons of money and living the life my parents wanted for me, but hating every second of it."

I think about my mom. The life she wants for me. Superficial normalcy. It's so different from the one I want for myself.

Why, then, am I letting her write *my* story? Why am I letting anyone, other than myself, write even just one page?

"We don't always know why certain things happen to us, April. Why we're led down paths we never anticipated walking. And I won't tell you that everything happens for a reason. But I do believe that there is reason in everything, if you really look for it. If you just let yourself see it."

I add that quote to my list of tattoos I'll never get.

"At the end of the day, it's much simpler than you think," she continues, her voice soft. "Figure out who you want to be, and be that. Figure out what you want to do, and do that. Unapologetically, and on whatever timeline works best for you. And I promise, everything else will fall into place."

"But...what if I don't know what I want? Or who I am?"

"You do know, deep down. You're just listening to the noise around you." She reaches out to touch my arm. "Only *you* have the answers, April."

But my life feels like a multiple-choice exam, and I've never been a good test-taker.

"How do I find them?" I ask her, desperate for someone else to take the pen from my hand, to fill in the blanks for me.

She smiles at me. "You trust yourself."

\*　　　\*　　　\*

I drive myself home early the next morning so I can have breakfast with my parents. They're sitting in the kitchen together, having their coffee, when I walk in.

"I didn't expect you home so early," my mom says when

she sees me. She raises her eyebrows at me as I get closer. "Rough night?"

My dad looks up from the book he's reading and meets my eyes.

"Are you alright?" he asks, shutting the book without marking his page.

He isn't referencing my baggy sweatpants and sweatshirt I slept in, or my greasy hair gathered in a messy bun, or even my blotchy cheeks streaked with last-night's makeup. Maybe that's what my mom notices, but it's not what my dad sees.

He sees the person beneath the facade, the girl who's struggling to grow into herself. He sees me.

I shake my head.

"What's wrong?" my dad asks me, and they both look at me like I'm about to tell them I'm ill. And I guess that's not so far off. I guess, maybe, *ill* is the right word.

Ms. Bailey's words flash back into my mind: "Figure out who you want to be, and be that. Figure out what you want to do, and do that."

*I want to get better.*

"I want to go to residential therapy," I say before I can stop myself.

My mom opens her mouth, then shuts it. She looks at my dad, who looks at me, questioning.

"I need help. But I don't want to go all the way to Houston," I add. "I was doing some research last night with Kat. There's...there's a really good place. In Boston. I think...I think it'd be a good idea." I clear my throat. "I want to go to that one. So, that way, once the program is over, I can hopefully transfer to Boston University. I'm gonna spend all day applying, and for my application, I'm gonna write about...all of this. This year, the therapy, everything. And just hope for the best, I guess."

Silence falls among us like a blanket of snow. I shiver in my sweatshirt, longing for a hot shower. But it can wait.

"Okay, honey," my mom says. "Then, you'll go to that one."

*    *    *

It's only the first day of the new year, and I've spent it lying in bed watching *Gilmore Girls*, trying not to think about the next few months. At least I have some sort of plan that might help me get better. Still, that doesn't ease the anguish.

My phone buzzes on my nightstand just as Netflix pauses, asking if I'm still watching. I grab my cell to see an incoming call from Colton.

"Hello?"

"Hey. Just wanted to check in. How are you feeling?"

I let out a long breath, sitting up in bed. "I'm okay."

"Yeah?" His soft tone strikes a chord with me.

My eyes sting. "Not really."

"I didn't think so."

Neither of us says anything, but we don't really have to. If Colton was here right now, he'd probably sit next to me on the edge of my bed and let me cry, and maybe even put his hand on my shoulder, if he felt like it. And it'd be enough. More than enough. Sometimes, all you need is someone to acknowledge your pain, to stick by you as you endure it.

"I'm sorry I ruined your party," I say.

"You didn't ruin anything. Plus, that wasn't exactly a 'party.'"

"Well, for you, it was," I joke.

He laughs. "Touche."

Sighing, I wipe my head over my forehead. "I'm so embarrassed."

"There's no reason to be," Colton tells me. "No one thought anything of it. We all just felt bad...and not in a pitying kinda way."

I groan, pulling the covers over my head as if that will help anything.

"I was a complete mess."

"Listen, April. We all have our shit, remember? No one's judging you for yours. And if they are, then they're not worth your time. Some people don't understand. They just can't.

They're not wired the same way. But that's not a reflection of you."

*He's right.* And as shitty as it sounds, I'm relieved Colton *is* wired the same way I am.

"I'm really glad I met you this year," I tell him.

"Aw, April..." he says, his voice soft. "That's cute and all, but you didn't meet me this year. We met last year."

For a second, I'm confused, wondering if I somehow met him before that night at the liquor store, if I somehow missed something. But then I realize today is New Year's Day.

I laugh. "You're the worst."

"I know." He pauses. "I'm glad I met you, too."

*   *   *

I'm half asleep with a book still in my hand when someone knocks on my door. Thinking it's my mom or dad, I roll over to face the doorway and tell them to come in.

When I notice it's Tristan, I quickly sit up and brush through my hair with my fingers. I can only imagine what I look like right now.

"Hey," he says. "Sorry if I woke you."

"No, you're fine." I pretend to yawn while covering my mouth, but really I'm checking to make sure my breath isn't deadly.

Tristan slowly walks over to my bed as I pull my knees up to my chest, making room for him to sit.

"How are you holding up?" he asks me.

I shrug. "I'm alright."

"I'm really sorry for everything. I never should've kissed you when you were drunk."

"You were drunk too. And I knew what I was doing. And I..." I meet his eyes. They're glistening bright green, like lush fields in the midst of winter. "I don't regret it, Tristan. You need to know that."

He perks up a bit. It's subtle, but I can read him like one of my mystery novels, so I pick up on it.

"You don't?"

Tears spring to my eyes as I shake my head. Tristan stares at me with confusion.

"Last night had nothing to do with you," I tell him.

As I start to cry, I try to wipe the tears from my eyes. But there are too many to catch, so Tristan reaches over and brushes a few off my cheek. I fight the urge to lie down with him, to rest my head on his chest. I want to be close to him. Because even though it makes me feel emotions I've been trying to resist my entire life, it also makes me feel alive.

Sometimes, to feel anything, you have to feel everything.

But right now, I can't do that. I'm just not ready.

Tristan looks away from me, rubbing his eyes like he's tired. I wonder if he slept much last night. I know I didn't. I woke up every hour, drenched in sweat, and stared at the ceiling, my stomach in knots.

Tristan sniffles, and I realize he's crying. Not obviously, but his eyes are red and wet with tears.

"I'm sorry," he says.

"Sorry?" I ask, concerned. "What are you sorry for? You didn't do anything wrong..."

"No, I'm just—" He shakes his head. "I care about you, April. It hurts me to know you're hurting."

"I'm okay."

He leans forward and kisses my forehead, lingering for a few moments. My eyes flutter shut, and I want to kiss him again, like last night. God, I want to kiss him more than anything.

Instead, I pull away from him.

Tristan studies my expression, his eyes flickering over my face.

"April, you've been my best friend for a while now. Every time I'm with you, I just feel so happy. And I just want *you* to be happy. So, yeah, I don't know what you call that, really, but...I just care so much about you."

He shrugs, and my heart swells, because I feel the same way about him. But I don't know what to call it either.

"You're my best friend, too, Tristan. You're more than

that. You're...you make me feel like I'm home. And I've never really felt that way anywhere, with anyone else."

I look down and blink back tears, knowing what I have to do.

"But...I need to think about myself right now."

Tristan inhales a long breath, his gaze fixed downward. Is he mad?

"I'm going to residential therapy, and I'll be gone for a while," I continue. "But this is what I need. I need to get better, to be happy with myself." I swallow a lump in my throat. "Before I can be happy with someone else," I add.

He meets my eyes and presses his lips into a small smile.

"That's amazing, April. Really." I can tell he means it.

He places his hand on my leg.

"I'm proud of you. Everything is going to be okay."

I nod slowly, taking it all in.

"I just, I don't know how long it will be. These programs last for months. I'll miss school and prom and graduation..."

"You don't have to explain yourself to me," he says. "You know that."

"I know. It's just...I feel this, too." I gesture between the two of us. "I need you to know that."

"I do know." He smiles softly, then takes my hand in his. "And I need you to know, no matter what, I'm not going anywhere."

# CHAPTER 45

Greg puts his arm around my shoulder as we carry my bags out to my dad's car. I feel the way I did when we were kids, like when he met me in the nurse's office the day I had a really bad panic attack. He sat with me and let me borrow his cell phone since the nurse wouldn't let me call my dad because I didn't have a fever. She didn't realize all I needed was to hear my dad's voice for comfort.

Part of me still feels like that little girl. It's like she's trapped inside me, begging to be seen and comforted. I'm ready to embrace her and all the other versions of myself.

"I'm proud of you, you know that?" Greg asks me.

"You are?"

He stops walking in his tracks, despite the fact that he's wearing my heavy bag of books over his shoulder, and I'm struggling with a box of goodies my dad baked me.

"Yeah, I am," he says carefully. "I know sometimes it seems like I doubt your strength, but it's only because you're my little sister. When you're struggling, I feel like, in some way, I've failed you. And I know that's dumb, because you obviously don't need protecting."

"You're not responsible for my happiness, Greg."

"No, I know that. It's just instinct sometimes. You'll always be my little sister, Ape, and I just want you to be okay."

I smile. "I will be," I say. "But I really wish you'd stop calling me 'Ape.'"

"Never." He laughs, then starts toward the car again. "I don't say it enough, but I am always proud of you, April."

He throws my bag in the trunk and takes my box from

me. Then, he pulls me in for a hug. It's a bit uncomfortable and forced, but I return it anyway. I love my brother—I really do.

Just as we pull apart and he heads back toward the house, a car pulls up to my curb, and Kat practically jumps out before it stops moving. Jenny and Tristan follow closely behind her.

Zach is in the driver's seat. He doesn't get out, but it's not lost on me that he's the one who drove them here. And the one who was there for me in the bookstore when I broke down about Tristan.

He waves politely out the window, and I think back to what Colton told me a few weeks ago. *We all have something.* I wonder what his *something* is, and I hope he knows he's not alone.

"We all chipped in and got you a going-away gift!" Kat yells as she tackles me in a hug. "From me, Jenny, Colton, and Zach. Tristan had to do his own thing, of course." She sticks out her tongue, then winks at me as Jenny and Tristan walk up. They smile at me.

Jenny hands me a red gift bag with a bow on it.

"Open it!" she says.

I do as I'm told. Inside is a dark leather journal with my initials engraved.

"Guys...this is beautiful. You didn't have to do this!" I flip through it slowly. So many blank pages to fill. My eyes well with tears as I look up at their grinning faces. "I don't even know what to say. Thank you."

We group-hug it out, and part of me wants to run back inside and tell my dad I can't do it—I don't want to leave. But I need to keep moving forward.

"I'm gonna miss you so much," Kat says, her face squished against mine.

"Me too!" Jenny says. "But I have a feeling I'll be seeing you around a lot more once you're home..." She winks as she pulls away.

"On that note, we'll let you two chat," Kat tells me. She gives my hand a squeeze. "Proud of you, girl. I love you, and I am always just a phone call—or car ride!—away."

"I love you, too," I tell her as she skips away.

Once it's just the two of us on the driveway, Tristan hands me an envelope. "What is it?" I ask.

"Open it."

I slide my finger under the seal and gently pull out two tickets. But not just any tickets. Tickets to the next Knuckle Puck concert, in New York, like last time.

"It's in the summer, so you should be home in time for it," he says as my mouth hangs open in shock. "I thought maybe we could have a redo on that date."

"Tristan, I—" I shake my head, at a loss. Some emotions, you just can't put into words.

"You don't have to say anything," he tells me. Then, smirking, he adds, "Just don't ditch me again."

Rolling my eyes, I swat his arm with my hand as he laughs.

"I wouldn't miss it for the world," I tell him.

"Oh, also!" Tristan exclaims, pulling out his phone. "Colton wanted to be here, but he had work. He said to tell you, and I quote"—Tristan squints down at the screen—"'Our friendship will always be...*mutually beneficial*?'" Tristan looks at me, questioning, and all I can do is smile and shake my head. "'I hope you know our deep talks are not just limited to my balcony. Call me any time. You'll always have someone who understands.'"

I look around me, at my street and the houses lining it, at the trees and the sky and the few white clouds. It all looks so different to me, in the best way. Tristan is safe, and I have friends who really care about me, old and new, and a family who isn't perfect but is willing to do more for me than I'd ever noticed. For once, I feel like maybe I do belong.

"I'm gonna miss you, Tristan," I tell him.

"I'm gonna miss you too, April." He hugs me tightly against him, and I breathe in his familiar scent, never wanting to let go. I wish I could pack up his warmth and take it with me. "You'll be home before you know it."

# CHAPTER 46

"Your mother wanted to be here," my dad says as we back out of the driveway. It's just him and me, road-tripping to Boston. "But you know how she is with work…"

"I know," I say, because I do. I know my mom. I know her unwavering loyalty to her career, and her inability to understand the things I go through. I also know she loves and accepts me anyway. Even if her way of showing it is through a last-minute "good luck!" text.

As if on cue, another text pops up on my screen:

**Jade:** Your mom told my mom about therapy…I wish you'd told me, April. I would have been there for you.

It suddenly dawns on me: my mom and Jade aren't much different, just like my relationships with both of them. Constantly striving to please them, but falling short each time.

My dad glances at me.

"You okay?"

"Yeah. Jade texted me." I read him what she said. "I kinda feel bad for not telling her myself."

"Maybe, instead of making this about her, she could have looked inward and realized she hasn't been the most understanding friend to you."

I've never looked at it like that. I've really only ever pointed fingers at myself.

"The most important thing you can do right now is put yourself first. Trust your own judgments and find your own strength." He turns to me, eyebrows raised. "It's in there, April. And you've got a hell of a lot of it."

A voice inside me taunts, *He's wrong. You're weak. You don't know anything.* But I choose not to listen this time.

"And I'm sorry if your mom and I have made this harder on you," he continues. "We just want what's best for our daughter. At the end of the day, we just want you to be happy."

"I know."

"This is gonna be good for you, April."

Inhaling a deep breath, I nod my head slowly.

"I think it will be, too."

Just then, a ray of sunshine beams out from behind the clouds, highlighting my face. Its warmth is like a blanket on a cold winter morning.

"No," I say. "I know it will be."

My dad smiles, focusing on the road ahead. I shuffle and we jam out to Knuckle Puck, in honor of their upcoming concert this summer. The first song I ever heard of theirs, *Untitled*, comes on.

*There's gotta be something more for me,*
*More than framework and furniture.*
*Free fall into foreign waters.*

I've listened to these lyrics hundreds of times. They're the reason I love the song so much. But I've never taken the time to consider just what they mean.

There *is* something more for me—for all of us. It's just a matter of finding it. And that might feel like free-falling into the unknown, unsure of how you'll stay afloat.

You might fall apart, realizing you're the only one who can put yourself back together. That's not to say other people can't pick up the pieces, or hand you the glue, or even hold you tight throughout the process. But you're a puzzle only you can solve.

And it's going to hurt. You're going to have scars from the shattered pieces, be jaded for a while, or maybe forever. You'll miss parts of yourself you might never find, never fill, and have ragged edges that don't seem to fit.

And you might never feel whole. And you might never *be* whole. But we are all broken, and we will all break again, and again, and again. It is only in these moments that we learn which parts of ourselves need keeping, and which parts we might let go, so the current might slowly take them away. So we can change and grow and become the person we are meant to be.

So we might find, within ourselves, some place like home.

# ABOUT THE AUTHOR

## Sammi Caramela

Sammi Caramela has always loved words and their power to connect humanity. When she isn't working as a journalist at her nine-to-five, she's writing, reading a YA book with a third cup of coffee or attending local pop punk concerts. Check out her blog at SammiSays.org, and don't be afraid to reach out-she loves hearing from her readers.

# METAL LUNCHBOX
# PUBLISHING

*www.metallunchboxpublishing.com*

Made in the USA
Middletown, DE
15 January 2021